# ESCAPE TO THE HIGHLAND RETREAT

ELAYNE GRIMES

Storm
PUBLISHING

Ebook ISBN: 978-1-80508-786-1
Paperback ISBN: 978-1-80508-787-8

Cover design: Rose Cooper
Cover images: Shutterstock

Published by Storm Publishing.
For further information, visit:
www.stormpublishing.co

ALSO BY ELAYNE GRIMES

**Loch Strathkin**

*Secrets of Swanfield House*

# ONE

Ruaridh Balfour was all things to all men. He was a ghillie, a gamekeeper, a mountaineer, a scout, a bar-hand, a husband, a father of five and a general factotum to all the villagers of the tiny hamlet of Strathkin in Wester Ross. Today he was also a chauffeur. He had come to the airport to collect the new owner of *the big house* – Swanfield – which had recently been sold by his childhood friend, Marcella Mosse. The huge baronial style house stood at the head of the village near a row of little white painted cottages and crofts that ran alongside the shoreline of Strathkin Loch. His own house, Lochside Croft, sat across the loch, directly opposite Swanfield. He shared the croft with his wife Dina and their four boys, along with the recent addition of a longed-for little daughter, Mari, who was, without a doubt, his pride and joy.

For Ruaridh, driving was a chance to escape from his extraordinarily busy life for a time and reconnect with nature, albeit from behind the wheel of his car. Today's journey took him through soft rolling hills, then spectacular mountains to verdant valleys and glens. Where people saw an inhospitable wilderness plagued with atrocious weather, this Highland native saw only dramatic scenery that had given him, from as far back as he could remember, an innate sense of place. Drawn to water, he would stop at a viewpoint if he had the time in his busy schedule and gaze in wonder at the dramatic inland waterways and vistas that surrounded him. The natural features of the landscape in this part of the world never failed to amaze him and it was a wonder that he had passed on to his children like a family fable. Stories of kelpies and sea witches had enchanted him since his own childhood and gazing over the grandness of a loch truly made him feel alive.

Always keen to tell a visitor about the history and topography of his forever home, Ruaridh, however, had not exchanged a single word with his passenger since he'd collected her almost an hour before. At the airport, Ruaridh had eyed her with some suspicion, this newcomer, dressed in clothes that weren't suitable for the vagaries of the Highland climate. Her heels might have been called *vertiginous*: white snakeskin stilettos. Ruaridh would simply call them *pointy*. Beneath her cream silk skirt and jacket was a tight, trimmed waist. Her surgically enhanced breasts were pert, if large for her frame, and drew the eye towards a taut décolletage where chains were entwined with the letters 'CC'. Her honey-brown locks were teased and curled across her shoulders in gently falling waves. He had found her with an assortment of luggage around her: large silver boxes, of various sizes, seven in total, stacked and piled high.

'Mrs San?' Ruaridh had asked as he approached her at the Arrivals area. Her head had turned around sharply in a way that reminded him of a barn owl.

'Ms,' she hissed with a scowl.

'Oops!' He smiled, and there was no smile in return. He glanced around at the other drivers waiting to pick up wealthy visitors to take them to the exclusive lodges dotted around this part of the Highlands: men dressed as chauffeurs; men in kilts holding iPads with names on them; ghillies in well-worn tweeds.

'Ruaridh Balfour,' he said in introduction, offering a hand to shake in welcome. Ms San almost recoiled in horror, a vision of disdain. She waved her hand in the general direction of the matching suitcases and turned on her thin heels to the door marked 'EXIT'. In that moment, Ruaridh was relieved he had listened to his wife's advice and brought his new black Range Rover for the occasion and not taken the family's beaten-up Land Rover, which was filled with the detritus of four young boys and a new baby. Something told him it would not have helped endear him to this new visitor.

Ignoring his suggestion that she sit in the front, due to the undulating roads on the long drive, Ms San chose to sit in the back. He watched her carefully in the rear-view mirror, knowing it was wise to keep quiet until his passenger started a conversation. However, when she sighed for the umpteenth time, and Ruaridh caught her eye, he had to give in.

'First time to Scotland?' he asked with a genuine interest.

'Yes.'

'You're moving to the most beautiful part of the world,' he responded, smiling widely.

'I hardly think so,' she replied disdainfully and pushed her wide sunglasses further up her nose.

Her response caught him by surprise. He genuinely believed where he lived had the most stunning scenery he'd seen in his entire life and was at a loss at what to say next.

'Do you play golf, Mrs San?' he probed, changing the subject.

'Ms,' she corrected him for the second time.

'Ah, sorry!' After a moment, Ruaridh decided to have another try. 'To be honest, we were wondering who had bought the big house after—'

'*The big house?*' she interrupted swiftly with air quotes.

'Yes, Swanfield. It's been in the same family for years, so we were all wondering who the new owner was.'

'We?'

'Yes, well, me, us, all the villagers. The house sits at the head of the loch looking down on all of us!'

'Hmmm.' Ms San turned towards the window as more spectacular mountain scenery flew by.

Ruaridh realised the conversation was over and resolved to keep silent until they descended into the village off the high ridge. The dramatic view of the Glen of Strathpine normally made his passengers gasp in delight. Ruaridh expected this to be the reaction today. He was proved very wrong.

In Strathkin, Heather McLeod and Dina Balfour, Ruaridh's wife, sat outside Lochside Croft. Both were anxious to hear what Ruaridh had to say about the new owner of the large house opposite.

'What if they decide to turn it into one of those exclusive hotels?' asked Heather before biting the inside of her cheek. As owner of The Strathkin Inn, she had a personal stake in who the new owner would be. The Inn was the only accommodation between this village and the larger village of Strath Aullt, some ten miles away, and had gone through some exceedingly tough times in recent years.

Dina, meanwhile, calm as ever, swirled what was left in her teacup.

'They had a toilet stop at The Aizle,' she offered. 'Ruaridh texted but I don't think he was that impressed.'

The Aizle had started life as a small tea room and toilet stop for travellers and locals alike. Over the years it had grown into a large café, gift shop and refreshment stop in the remote western Highlands. It was a regular pause for Ruaridh on his frequent trips and he had used it as an excuse to glean information from passengers and locals alike. It was a joke amongst family and friends; his famous ruse to suggest a comfort break and then chat over a drink which to unsuspecting tourists was in effect a Strathkin interrogation.

Heather sighed heavily. It wasn't what she wanted to hear. She wanted Ruaridh to update his wife with a text that simply said, *It's going to be a family home. No worries.* If they turned her friend's childhood home into a secret luxury escape for the wealthy, it could ruin her. She got up from the old blue painted bench that sat up against the cottage and strolled down to the shore, where Dina's youngest son, Douglas, was wading, collecting some of the flotsam and jetsam that drifted towards the sand and shingle beach.

'What's going down here, doll?' Heather asked the seven-year-old.

'Nuthin' much,' the youngster said, shells held tightly in closed hands. A pebble fell from his pocket and gently splashed back into the water.

'You must have some collection?' Heather asked, and the boy shrugged. For years now, Dina had kept her son's collection of shells and pebbles stored in large glass vases throughout the house, displaying his most loved items on a wooden shelf in his bedroom.

Heather followed the young boy's gaze as it turned to the large house across the loch, where the noise of drills and banging disturbed this otherwise quiet day. For months now, the constant droning of building work had disturbed the peace in their tranquil village.

'Is Marcie coming back?' Douglas asked.

Heather patted his shoulder. 'Don't know, doll.'

To their left, a bevy of swans took off low and slow from a nearby reed bed, leaving a shimmering ripple across the water.

. . .

When Ruaridh pulled the car off the small single-track road that ran in front of Swanfield, it was only his very quick reaction that stopped him slamming into two men standing dead centre in the driveway.

'Jeezo!' he yelled out in his elongated tone, and he heard his passenger tut-tut behind him. 'Oh, sorry about that Mrs, er, Miss, er, Ms San, apologies. I'll go and see what the problem is.'

'No need. It's just my men, they won't be here long.'

In the rear-view mirror, Ruaridh saw her lips curl into a smile. The men continued with their work, not giving Ruaridh a second glance, and he continued down the driveway and headed to the rear of the property.

'STOP!' Ms San commanded. 'Where are you going?'

'Oh, I'm sorry, just force of habit. I'd normally drive round the back, to the back door.'

He pulled the car around in a tight circle, stopping at the front entrance, and leapt out of the driver's seat to open his passenger's door. He waited as she shimmied across the rear bench seat, easing herself out of the car and onto the gravel where her heels sank between the pebbles. She gave him a sneering look once more as she examined the damage to her expensive shoes.

'That'll be next to go,' he joked, nodding at the driveway.

'Next week.' She walked to the wide wooden door and extended a gloved finger to push it open.

Leaving the luggage in the car, Ruaridh was on her tail, quickly entering the house after her. As he saw how Swanfield had been transformed, he managed to keep his exclamations of surprise to himself. The room was almost bare save a few key items; the old Caithness stone fireplace still glowed with its golden stone, but the grate was empty. A mid-century sideboard was thrust, drawers first, against a wall and an ancient lamp, with a frilled shade, stood sad and forlorn in the corner. The tartan reading chair that would normally have sat before the fireplace in the kitchen was covered in dust.

'What is that still doing here?' Ms San asked, extending a gloved finger to the dejected and abandoned chair.

'Er, dunno, Mrs San.' A workman shrugged with a look of slight fear.

'I'll take it. I'll get rid of it for you.' Ruaridh made a beeline for the chair, covering himself with dust as he lifted it and heaved it outside to place it next to the Range Rover.

'Do you want me to unload your stuff?' Ruaridh asked Ms San when he returned.

'Good grief, no!' she said in abject horror. 'I've booked a room at the Inn across the road. I'm only here a day or two, and I wouldn't stay in this mess. Wait outside.'

Ruaridh whistled as he strode to the car, pondering how he was going to get the old chair back to his own house with all the cases in the known world stacked in his vehicle. He approached the men with the digger near the entrance, who he recognised as a joiner and part-time ghillie from the neighbouring village of Strath Aullt.

'Hey, Fraser,' Ruaridh shouted.

'Aye, aye, Ruaridh ma man, how's it hingin'?' greeted Fraser MacRae.

'Aye, the usual, big job here, eh?'

'Aye, it is that son, it is that.'

'What's doing then?'

'Och, just a big job, son. How's that new wee bairn of yours?'

'Aye grand, aye – growin' up, fillin' out!'

They then stood, as men do, staring into the large hole in the driveway.

'So, big job, eh?' Ruaridh repeated, hoping Fraser might take the bait.

'Aye, son, big job.'

Ruaridh waited for more details, but none came. With a smile and a nod, he turned and walked back to his car.

*Well, well, well, Fraser MacRae, normally we cannot get you to shut up. 'Look what I'm doing. Look who I've fleeced from the big city.' Normally you're awash with information and gossip and here you are – quiet as a church mouse.*

Ruaridh glanced backwards over the water to Lochside Croft. There, as usual, his children were out on the grass that ran down to the loch. He noticed that his wife and one of her best friends, Heather, were sitting on the bench outside the house.

'Have I got news for you,' he muttered under his breath. Ruaridh knew that within minutes of imparting this information about the new owner of Swanfield, both women would be in a race to call Marcella, who had recently become Mrs Grainger.

# TWO

Marcie was sitting in the living room of her new house in Southfields, London. A tennis fan from a very young age, she had long coveted an SW19 postcode. However, she had settled for one digit less to save several hundred thousand pounds, which meant a walk to The All England Lawn Tennis & Croquet Club at Wimbledon, though it was still near the Tube.

Teetering boxes were piled high in one corner, neatly labelled. She liked a minimalist style, one her new husband had grown used to over the years. Neatness was a family trait. Like her uncle Callum, Marcie preferred order to mess, even though some would argue it was less homely. After selling Swanfield, her family home, for well over the asking price, at an amount that was frankly staggering, she could now indulge in some little luxuries. Their new house was one such indulgence. First, she'd deposited a healthy amount to Callum, her only living relative, who had taken care of her after her parents' deaths. She had encouraged him to travel now he had the chance and the freedom to explore. His trip had commenced in the Maldives, with its powder white sand and warm, pale blue sea, and now extended to St Lucia. He was thinking already of his next island hop. Marcie caught up with her uncle weekly and his broad smile always told her he'd made the right decision.

Marcie's inheritance had also enabled them to have the most fabulous wedding in Strathkin Village Hall and a dream honeymoon in Italy. Even today, on this cold but bright day in south-west London, the memory brought a smile to her lips. She had spread her money out amongst her best friends in her little hamlet, too, to allow them to enjoy a bit of freedom after the trauma they had gone through together. Strathkin had been in danger of becoming another abandoned Highland settlement until an injection of money from Marcie paid to refurbish Heather's hotel, provided new glamping pods, and an upgrade extension to attract new visitors. 'The Snug', built in the new side return, offered the hotel guests a taste of local delicacies and patrons could experience what Heather had called *a taste of Highland culture in liquid form*. The owners of the local distillery were delighted. It had been a huge success.

As a result, the area had started to appear on the tourist map once again.

Marcie had pulled in favours from a friend who wrote travel articles for airline magazines. Picking up on it, high-end newspapers had followed with articles of their own. Now, Strathkin was firmly planted in the minds of travellers wishing to sample everything this area of Scotland had to offer, from spectacular scenery to incredible eating experiences. With an enviable larder of abundant highland produce, and friendly locals, Strathkin was beginning to thrive again. With Marcie's help, Heather had engaged the services of a bright young chef and now, rather than being a one-night stopover on the way to somewhere more interesting, the hotel had itself become a go-to destination. Suddenly a sense of pride had returned to the world-weary villagers of Strathkin along with a smile on their faces.

Presently, Marcie held the phone up to her face as her two best friends squeezed into the small screen.

Heather gave a beaming grin. 'Well, well, well, someone is all tanned and gorgeous.'

Marcie held the phone up to show her friends the boxes piled in the corner. 'That will fade by Monday, I can assure you – and look at this I've got to get through!'

'Pah! We know what you're like. You'll be in your element. You're a clean freak – that'll be gone by teatime!'

'So, what's prompted this call from you pair?' asked Marcie, sitting down on her Eames chair, lifting her feet on to the ottoman.

'Where do we start?' asked Dina as the two women sat down on the large, battered leather sofa in Dina's comfortable cottage. 'Ruaridh has met the new owner of Swanfield.'

'She seems a bit nipped and tucked according to him. He picked her up earlier from the airport. Flew in from Amsterdam.'

'She's staying at the hotel tonight so full update tomorrow,' explained Heather.

'Interesting. Family with her?'

'Husband arriving tomorrow,' stated Dina, 'and someone else the day after.'

'It's all go, go, go here.' Heather laughed. 'You don't know what you're missing!'

'Go, go, go in Strathkin? Hmm, that'll be a first. Is there still building work going on?'

'Gawd almighty, Mars, at one-point last week, I expected to look over and see the place demolished. The noise is incredible. I've no idea what they're doing. It starts early in the morning until late at night. There are two of those mobile caravan things, too, so people are living on site and can work inside till God knows what time. Plus, Ruaridh texted. He met old Fraser MacRae. He's working over the way. Not saying a thing about what they're doing over there,' concluded Dina with a gesture of her hand zipping her mouth closed.

'Fraser MacRae? Old *Foghorn Leghorn*? He normally can't shut up! What's going on? Heather, it's your job to get him plastered in the pub and wheedle it out of him! Find out what's happening at my old gaff.' Marcie laughed to her friends.

'He's not been in. He and the lads are keeping very much to themselves these days.'

Marcie sat back, her curiosity pricked. 'That's a bit odd.'

'Oh, that's another thing. The sign is down,' added Dina.

'The sign?'

'The sign for Swanfield, the one on the road to the village, at the junction. And Ruaridh said the gate posts, too.'

'The posts?' Marcie queried, now very much intrigued.

'Yes, the big gate posts at the end of the driveway. You know, the big stone gate posts that had "Swanfield" carved in them. Ruaridh thinks they're away. Gone.'

'The stone gate posts? Wow!'

'Everything.'

'What do you mean, *everything*?'

'Well, the gate posts, the old gate that was always open, and the drystone wall. He thinks it's all gone,' explained Dina.

Marcie was perplexed. It was clear the new owners wanted to put their own stamp on the new purchase, but the extent of the renovations was startling to everyone – except perhaps Fraser MacRae.

'When are you coming up?' Heather asked.

'We're thinking a week on Saturday or so. Could come up on the Friday night?'

'Okay, we'll keep in touch, and I can nip over to Sweet Briar and refresh and open the house for you,' Dina reassured her.

Marcie had, after a lot of persuasion, talked her husband Simon into taking an extended break from his work in the hospitality industry. *Why not take advantage of their newfound wealth?* They had the means and the opportunity to do something at a time in their lives when they weren't yet tied by family or children. Rather than a usual brief weekend break, she would spend six weeks in Strathkin. This was the longest she would stay in Strathkin since she had originally left the place, and she knew that to spend it in Sweet Briar would be bliss. The cottage, which sat in the shadow of Swanfield, had belonged to her uncle Callum until her grandmother's death. Marcie had given Dina a healthy budget to refurbish the cottage and allowed her eye for detail to change it into a modern-day masterpiece. Known for her stylish interiors, Dina had used her imagination to transform the cottage into a magazine ready and comfortable holiday cottage. From Lochside Croft, however, Dina's eyes, were increasingly drawn to the house across the water and she wasn't the only one in this small hamlet to gaze over the loch and wonder. *Would they fit into this small and close-knit community? Would they have children who would become fast friends with her own? Would they simply be once a year holiday visitors like so many of the tourists who dropped by?*

After the call from Strathkin, Marcie sat back and smiled. The thought of breathing in the clean, clear mountain air, riding fast horses on the shore and taking outdoor picnics filled her soul with joy.

Keeping Sweet Briar was only the start of her plans. When selling part of the estate, including Swanfield, she had been careful to keep most of the tied crofts and cottages, many of which also needed modernisation. Callum had made an agreement with her that she could upgrade his old abode, stay in it as long as she needed, and start the refurbishment of all properties on the estate, as soon as she wanted. And now, she thought, was the time. Dina's taste and sense of style would be ideal for each of these little houses. They had spent long video calls discussing colours and budgets and timescales and planning. Whilst the money being spent at Swanfield was obviously to create a high value house, both women decided that less was more when it came to their renovations. Single pieces were discussed rather than vast swathes of expensive carpets and wallpaper, and colour coded mood boards swung back and forth up and down the country. Gossip was still rife in the village about the unseen owners of Swanfield and the money being spent and Marcie was more than keen to gather her family of girlfriends around her for her own take on the proceedings. Though Marcie had told her solicitor in Inverness that she did not want to know who had bought Swanfield, now she was as intrigued as her girl-friends about its mysterious new owner who already seemed to be making quite a stir.

While she was scanning for flights on her phone, she was already planning how she and Simon would fill the late spring days as they bled into summer in the sweeping landscape of the Highlands. And she was also hoping against hope that things would improve in these difficult early days of her marriage. The never-ending visiting mother-in-law and her talking incessantly about grandchildren. The long weekend trips from her home in Yorkshire that seemed to stretch longer and longer. The way Simon changed when she was around as if he was reverting to a child waiting to be praised. It was something she wished she could discuss with her girls, but Marcie had never really failed at anything, and she imagined they would tell her she was being overdramatic. She wanted an injection of normalcy back in her life and Strathkin was the place she knew she would get it.

# THREE

'How pointy?' Heather asked Ruaridh in the kitchen of Lochside Croft.

'You'll see soon enough. I'll be heading back to pick her up shortly,' he replied, peeling a mandarin orange and devouring it within seconds.

'I mean, did they look expensive?'

'Put it this way, I don't think either of you could fit your feet into them, never mind be able to afford them. Not that you have big feet, Dina, just that she's really, really thin. Ah, now, what I mean is...' Ruaridh was trying to dig himself out of this particular hole when his wife raised her eyes to the ceiling and shook her head.

'Did she smell expensive?' asked Heather, firing quick questions at the only person in their close quarters who had seen the new owner.

'I dunno, what do rich people smell like?'

'I don't know but whatever it is, they reek of it. They must have all their clothes washed in it. Bet she was wearing white or cream or something. They always wear light-coloured stuff.'

'Oh, they don't have their clothes washed. They have everything dry-cleaned and if it can't be cleaned then they simply get rid of it.' Dina gave a confident nod of someone who had read about such things. Her knowledge was updated every six months in the discarded magazines in her hairdresser's salon in Inverness.

Ruaridh was wiping citrus juice from the front of his fleece until Dina came over to him with a wet microfibre cloth. She swabbed him down like she would one of her five young messy children.

'And they don't eat,' Dina went on. 'These people with money, they just smoke and drink cocktails. They don't eat any food. Well, not *real* food like us.'

'You don't eat!' stated Ruaridh. 'Not anymore.'

Dina caught his eye and then turned away, gazing out the window to the house across the water.

'Right, time for me to hit the road,' Ruaridh said. 'And you, Heather, better get back to welcome your new guest.'

Ruaridh kissed his wife's cheek and headed out to his vehicle to taxi Angelina San to The Strathkin Inn.


Shortly afterwards, the woman slithered out of the back seat of the vehicle. Heather outstretched a hand and then, without any reason, gave the woman a small curtsey, much to the amusement of her driver. Heather gave Ruaridh a look that said, *I have no idea why I just did that*, and he laughed.

Striding into the newly refurbished hotel, Angelina San gave an approving look as she glanced around.

'It looks nicer on the inside,' she stated and headed straight to the reception desk, which saw Heather scurrying around her to be on the serving side within seconds.

'I've put you in Lochside View,' said Heather. The room was the biggest in the hotel and, up until recently, had been two rooms, taking over an entire corner of the first floor of the building. Considerable planning had gone into the room's décor and huge bathroom suite which meant it could now be sold at a premium price and was a sought-after destination for returning guests. Heather handed her a room proximity card and the woman stared at it disdainfully.

'Lift?' she enquired.

'No, it's only one floor up so there's no lift here.'

The woman gave her a look with what was akin to a snarl then turned and headed towards the broad staircase.

'Will you be having dinner?' Heather called after the woman, but the question went unanswered. She turned to Ruaridh who was standing in the vestibule in front of her surrounded by cases.

'No lift!' he mouthed to his old schoolfriend and lifted his palms to his cheeks in mock horror. Heather shrugged, and watched on as Ruaridh made the first of several trips up the stairs to Lochside View.

The next day, Ruaridh found himself once again at Inverness Airport waiting for the daily KLM Embraer jet to touchdown from Amsterdam. He was early this time and had a sign that said,

### Dr Louis De Groot

He had written it on a piece of paper at the kitchen table earlier that morning, and his four boys had thought the name hilarious.

'Oh, hello, Mr De Groot, is Mrs De Groot with you? Do you go *oot* Mr De Groot? When you eat beans do you toot, toot, toot, Mr De Groot?' They giggled themselves into hysterics.

'If they had an owl as a pet, would it be Hoot De Groot?' said the youngest boy, Douglas, with a laugh as the other three howled with laughter, before their father shouted that he couldn't hear himself think.

Now, standing in the small Highland airport, Ruaridh saw a man read his sign and approach, and thought he must have been mistaken. He was not anything like the De Groot that Ruaridh had expected to be transporting back to Swanfield. He was a short, bald man, barely over five foot tall, stocky in appearance, with thick round glasses and only a briefcase as luggage.

Ruaridh extended his hand, and the man shook it firmly.

'Welcome to Scotland, Mr De Groot,' he offered with a smile.

'Doctor De Groot. Thank you, I have no luggage,' said the man with a hint of a Dutch accent.

They walked in silence to the car. When they got there, the man insisted on sitting in the front passenger seat next to the driver.

'Any request stops enroute? It's about an hour and a half,' asked Ruaridh, but the man shook his head.

'It's better if you say eighty-five, ninety minutes or so,' suggested Doctor De Groot. 'That way it doesn't seem as long as an hour and a half. That seems interminable. A long and tedious drive. But when you say it quickly and in minutes it doesn't seem quite so bad. Don't you agree?'

'Aye, aye,' agreed Ruaridh and pulled the car out of the car park of the airport for the ninety-minute drive to Strathkin.

Doctor De Groot sat motionless in the passenger seat, hands clasped over his lap. At least he was chattier than his wife, thought Ruaridh. Their conversation that followed was mostly about the scenery and history of the area, and the old standby conversation filler, the weather. It was all very general and safe until Ruaridh mentioned the building work at Swanfield.

'So, there's a lot of building work going on – we live across the water, you see – so we're intrigued as to what you guys are doing. Do you plan to live here?'

'That's entirely up to my wife,' responded the doctor.

'I met your wife yesterday. She's very...'

'Expensive.'

'Aye, I'd say that,' agreed Ruaridh. With that, the conversation was over, and they fell into silence for the next fifty-five minutes.

When they reached Strathkin, Ruaridh pulled the car *slowly* into the long drive, following the near miss the day before, and drove up to the front door. There, Doctor De Groot got out and collected his briefcase from the footwell.

'Thank you, Mr Balfour,' he said with an outstretched hand, and Ruaridh realised that a folded piece of paper had been exchanged in the handshake.

Once his passenger was in the house, he unfolded it to reveal a £100 note.

'Wow!' he said to himself and put the polymer note into his pocket. He left the car and strolled down to the men still working at the entrance.

'Aye, aye, Fraser,' he said to the foreman.

'Ruaridh,' the man greeted in recognition.

'Another busy day?'

'It is that son.'

'I see the posts are away, the wall, the gate?'

'Aye, son, indeed, they are,' agreed the older man in his blue boiler suit.

'So, you're putting in another gate?'

'There'll be another gate, son, aye.'

'You putting it in then?'

'Oh no, we're off-site end of play today. There's another team up from down south arriving tomorrow to carry on the rest of the work. We're only here doing the heavy lifting, Ruaridh, as they say.'

Fraser MacRae turned, walking over to where the digger driver was climbing out of his cab. *Conversation over then,*

Ruaridh thought to himself and walked back up to his car so he could head home to impart this latest information to his wife and Heather McLeod. They in turn would pass the information to Swanfield's previous owner, and more intrigue would no doubt follow.

# FOUR

'Wholegrain toast and honey, no butter. Earl Grey tea, no milk,' said Heather to Dina sitting in the window seat of the lounge at The Strathkin Inn. 'How can you have toast without butter? I get mine for the hotel from the Black Isle Dairy. When you drive there, you can virtually see the *moo-cows* making it. Best you can get. Bright yellow. Fresh as anything. But Ms San pushed it away like it was contaminating the breakfast table.'

'Interesting,' said Dina as she adjusted her top to allow her daughter Mari to continue with her own breakfast. Both women gazed across the water, where the building work had subsided. Large items were being packed away into a stream of vans that were lined up on the driveway and into various cars dotted along the shoreline.

'Plus, her toiletries are all high-end stuff. Crème de la Mer and the like.'

'Surely you shouldn't be going through her personal stuff?' queried Dina.

'Oh, I wouldn't do that, it was all out on the bathroom counter. One of those face creams costs the same as you'd pay here to stay the night. Certainly, got plenty of dosh that one. Bet her husband is gorgeous. Bit of a silver fox, I'd say. I bet he's a Swiss banker or something. Could be German, no, Austrian. Couldn't put an age on her. All very tight.'

'Honestly, this wee one feeds more than the boys ever did. I'll need a tuck myself after this, H. My boobs are beginning to look like a couple of old windsocks,' Dina complained. 'And don't get me started about the pain in my back.' She stopped as Heather reached out and placed a comforting hand on her knee.

Ruaridh strolled casually back into their conversation.

'Aye, aye,' he said with the wicked grin of someone who knows a secret.

'What's set you off?' Dina asked.

'I've just met the husband. What can I say...?' He grinned and pulled a seat up beside the two women. He indicated to his wife to unhook his daughter so that he could take her in his arms, and she handed over the small child. Heather watched as his eyes lit up with unconditional love for this young bundle, the undisputed love of his life.

'So, what's he like? I'm thinking a George Clooney type with absolutely dazzling blue eyes, grey hair like silver strands and a light stubble?' suggested Heather.

'Er, nope,' said Ruaridh with a shake of the head. 'He's Dutch.'

'Ooh, like that guy in *Van der Valk*, the blond guy with the leather jacket – an older version of that? He's a bit tasty!'

Ruaridh shook his head. 'What's that thing we sometimes watch on Netflix when the boys have gone to bed, D? The comedian guy in the house. The neighbour that slides in the door.'

'Seinfeld?' suggested Dina after a moment's thought.

'That's the one.'

'The neighbour? The big lanky guy? Kramer?'

'Nopesies.'

Heather tapped her fingers against her lips, deep in thought. 'The friend? The wee bald guy?' she asked finally.

'The wee bald guy,' confirmed Ruaridh.

'You're winding me up?'

'Bald as a coot.' He stood up to take his daughter out into the bright sunshine.

The two friends caught each other's eye. 'Surely not?' Heather sighed, her face filling with deep disappointment.

'I'm not sure he'd joke about that, would he?'

'It's Ruaridh, who knows?' Heather nodded to Ally, her bar manager, who came to take away their plates and refresh their coffee.

For the third time in as many days, Ruaridh Balfour was at the airport Arrivals. Today he held up a sign that read:

MAUREEN BERMAN

The clickety click of heels made him turn around sharply from staring at the Arrivals board – that and being prodded in the back with something sharp that turned out to be a long umbrella.

'Are you Rudolph Belper?' asked a woman with a heavy Cockney accent, and perfectly coiffured high hair.

'Ruaridh,' replied her driver, 'Balfour.'

'Roo-ray?' Maureen quizzed, her mouth trying to fit around the name.

'Ruaridh,' he repeated slowly in his soft Highland burr.

'Roo-ray, that's what I said,' she repeated and pulled her leopard print suitcase up to join them. 'I've never really understood the Scotch accent.'

'Scottish.'

'My second husband, Brian, had a Scotch cousin. She was

from Glasgow, and I used to say, Bri, I used to say, I can't understand a word that woman is sayin',' Maureen continued in her
Cockney accent. 'Bri, I'd say, you're going to 'ave to translate for
me 'cause I 'aven't a bloody clue. Know what I mean, love?'

'Er...'

'I expected you to turn up in a kilt, I did. Isn't that what
they wear here? I've never been this far north, me. Bet it gets
cold here in the winter. Couldn't stand it, me. I 'ate being cold.
My Brian used to suffer *really* badly from cold feet. Bri, I'd say,
get them away from me, I'm freezing already, even when we
was in the Canary Islands. Know what I mean, Roo-ray?'

'Er...'

'I've only got this bag, son. I didn't really bring much this
trip but it's good to know it's not as cold as I thought. I don't
want to be going buyin' more clothes when I'm 'ere. My Bri
used to say, don't buy anythin' else until you throw something
out or I'm going to have to build an extension, so I didn't. Have
we got far to go?'

'Er, about ninety minutes.'

'Ninety minutes? That's an hour and an 'alf. Why can't you
just say an hour and an 'alf? I'm going to have to go to the lava-
tory. Wait here.'

Ruaridh watched as this new passenger in her leopard print
knee-length boots shimmied down the concourse to the toilet.
He put her age at around seventy plus. She was well turned out,
snazzily dressed in mostly browns and animal print. Her heady
aromatic perfume was reminiscent of one his mother wore at
Christmas. He took her case out to load into the car and met her
on his way back in.

'I thought you'd done a runner with me bag then, Rudy!'

'Ruaridh,' he corrected.

'Oh, I'm sorry, love.'

He led her to the car and opened the rear passenger door.

'I'll climb up front with you. You're a bit of a handsome

bugger. I miss male company. Have done ever since my Brian passed away. But I talk to him all the time, don't I, Bri? Give me a shove, love, I'm a bit stiff sitting down in the plane for too long. That's it.'

'What did Brian do?' asked Ruaridh when a gap emerged in the one-way conversation.

'He was an 'airdresser. Best in the business, was my Bri. Did all the old duchesses and what not 'cause they knew 'e never put a foot wrong. Cutting the 'air of the great and the good, 'e was. Making a fortune. Well, that's how I met Angelina, wasn't it? Someone recommended my Bri to her and that was it. Stunner, she was in her younger days, but she's still a beauty. What do you think, Roo, Ru, Ru... you know, I can't get my mouth round your name. Don't you 'ave a nickname I could use, son?'

'Well...'

'She's been so good to me. So good,' she said with a quivering lip and a hand on her heart. 'I'd do anything for that woman, *anything*. She 'elped me with Bri right up until the end. She looked after 'im, you see. Wouldn't take anything for it. Frank Sinatra in the background, glass of champers. It's 'ow we'd all like to go, you know. What a send-off for my Bri.'

'And what about her husband, Doctor De Groot?'

Her expression soured. 'Can't stand the little shit.'

# FIVE

'I think the word is eclectic. I've never *met* a more eclectic bunch of people. Wait till Marcie sees them,' said Heather, shuffling glasses and cutlery on a long wooden table that was balanced precariously on grass.

'I prefer the word, *odd.*' Ruaridh dished out spaghetti straight from a large pot onto waiting plates. They were sitting outside on the front lawn of Lochside Croft around a long trestle table covered in a red gingham tablecloth.

'They're in a wee huddle every breakfast. Ms San is checking out in the morning. Hardly eats a thing. Smokes those long brown cheroots out in the car park. The husband only eats salmon. The English woman eats everything in sight but there's not a pick on her. Never stops talking. Even at breakfast this morning, I don't think she took a breath. The other two just nod in agreement or, occasionally, in disagreement.'

'What do they disagree about?' asked Dina, intrigued.

'No idea, there's only so much hovering you can do at a table.'

They sat in silence for a moment as four of the Balfour children slapped each other with strands of spaghetti. Their father was about to intervene when his wife nudged him and shook her head. She was more willing to let them get away with nonsense than their father. He sighed, sat down, and pulled the baby's pram close to him, rocking it while he ate his pasta with his free hand.

'You need to get an invite over for a look. I'm desperate to see what they've done to the place,' suggested Dina.

'Fraser MacRae is still not saying a thing,' Ruaridh replied. 'They must have paid him well otherwise he'd be shouting the odds about how much he's made.'

'Not seen hide nor hair of him at the bar in weeks and that's not like him. I'm usually forcing him out the door at midnight. I've lost count of the times I've had to call his Katie to pick him up – literally.'

That moment they were all distracted by the sound of a helicopter flying low over the water and then hovering above Swanfield on the other side of the loch. The four boys were up and away from the table and down to the shoreline in seconds with whoops of 'look at that!' and 'land here!' The helicopter dipped then took off along the loch and disappeared over the hills beyond. The three friends glanced at each other, curiosity spreading across their faces. They were still looking perplexed when the same helicopter returned and did the same again, only in reverse order.

'Imagine owning one of them. You'd be able to get to the airport in no time,' said Ruaridh, as he went back to rocking his baby asleep.

Dina stroked her husband's arm. 'You'd do yourself out of a job, Mr Chauffeur.'

'Aye, true. But I'd look great in a pilot's uniform.' He winked at her before shoving a huge forkful of spaghetti into his mouth.

Dina raised her eyes to the sky. Ruaridh's biggest cheer-leader was Ruaridh himself. But Dina secretly had to agree; her husband would look fabulous in any type of uniform.

. . .

An hour later, Ruaridh, mostly out of nosiness, found himself at Swanfield. He became annoyed as he watched workmen turn over what remained of the beautiful lawn at the front of the house. They unloaded well-wrapped furniture and white goods into the house. Angelina came out and shooed some of her workforce around the back and directed others in and upstairs. Hands in pockets, whistling, Ruaridh strolled up to her with a smile.

'Aye, aye, Ms San, what time did we say today?' he enquired.

'You're several hours too early.'

'Just wanted to make sure you hadn't changed your mind, and you were still planning on leaving at the same time?'

'If I had changed my mind then I would have called you, Mr Balfour. Be here at four.' She went back into the house, closing the door firmly behind her.

He made a face and decided to take a chance on looking behind the house. What had previously been a long lawn and rose garden were completely pulled out. A paved area stretched down to the far end of the garden, and there was no longer a flower-trimmed arbour, or well-planted seasonal country garden. At the end of what had been the garden, two diggers were hard at work at what had been the start of the wood that led to the old Drovers' Road, which had now been cleared and flattened. An industrial-sized cement mixer was slowly and nosily churning.

Ruaridh recognised the local planner among the workers. He was sure this was the same man who had come out for a final inspection of the four glamping pods which now stood on the land behind Heather's hotel with spectacular views of the water in front and the mountains behind. Ruaridh had also agreed to have two on his land to ensure a little extra income. As he approached, the man quickly folded the plans and put them on the table.

'Mr Balfour, isn't it?' asked the man, hand outstretched in welcome. 'Charlie Mackintosh.'

'Aye, well remembered!' Ruaridh smiled as they exchanged a handshake. 'Busy here, eh?'

'Indeed,' said Charlie as he surveyed the work that was being carried out all around them. One of the local town planners, Charlie was well known for his *extras* and maybe a signature or two if the price was right. He could draw you a plan, critique a plan and approve a plan all at the same meeting.

'So, what's happening here?'

'Just a bit of modernisation and long overdue in my opinion.'

'Swimming pool?' Ruaridh nodded to a large circular area being dug at the far end of the garden where trees had been felled to make a large clearing. 'I mean, what kinda size is that?'

'About thirty-five metres diameter, according to their plans,' explained Charlie, just as the small helicopter that had swooped over Lochside Croft earlier made another appearance. When Ruaridh turned around, he was surprised to see Louis De Groot at the window of the helicopter with an extraordinary long lens, taking an aerial photograph.

'Doesn't like the drive from the airport,' explained Charlie. 'Thinks it's too lumpy.'

Ruaridh shook his head incredulously as the helicopter swirled low over them, scattering leaves and bits of cardboard around like a tornado. Then it took off again and disappeared.

'Must have money to burn if you ask me,' stated Ruaridh.

Not far from them, the large mixer was churning cement, presumably for a helicopter pad.

'Absolutely no expense spared here,' replied Charlie, heading off to continue his work, 'none at all.'

Hands in pockets, Ruaridh strolled back to his car. He felt

another text conversation coming on. Marcie was the third person at the top of his WhatsApp list.

> Hey you! How are things in sunny London?

he texted to Marcie. He watched as reply bubbles appeared on screen.

> Hey you back! All well here, looking forward to coming up for some R&R. How's the weather?

> Dusty

> Dusty?

> All the work going on in your old pad has covered the whole of Strathkin in a layer of dust and concrete.

> ?

> Place is being gutted.

> Yes, the girls told me. Have you seen it?

> Oh, yes! #startledface

> And??

> Oh, it needs to be a surprise!

> Spoilsport!

> You know me.

> See you at the weekend?

> Looking forward to it.

# SIX

On this bright spring day, Marcie and Simon's hire car swooped back and forth as the camber of the road changed on the long drive to Strathkin.

'How long would it have taken if we'd driven the whole way?' asked Simon as he gazed out of the passenger window.

'Days, probably. If you were driving,' responded Marcie, only half joking.

'I like to take in the scenery. The whole experience, it's beautiful – not as beautiful as God's own country, but fine for what it is.' He waited for either something to be thrown at him or a barbed response, but Marcie was too engrossed in her homecoming to even rise to the occasion.

A boy from Yorkshire farming stock, Simon had also grown up in a beautiful wilderness of undulating hills and spectacular coastlines. Even so, he knew there was something special about this part of the world. Not just because it was where his wife was born and raised, but because of the fact Marcie changed when she came here. In the Highlands his wife was a relaxed and calm Marcie, a carefree Marcie away from the confines of her legal career in London. Here she reverted to a sunny, easy-going disposition, far from her London demeanour.

Almost ninety minutes later, Marcie pulled the car into the viewpoint known as the high ridge, a promontory that jutted out of the headland and looked down over Strathpine Glen to Strathkin Loch and the village that encircled it. Swanfield and the wider estate sat on the left with her own cottage, Sweet Briar, sitting in its shadow. Escaping the car, they gazed out at the spectacular scenery opening beneath them as they both absorbed this beautiful day. Marcie's eyes were drawn again to Swanfield and instantly she saw what her friends had been teasing her about. She was suddenly aware of the amount of traffic consisting of trucks, vans, and machinery all around the house. As curiosity got hold of her, she grabbed Simon's hand and raced back to the car. She was both excited for, and slightly dreading, what she would do when she arrived at the house. It had meant so much to her when she was growing up.

'C'mon! I gotta see this!'

Soon afterwards, they arrived at a huge gate that now blocked the entrance to Swanfield. A high wall had been constructed on both sides of the property. The clearly electric gates ensured there would be no casual entry to what now appeared to be a fortress. Marcie climbed out of the car and could hear someone speaking. She initially thought it was coming from behind the twelve-foot-wide gate, and she shouted a 'hello' to whoever was speaking. But then she heard the voice again and realised it came from an intercom panel on a tall post.

'Hello?' she shouted again.

'Hello, can I help you?' asked the remote voice.

'Er... I'm trying to get in?' said Marcie and shrugged her shoulders at her husband, who had got out of the car and stood beside her.

'We have no more deliveries scheduled for today,' said the voice from the panel. 'Goodbye.'

'Er, no, not goodbye. I'm trying to get into *my* house. It's Marcella Mosse. I'm trying to get into Sweet Briar cottage. The house next door?'

'Marcella Grainger,' stated Simon, only half joking. 'You're going to have to get used to it no matter how much you like your own name.' There had been a tussle over the name with Marcie keeping her previous name professionally but had agreed (albeit reluctantly) to take Simon's name for legal documentation.

The gate creaked then smoothly opened, sliding to one side. Marcie and Simon both hastily ran back into the car. As soon as the gate was clear, Marcie put her foot down and took the car into the driveway. She gasped. The front lawn was gone. It had been replaced with several parking places with low lights, all switched on despite the brightness of the day. Individual spaces of light-coloured paving stones each surrounded by low shrubbery now lay where there used to be heathers that signalled the end of the lawn and the start of a gravel path in front of the house. Even from this distance she could see that they had been designed to have low sedum grow over them to disguise them as parking spots but her shaking head and tutting made it obvious that this was not the case. In Marcie's eyes it was simply hideous. A man in a blue overall near the front entrance signalled her to drive forward as if he was marshalling aircraft to a stand. Marcie drove along the side of the house and went to make her way towards Sweet Briar but soon realised that was impossible. A large wall had been built, effectively blocking her tied entrance.

'What the actual...?'

The man in blue overalls pointed her towards a newly constructed road that took her well past Swanfield. She came off this road at the rear of both properties and drove into the back yard of Sweet Briar.

'Flipping heck,' she heard herself say, and then apologised to Simon.

'No need, love. That is properly insane.'

They stepped out of the car and strolled around the yard.

'Well, I knew the guys said there had been changes, but gawd almighty.'

Simon reached deep into the old hydrangea pot to dig out the back door key and they made their way into the kitchen. On the table was a bottle of champagne, and a piece of paper sat between two mugs that said, '*MR & MRS*'.

'Welcome Home' read the note, clearly written in the hand of a young child. There was also an official-looking letter on the table which had been separated out from the usual junk mail. Marcie picked it up and opened it. It was from the solicitors representing the limited company she'd sold Swanfield to, about their plans for refurbishment, highlighting potential noise issues and the fact that the shared entrance was now rescinded. It further stated that if the owner of Sweet Briar wished a new entrance and driveway off the single-track road that ran in front of both houses, then this could be arranged with no expenses incurred by the owner. It was offered as a gesture of goodwill by the new owners of Swanfield, which would soon be known as 'The Retreat'.

'*The Retreat?* What kind of a name is that?' asked Simon over Marcie's shoulder.

'Something that sounds expensive. But why change it? Everyone knows it's Swanfield,' said Marcie, somewhat aggrieved, 'and I don't want a road at the front of my house.'

'Our house,' corrected Simon.

'I like my view!'

'Our view?' Simon sat on the edge of the long kitchen table and pulled his new wife towards him.

'I'm sorry, darling. I'm still in me, me, me mode,' she apologised, and kissed his lips quickly. 'Let's see what our interior designer has done in our new bedroom.'

Marcie smiled and started to race to the stairs. But her new husband made his way back to the countertop.

'I was just going to put the kettle on.'

Marcie shrugged and went to discover what had changed in the rest of the cottage.

A few hours later, Marcie was sitting with her friends around the large table in the alcove of the dining room at The Strathkin Inn.

'It's absolutely gorgeous,' enthused Marcie to Dina, who had been given carte blanche and a large budget to transform Sweet Briar into a stunning country retreat. The house had always been neat but sparsely decorated with nothing frivolous or impractical and desperately needed an injection of both colour and imagination. Dina had well and truly ticked boxes on both counts.

'It's just the way I would have decorated it myself – if I had any imagination,' continued Marcie, giving her friend a tight hug of thanks. When Marcie leaned back, she was struck by a faraway look in her friend's eye. 'Are you all right, Dina? Mari taking it out of you?'

'In truth, I'm exhausted!' Dina sighed. 'Just tired all the time.'

Marcie noticed fatigue in her friend's face and wondered if she could persuade her girlfriends to take Dina's boys to the Balfour lodge at Achmelvich, and perhaps Dina's mother would take Mari overnight and give her friend a rest. She took a mental note and clasped Dina's hand tightly.

Ruaridh sat forwards at the table. 'But you still haven't seen anyone yet?' He directed the question to Simon, sitting opposite him.

'No one, apart from the headless voice that opened the gates for us,' said Simon with a shrug.

'Why do they need big gates like that up here?' asked Heather. 'It's like Fort Knox. I haven't locked my door in who knows how long. Mind you, there's nothing to steal.'

'And what's with a flipping helicopter pad? Trying to do me out of a job!' complained Ruaridh.

'What kind of money are these people making? Have you found out what they do yet?' asked Marcie.

'No idea, but they're due back this weekend. Only Maureen is currently here,' explained Ruaridh.

'Maureen? Who's she?'

'Don't know what Maureen does, to be honest, or why she's involved with the new owners. I can't make head nor tail of where she's coming from, where they're *all* coming from. She was all "my Brian this, my Brian that". I think he died and left her a fortune, something to do with duchesses and stuff,' Heather went on, 'but I switched off after a while. They're just an odd bunch.'

'He was a hairdresser,' said Ruaridh.

'A hairdresser?' asked Marcie. 'How could a hairdresser afford a house like that?'

'Well, it's not hers, is it? She works for them or something. I dunno. I switch off too when she talks but you must admit it's all a bit secretive.'

Silence fell upon the table, until Marcie broke the silence with, 'I'm going in.'

'You're going in?' asked Simon in horror.

'Tomorrow. D-Day. If this Maureen is the only person there now, then I'm going to ask her for a tour. I'm going to knock on the door and I'm going to find out exactly why Swanfield is no longer Swanfield but the flipping "Retreat".'

The friends all shared glances around the table. If Marcie

Mosse was sticking her nose in where it was not wanted, then her friends knew that they would soon be the reluctant participants in whatever scheme she was planning.

# SEVEN

Marcella Mosse had lived in Strathkin all her life. From an early age she knew every nook and cranny of the village. When she moved away, her first stop was Edinburgh University to study law, and then London to be seduced by the bright lights. Her stellar legal career, however, had so far been a series of fits and false starts. She had settled, finally, into a partner position in Steyn and Company in the city and was grateful to her boss Henry for his patience and tolerance over recent events. When she'd taken leave to attend her grandmother's funeral, Marcie and her friends in Strathkin had unfortunately become caught up in a scam to take over her grandmother's estate and manoeuvre her uncle out of his inheritance by both deceit and a sham marriage. In the fall out, one of their friends, Isabella Forrester, Bella, had endured a custodial sentence at the hands of the Scottish justiciary. If there had to be a positive outcome, it had culminated in Marcie and her former schoolfriends becoming closer, if just a little more suspicious of outsiders and, occasionally, of each other.

So, it was with a curious mind that Marcie found herself at the front door of Swanfield the next morning, where she was confronted with an elaborate entry system. She had walked the long way around from her next-door cottage, Sweet Briar, whereas previously she'd have skipped along the back yard where doors always remained unlocked. Village visitors were welcomed with tea, cake and sympathy, no matter the time of day or the issue at hand. Now a startlingly high drystone wall had been constructed, and there was a clear indication from the new owners that unwelcome visitors would be ignored or dismissed.

Marcie pressed a button marked 'E' – could that be for *entry*? – and then she waited and listened. There was no answer. She ran her finger over her lips – a sure sign she was deep in concentration – and pressed the next button marked 'R' – could that be for *reception*? Smiling to herself at her ingenuity, she heard a *click, click, click* of high heels. She was alerted to a whirring sound. She gazed around, then up, and saw a CCTV camera move to take in her full view. For some reason, she waved. While she cursed herself for being stupid, the large new modern door pulled open, and she was faced with a glamorous, but slightly stern-looking woman. Maureen Berman was dressed in a leopard print jumpsuit, cinched at the waist, with an elastic belt that fastened with a large Gucci clasp. Her feet bore matching leopard print high-heeled shoes. Her white hair was immaculately styled, while brown Bulgari sunglasses protected her eyes from the glare of the sun which, Marcie pondered, surely wasn't so bright you needed them indoors.

'Yes, dear?'

'Er, hello...' Marcie realised as soon as she opened her mouth that she hadn't prepared herself for what to say when confronted with her new neighbours. She found her normally agile mind searching for words.

'Macular degeneration,' stated the woman as if reading her visitor's mind.

'Pardon?' replied Marcie.

'My glasses. I have macular degeneration. Dry. And my doctor said I 'ave to protect them at all costs. So, I'm always wearing my glasses. My Brian used to say I was like a film star hiding from the paparazzi day or night. What did you say you wanted?'

'Um, well, I'm Marcella Mosse.'

'I know who you are, dear, though I thought you were Marcie Grainger. Now, what can I help you with?'

Marcie noticed that she had closed the door ever so slightly as if protecting what lay beyond. She was tempted to step forward and put her foot in between the door and the jamb, but something told her this would not endear her to the glamorous Maureen Berman. Instead, she decided on the sympathetic approach, though it didn't come naturally to her lawyerly demeanour.

'I used to live here, you see. Now I'm next door in Sweet Briar.' She noticed Maureen Berman's fixed smile didn't move, though her eyes, behind the glasses, had an expression that said, *hurry up and get this over with.*

Marcie gave a beaming smile. 'I'd just love to see what you've done to the place.'

'Wait 'ere,' ordered the woman on the threshold before she closed the door with a resounding 'thud'.

Marcie listened as she heard the woman's footsteps click away from the door. Next, she heard a one-sided conversation. Could it have been with Angelina San by any chance? She was a woman Marcie desperately wanted to see in the flesh. A few seconds later, she heard the footsteps returning and then the wide door was flung open. Maureen gestured for Marcie to enter the house. She gingerly took a step forward. Once inside, she had to stop herself from releasing a loud gasp.

She stepped into what had previously been a dark vestibule, with a heavy carpet and dark wooden panelling. Now it had a light wooden floor. Instead of dark spindles, a balustrade led up to the first floor. The walls were painted in light vellum, and huge modern pictures and paintings adorned them, with silver framed mirrors casting more light into the hallway than Marcie would ever have thought possible. She followed Maureen Berman into the impressive front room and, this time, she did gasp aloud.

Two huge low-back blue velvet sofas sat on either side of the newly refurbished fireplace. At the window, there was no longer a window seat, but a baby grand piano. Two small tables sat either side of the sofas with huge Chinese-style patterned lamps on each. A fully stocked drinks trolley sat against the wall, which was decorated with embossed gold paper. The room felt vast, stylish, and very expensive. It was a million miles away from the dark and sometimes dreary house she had known since birth. Each piece of furniture had obviously been carefully curated by an expensive interior designer. In fact, money seeped out of every pore of this old house. Marcie was stunned into silence when she gazed around. She was conscious she had not spoken a word to the woman taking her on the tour, and her face obviously relayed the shock that she was experiencing in her old home.

'Can't believe it's the same place, can you?' offered the host of the tour. Marcie watched as she ran her hand along the back of an expensive chair, then brushed her hand the opposite way to ensure absolutely nothing was out of place.

'No,' was all Marcie could manage before Maureen spoke again.

'It's stunning, and I'll be honest, dear, how you could have lived in a place that was straight out of the Victorian era, I'll never know. Mind you, I only saw the pictures. My Brian always said if you surround yourself with beautiful things, you'll feel beautiful inside. He was all for the modern, you know, my Bri. Now, is there anything else, 'cause I'm a busy woman, you see?'

Marcie wondered what was keeping this woman busy. Strathkin was hardly a bustling metropolis.

'Is there any chance of seeing upstairs?' Marcie asked with her pleading eyes and wide smile.

'Hmm, well, I'm not sure. I mean, only this part of the 'ouse would be considered *public*, if you know what I mean.'

'Public?' queried Marcie, intrigued.

'Well, the bedrooms, they're private. I wouldn't let any Tom, Dick or 'arry into my private space. Not since my Brian passed away.'

Marcie imagined there was a wide theatrical wink behind her obscured glasses. She was determined to stand her ground, crossing her arms lightly in defiance.

'Wait 'ere,' demanded Maureen, and she turned and walked purposefully along the corridor.

As soon as the woman walked into what used to be the kitchen, Marcie gingerly placed her foot on the second step, knowing from her teenage years that the first one had a squeaky plank. It was on the third step that Marcie heard the kitchen door suddenly swing open and she sat down on the heavily carpeted stairs with a thump.

'Wot you up to?' quizzed Maureen as she headed Marcie's way, quicker than expected. 'It's private. Upstairs. No go. Cerrado. Wot you doin' sittin' there?'

'Stupidly went for a run this morning and turned over my ankle. Should really see Doctor Mooney while I'm here.' Marcie rubbed her ankle, still sitting on the step. 'Probably needs to be strapped.'

'Oh, you better go soon if you want to see 'im. He's leavin',' said the woman on the bottom stair, eyeing Marcie with some suspicion.

'Leaving?' repeated Marcie. She'd known the family doctor all her life.

'Retirin'.'

'I didn't know.' Marcie wondered if any of her friends knew this information as it certainly hadn't been discussed at their recent get-togethers. As she pondered this news, Maureen let out a heavy sigh, and Marcie decided she should take her leave.

'Well, thank you so much. It's been, er, a revelation.' She forced a warm smile and outstretched her hand to the woman who gave her a weak handshake in return.

As she made her way from the bottom of the stairs, she instinctively turned left to head through the kitchen to the back door, until her guide coughed. Maureen pointed her expertly manicured nail towards the front door.

'Force of habit.' Marcie pulled open the heavy door and stepped out onto the porch. She was about to turn to offer her thanks when she felt the door slam loudly behind her.

Halfway down the new road at the rear of Swanfield, she glanced back to see Maureen watching her from what had been one of the spare rooms at the rear of the property. Marcie suddenly remembered the excuse she'd given and began to pretend-limp. Something strange was definitely going on at Swanfield.


A couple of hours later, in the bar of The Strathkin Inn, Marcie and her two friends sat at a window seat, while out in the car park, Ruaridh tried to calm down his screaming daughter.

'I have to say, it's absolutely stunning and I've only seen the hall. It's so bright. All that dark Victorian wood panelling has gone.' Marcie dipped warm bread into cooling soup. 'You'll not believe it's the same house, D – it'll give you loads of ideas. It's astonishing.'

'Ideas? Looks like I'd need a bank balance to match if I wanted to do anything else at Lochside.' Dina sighed as she stretched out and rubbed her back before leaning forward. 'What else?'

'She's a strange fish though,' said Marcie.

'Angelina San?' asked Heather.

'No, the English woman. There's something odd... can't put my finger on it. But here's the thing, two things, in fact—' She stopped as Ruaridh crept in with his now sleeping child and slipped her into the pram that sat next to his wife. 'Glad you're here,' Marcie whispered. They all leaned in while Marcie disclosed what had been revealed at her visit to Swanfield. 'I think there's something odd going on. She almost barred me from going upstairs. So, we need to get in—'

'What?' asked Dina.

'Ah! Ah! Ah! Whatever you're planning, I'm not getting involved. I was up to my *arsicles* last time in all those strange goings on here and it's not happening again. Nope. No way. I'm out.' Ruaridh sat back, eating the rest of the bread left on his wife's side plate next to her half-eaten soup. He crossed his arms defiantly, shaking his head indicating a resounding *no*.

'I'm just saying what I saw,' explained Marcie as Ruaridh continued to shake his head. 'We need to find out what else they've done.'

'*We?*' repeated Ruaridh.

'I'm desperate to see inside now,' said Heather enthusiastically.

'We need to cultivate an invite and spread out while Maureen Berman is there herself and no one else is around.'

Ruaridh sighed. 'You're doing it again, off on your Miss Marple exploits. Strathkin is just getting back to normal after all that happened and now, you're trying to turn it into *Midsomer Murders*, dare I say, again?'

'You're getting your detectives mixed up, darling.' Dina smiled and patted her husband's hand.

'What's the number two?' asked Ruaridh, resigned.

'Doctor Mooney is retiring,' said Marcie, and from the looks around the table she realised she was imparting news that was a genuine shock to them.

'Stuart Mooney? You're joking?' asked a stunned Heather.

'He did say something about knowing the right time to go last time I saw him,' said Dina, 'but I really didn't take him up on it.'

'When did you see Stuart Mooney?' queried Marcie.

'Oh, couple of weeks ago.' Dina exchanged a glance with her husband and gave him a slight shake of the head.

'Ooh, we could get a gorgeous young thing,' continued Heather excitedly, all thoughts of a raid on Swanfield replaced with a new (*hopefully single*) General Practitioner.

'Focus, people! What do we think is going on in Swanfield? A hotel? They don't look like people who are making it into a family home.'

'No idea. Count me out,' stated Ruaridh, stretching his full frame from the banquette and shoving his hands in his pockets.

'They'd need planning permission to change it into a hotel or something, surely, so I'm sticking with a private home, probably,' said Dina, and they all sat silently for a moment.

'I'd even settle for an older GP, a George Clooney lookalike. Oh, can you imagine?' Heather smiled, chin on her palm, elbow on table.

Marcie, however, was not lost in any reverie. She was wondering one thing: how she was going to get all her friends on board to find out what was going on in her former childhood home. She would not have to wait too long.

Later that day, Heather was still thinking about the retirement of their local General Practitioner as she slowly cleared away empty dishes. The Strathkin Inn was rarely busy on a Monday. It was usual for the chef to have a well-earned rest, leaving pre-prepared meals either blast frozen or refrigerated for anyone who cared to eat either lunch or dinner. Heather retired to the office and peered at her mountain of paperwork. Ally, Heather's right-hand woman, had told her there was only one check-in after eight check-outs that morning. As she twirled her pen through her fingers, her lead bar woman, manager, chambermaid and housekeeper, peered around the door.

'Potential at the bar.' Ally winked, and Heather was off her chair like a greyhound out of the traps, and straight to the counter.

'May I help you, sir?' offered Heather to a man who turned to her.

'Ah! I was looking for a bell or something. I thought you were maybe shut.'

Heather recognised the accent as Irish, soft, with just a gentle lilt.

'Just quiet. Mondays are usually fairly peaceful, as most people will have arrived at the weekend in the Central Belt and will be driving up.'

'Ah, I see, it's too beautiful a place to drive by now, is it not?'

'Well, we're lucky enough to have a great chef so we're more of a destination than a drive by these days.' She found herself tucking her stray hair behind her ear and cocking her head to one side. 'Are you just staying the one night? Ally checked you in okay?'

'Ah, yes, just the one night this time. A flying visit, you could say.'

She noticed a small smart black case sitting at the window table with a jacket over the back of the chair.

'Pilot?' she queried, with an unnoticed glance at his ring finger.

'Oh, no, no, nothing as glamorous as that,' he said with a smile, and she noticed how his eyes creased at the edges. Heather deduced he was in his mid to late forties, even early fifties. He had a well-toned body, well cared for skin and his hair was short and greying.

'I'm a doctor,' he offered, and Heather felt her heart leap. *Well, he certainly could replace Doctor Mooney this afternoon.* She tucked away this piece of knowledge for her next girls' catch up. Getting an early look at Stuart Mooney's replacement would raise her Strathkin currency when she also shared this vital piece of village gossip at the bar later.

'Can I get you anything to drink – orange juice? Sparkling water?'

'Ah, now, I'm not that good, don't really practice what I preach, so I don't. Do you have a local beer?'

'I can give you something from the Black Isle Brewery?'

'Perfect. And can I get you something for yourself?' he offered with a tempting smile.

'Thank you but I'm still trying to get rid of the lockdown poundage.' Heather laughed and slapped her expanded thigh.

'Now, I wouldn't say that. A well-rounded woman is much more appealing.' He winked as Heather handed him a pint glass of Goldfinch, then he turned to head to his table. Heather watched as he pulled paperwork out of the briefcase while he sat down. She smiled to herself, clasped her hands together in prayer, and silently said, 'Thank you, God.'

Heather was disappointed when Ally told her their guest would not be in for dinner, though she imagined that he would be heading to Strathdon to dine with the soon to be retiring local GP and his wife. She'd get a chance to chat with him over breakfast and find out not only his actual start date, but his true marriage status, whether he'd be sharing the tied surgery house with a wife, girlfriend or other, and how many children he'd like to have.

The next morning, Ally was eyeing her boss with suspicion.

'Are you wearing make-up?' she queried.

'Me? Oh, just a wee bit, I felt I was looking a little pasty this morning,' explained Heather, freshly showered with her hair pulled up into a loose bun.

'Shouldn't have bothered. He was leaving when I got in at half seven,' said Ally as she examined the optics closely to see where top-ups were required, with a wry smile at Heather's expense.

'Bollocks.' Heather pulled out the clip so that her hair fell loose over her shoulders and her newly washed and ironed silk top.

'A looker this far north. We should get Jamie to stop him on the road out.' Ally laughed, and Heather joined in while thinking whether she still had local Constable Jamie MacKay's number in her phone. Getting Jamie to do the questioning would save her a lot of time, while she could go straight to the general store for a dusty copy of *Brides* magazine.

Heather was about to head to the kitchen when she heard the back door open. The tall broad figure of Ruaridh Balfour cast a shadow as he entered the hotel carrying a tool belt.

'Your window fixer is here, and it would be a great start to the day to have one of your finest bean-to-cup cappuccinos. Or anything that goes with a bacon roll to be honest,' he pleaded as he affixed the belt to his waist, 'and brown sauce.'

'Thistle and Tweed rooms,' said Heather, 'they're still jamming. I'll bring something up in five.'

'You got make-up on?'

'Yes! I put a bit on this morning to cheer myself up.'

'Just yourself?' asked Ally as she passed with a tray of freshly ironed napkins. 'New man in town.' She winked to Ruaridh.

'Oh aye! New contractor over the road?' he asked, leaning on the lintel of the office door.

'No, I think you'll find he's Doctor Mooney's replacement. New doctor. Sounds Irish.'

'Oh aye, sounds interesting. I'm taking Dina over to the surgery at Strathdon in a wee while, I'll find out the gen. What's your opinion?'

'My opinion is... looks single.'

'Oh, a potential! Age?' said Ruaridh, folding his arms.

'Mid to late forties, could be early fifties, hard to say.' She put her elbows on the desk and cupped her face in her hands. 'Clooney-esque.'

'I'll get the gen from Stuart,' said Ruaridh.

'He wasn't here for dinner, maybe he went over to Strathdon. Left early so he's either over there again or he's heading back down the road. Everything okay with Dina?'

'Och, you know. What can I say?' said Ruaridh and headed to the stairs to get to work on the sticky windows of the Inn.

At the surgery in the small town of Strathdon, Ruaridh was leaning over the surgery counter talking to the receptionist and practice nurse. They were extremely happy to shoot the breeze with the handsome bearded Ruaridh while his wife was with the soon to be retired Doctor Mooney.

'So, you've no idea?' he asked as they eyed him quizzically.

'I thought we were getting a locum from Inverness for the short crossover, but as far as I know it's not been decided yet. I bet we'll probably be the last to know, to be honest,' said the receptionist with the short pink and purple hair whose new look had certainly caused a stir in the Strath. She called to the nurse. 'Trish, did you get a name?'

'Not a peep, but as you say, we're the last to find out anything,' replied Trish with a shrug of her shoulders as the GP's door opened. Dina came out with Stuart Mooney.

'Ah, Ruaridh,' Doctor Mooney greeted with an outstretched

hand, 'good to see you. Any chance of fixing that fence I mentioned to you, at the back of the cottage? Just when you have a minute, of course.'

'Not a problem, doc. I'll get that done before you go. When is that?'

'Well, as far as I know, they're still advertising for my replacement, so I'm not sure it's going to be any time soon! But... who knows!' he said, almost secretively.

'No new doctor heading this way, then?'

'Not that they've told me. It'll be a locum, I'm sure, before we get a permanent GP in the practice, but I keep telling them it's all about fit. You can't just dump anyone in Strathkin. It's a long, long way for a lot of people, a bit far from civilisation for some, so it wouldn't suit everybody. Someone with a family that can settle fully into the area would be the best option.'

'Hmm,' said Ruaridh. He was going to have to break the sad news to Heather that her *potential* was not going to be examining her any time soon after all.

Ruaridh took his wife's hand and squeezed it as they walked to the car at the rear of the surgery. They stopped for a moment, and he scooped her up in a tight embrace.

'Shall we wait till we get home, eh?' he asked close to her ear.

Dina simply replied, 'Let's go to the high ridge,' and opened the car door opposite him. Ruaridh looked over at her beautiful pale face and a tight knot began to form slowly, deep in the pit of his stomach.

# EIGHT

The Retreat classed itself as many things. A respite centre. A sanatorium. A quiet place of reflection. Words meant so many things and it was important to reflect the right tone. Maureen had read that in a marketing book and took to repeating it whenever appropriate and in company she could impress. Presently, as they walked out of the door into the bright sunshine, Maureen had her arms around the shoulders of a woman who had arrived the previous day. She couldn't admit to the woman that she and her husband had been chosen for The Retreat's *soft launch*. But Maureen, ever pragmatic, knew these things had to be done before any *real money* arrived. The woman had been crying but had been calmed down by Maureen's reassuring manner. Maureen released herself and headed back inside, where she met with Doctors De Groot and Moran Maguire in the hallway.

'Well, that was a bit of a surprise, eh? My Brian used to say, always expect the unexpected, Maureen, and you won't be disappointed, and 'e was right.' She crossed her arms and pushed her large dark glasses up her nose.

Moran pushed his hands into his pockets. 'I've dealt with

the paperwork, so, if there's no more required of me, I'll head for a bite of breakfast across the road.'

'How can you eat?' asked Maureen with a look of disdain to the Irishman. 'My Brian 'ad the appetite of an 'orse but even 'e had times when he couldn't eat.'

Doctor De Groot stood silently with his hands clasped behind his back and observed the exchange.

'Well,' replied Moran, 'you see all sorts of things in my profession, Mrs B, and there's not been a moment yet when I've refused an Ulster Fry after a difficult morning.'

'And was this difficult, doctor?' asked De Groot.

'Oh, far from it. All went a bit quicker than we expected so no, not difficult at all. In fact, I'm in no rush to get away this week if you want to tell me when your next arrival is?'

'Maureen?' asked the small bespectacled man.

'Thursday. I think 'e's from your neck of the woods, too.'

Maureen gave a nod to Doctor Maguire. She handed the Irishman a sheet or paper. He took in what it said and handed it to Doctor De Groot.

'All in agreement?' they muttered in confirmation. The elder of the two doctors then turned sharply and walked along the hallway to the dining room, where a light breakfast had been laid out on the sideboard. A young woman dressed in a white nurse's uniform came along the corridor, and Maureen caught her eye.

'Sissy, head up there, will you, darlin'? We need to get the team in, then the 'ousekeeper needs to get clearin' up.'

'That's a bit harsh, is it not?' asked the Irishman as his wide eyes followed the figure of the shapely young nurse heading up the stairway.

'You won't think it 'arsh when you're checking your bank account later, will you, Doctor Maguire?'

'Touché, Mrs B, touché,' he responded with a smile and a

wink, his Irish eyes shining. He picked up the case that was at his feet and headed for the door.

It only took moments for Moran to drive the short journey back to the hotel on the other side of the loch.

'Well, that's a sight for a man of a morning.' He observed Heather McLeod leaning over the bar to pick up her glass of water. She jumped back, red in the face at his comment.

'Oh, thought you'd left!' she said quickly, but her eyes showed that she was pleased to see him returning to the hotel. 'I wondered if you'd simply gone without checking out.'

'Oh, no, no, just a bit of early business. I hope I'm in time for a bit of breakfast?'

'Absolutely, you're the only one here so I'll have the pleasure of cooking that for you. If you want to head to the dining room?'

'I'm quite happy to stay in here.' He walked over to the same seat he'd had the previous day, in the window nook, with a view of the loch and the hills that rose up behind what was now The Retreat.

'I'll get you a menu.'

'I'll save you some time. Don't suppose you have fresh kippers?'

'The freshest!' Heather smiled and headed behind the bar as he slung his jacket over the back of the chair. When she returned, she was carrying a tray of cutlery and crockery and set his table. His eyes were drawn from the house across the water to the woman setting his table.

'So, I didn't catch your name last night apart from "owner"?'

'Heather, Heather McLeod.' She outstretched her hand. He took it and began to shake it, then lifted it to his lips and kissed the back tenderly.

'Pleased to meet you, *Miss* McLeod?'

'Oh, definitely Miss,' she responded before realising she was sounding a bit too eager in her reply.

'Moran, Moran Maguire,' he said softly, and Heather watched as he rearranged his cutlery.

'A leftie?' she remarked.

'Ah, yes, it is indeed a curse, swimming against the tide.'

She smiled at him. 'Back in a sec.' Heather turned to head into the kitchen before stopping and shouting over her shoulder, 'Tea or coffee?'

When he didn't respond, she headed back to his table where he was playing on his phone, and she saw the familiar red page of the bank *HSBC* flashing to life on his device. Her sudden arrival at his side made him jump slightly and he turned his phone around and set it screen down on the table.

'Coffee or tea?'

'Is there a problem with Wi-Fi here?'

'Er, not normally, just been upgraded. Out there, yes, but here, not so much.' She gestured to the hills and mountains beyond the window.

'Hmm,' he said thoughtfully, glancing back across the water to the house that sat near the bank of the loch.

'So, tea or coffee?'

'Just tea, please, Heather, I'm not a coffee person,' he replied and absentmindedly picked up his phone again.


Moran had decided that if the money promised in payment of his services was not in his bank by ten a.m., he would be back around the loch to The Retreat with strong words for Maureen Berman and an ultimatum for Doctor Louis De Groot.


On the other side of Loch Strathkin, Marcie was hunting through a large cardboard box in her newly refurbished kitchen that was full of miscellaneous items that had yet to find a home. When she finally found the black box she was searching for, she pulled out a pair of ancient binoculars and headed back up the stairs to the window at the end of the hall from which she could see a helicopter, albeit from quite a distance. Its arrival had disturbed them both in bed and Simon had decided to go for a run. Marcie watched a group of people as they carefully exited the aircraft, ducking down as the rotor blades slowly ground to a halt. She noticed that leading the party down the newly laid road was Maureen Berman, walking with a short bespectacled man back along the new road that led to the house next door. After disgorging its passengers, the helicopter lifted off and rose up steadily to head back to its base at Dalcross near Inverness. As this new group neared the back of the house, Marcie strained to hear them talking, opening the window slightly, but the words were taken up by the breeze. She had a flashback of the last time she'd stood observing strange goings on from a window; goings on in this small village that resulted in the untimely deaths of so many residents of Strathkin and the imprisonment of her best friend. Con artist Poytr Medvedev had fled when his deeds were exposed, leaving behind a trail of death and devastation that was still affecting villagers and law enforcement alike. He, the blond and charismatic interloper, posing as Brodie Nairn, had wheedled his way into the lives and dreams of this quiet hamlet and caused havoc. He revelled in sowing division amongst villagers and was still being talked about in hushed tones throughout this part of Wester Ross. Marcie felt a shiver run through her at his memory and shook out her shoulders.

And what of these new neighbours now living next door to her, in her old home? It felt as if there was a new secret society being created, rightly or wrongly, in this quiet part of the Highlands. Marcie wasn't prepared to go through another terrible time of suspicion and deceit. She placed the binoculars in their box on the low dresser and headed back to the front of the house, where she caught sight, through the front window, of a black car heading along the road from Lochside Croft. Probably Ruaridh off to pick up someone from the airport, she mused. It was early, and Marcie thought nothing more of it, heading downstairs to make breakfast in her smart new kitchen.

On the other side of the loch, Sweet Briar was bathed in sunshine on this gentle summer's morning as Dina glanced over the water from the window of her car. On her long drive to Inverness, she thought to herself, how odd it must be to live in a house directly next door to your old home, now full of strangers. That morning, the young children of Lochside Croft had excitedly watched a helicopter arrive and depart from the rear of the property, jumping up and down with glee. Dina had convinced herself that these people were wealthy with celebrity-like status and that's why they could afford to live in such luxury. Her husband had driven them to and from the airport, before they had installed their own air transport hub, and had commented on what an odd bunch of people they were. He'd used the word 'eclectic' – an unusually erudite word for him – but she was too busy in her own thoughts to mull it over too much. Dina was harbouring secrets and that was not normally in her nature; she was usually always open and transparent.

When they'd found out that the most upfront of their quartet of friends, Isabella, had been helping and assisting their Russian invader, Brodie Nairn, it had shocked them to the core. It was Dina who'd stayed connected with Bella when she was sentenced for *Attempting to Pervert the Course of Justice*. Bella had helped Brodie execute his plan without knowing or understanding the full extent of his crimes. He'd evaded justice, but Bella had been given a custodial sentence. Dina had gone to court to see her friend before she was sent away and had supported her with letters and supplies during her incarceration. She'd only made a few visits to the facility that held her in Stirlingshire; Dina was a new mother, and it was just too far away to visit regularly. She knew that Heather had visited once, and Marcie never, making all dealings with her friend through her lawyer, Richard MacInnes.

Before her incarceration, Bella had run the successful Strathkin Trekking Centre. When her prison sentence was delivered, Marcie stepped in to buy the facility. Despite their differences, Marcie must have known in her heart of hearts that if she didn't do so, her best friend's life's work would end up as another derelict and forgotten business. Additionally, this loss of income and loss of local employment would be more acutely felt in the small rural area than it would have in a larger conurbation. Marcie's purchase meant Bella's few staff had been kept on and the business continued, not to flourish, but certainly to keep the wolf from the door. It also meant that Bella could come home and have a job while she settled back into the community having served half of her custodial sentence.

Dina had praised Marcie for this selfless act and, when Bella returned, she hoped they could continue their lives as before as best they could. Dina and Bella had agreed in their last phone call to meet at the station at two o'clock. All her friend wanted as a special request was a McDonald's takeaway before they drove back to Strathkin, and a night in her own bed. It wasn't much to ask, and Dina had agreed to meet her in Inverness, making other secret arrangements for herself during the same trip.

As she pulled into the car park of the large sprawling hospital building just before midday, she steeled herself for what lay ahead and the immense changes she may have to make in the coming days and weeks.

· · ·

Later, when she stood on the concourse at Inverness Railway Station looking around at the concession stands and the shops, as busy, tired travellers milled around her, it was immediately obvious that Bella had changed. She had lost the long mane of hair which had always seemed to define her. Her flowing auburn locks, which had been pinned tightly under a riding hat as she picked up rosette after rosette as a young girl, then medal after medal as she grew up, were now cut short. It had been clear from a young age that she would spend her life in the saddle. Like many brought up in picture-perfect Strathkin, she loved nothing more than an early morning canter along the shore, water splashing up to her bare feet as her horse kicked up stones and pebbles, her own mane catching in the wind.

Now, outside of her recent confined existence, Bella was overwhelmed by how busy the station was. Young travellers with backpacks met couriers that would whisk them away for a hoped for glimpse of Nessie in the deepest loch in Scotland. Older people met relatives with hugs and embraces of joy. Bella checked her watch and decided to walk out to the car park just as she saw Dina make her way towards the information board. They caught each other's eye and Dina rushed over, throwing her arms wide to welcome her friend. Bella responded with a weak cuddle. Dina linked their arms and guided her out to the car park at the rear of the building.

'Couldn't get parked! Isn't that always the way? If you've plenty of time to waste, there are hundreds of spaces!' she said with a broad smile. Bella blinked against the bright sunlight. Dina handed her friend a pair of sunglasses with scraped lenses and a broken arm.

''Fraid it's all I have – can't keep anything good in that house,' she explained of her life with four boys, a new daughter and a clumsy husband.

'Thanks,' offered Bella weakly.

'I hope you don't mind, Bells, but I want to get a big shop while I'm here then we can go and get something to eat?'

'Whatever,' responded Bella, swallowing hard. 'Listen, thanks for coming all this way, I know it's a bit of a trek. I'm so sorry.'

Dina lifted her finger to her lips. 'Ssh. No worries.' Dina smiled then stopped and threw her arms around her friend tightly. This time Bella returned the embrace, and they clung to each other for a moment. When they parted, both had tears running down their cheeks: Bella in relief, Dina in fear.


It wasn't long before the pair found themselves in the car park beneath the golden arches tucking into fast food and dry French fries.

'Was it just awful?' asked Dina, slurping on a milkshake, something she would normally never touch.

'Overall, it wasn't that bad, to be honest. I wasn't in for as long as some of the other women, so I just put my head down. Did a hairdressing course as you can see.'

'Suits you. Trendy,' said Dina, trying to sound convincing at her friend's new style.

'Cornton Vale... it sounds like you're going to a seaside version of Center Parcs, not a women's prison.' Bella sucked on her straw. 'But I just feel so sorry for some of the women who have had such tragedy in their lives and have ended up in a prison for years.'

Dina thought she sounded melancholic and watched as Bella gazed out the window at the cars lining up to be served food through a hatch. 'I don't even like this stuff but all they can talk about is the little things they miss. Taking their children for a Happy Meal as a treat or seeing their parents on a Sunday. I never knew such a place existed, Dina, and certainly never thought I'd end up in one.'

Dina watched as her normally boisterous and entertaining friend sat in silence and divided her fries into little bundles of four.

'I hear Marcie's back,' Bella said finally.

'Yes, just for a holiday,' said Dina simply, realising the concern this must be causing her. 'Look, it's all fine. I didn't tell her I was coming to pick you up, but it'll be okay. I told Heather and she's going to do a nice dinner at the hotel tonight.'

'I don't think I could meet—'

'What did we always say? Rip the plaster off? You're going to have to face her some time – better that we're all there together, is it not? And once you get a glass of sparkle in, it'll be pain free, guaranteed!' joked Dina.

'Haven't had anything to drink in almost a year. I'm better staying off it!'

Dina noticed a tiny spark of her old friend returning. She leaned over and nudged her. Bella took her hand, and they locked eyes.

'I don't have words, Dina, I really don't,' she said with tears in her eyes.

'How about just, *I'm back*?' Dina smiled, and Bella's broken face gave a wide grin in return. Dina held open the paper bag and they threw in their half-eaten meal deals and decided it was time to return home.

# NINE

The high ridge that took in Strathpine Glen overlooked the entire village of Strathkin. The loch that sat at the middle of it, and the mountains beyond, were more spectacular than Arshia Brahmins had expected, and she was glad she had taken the advice of the person who had persuaded her to stop there before driving into the village.

Arshia held her phone up on *panorama* mode and slowly drew it around to capture the vista in front of her. She had experienced several *wow* moments on the drive from the airport and had made several unscheduled stops along the way. She had visited the touristy lunch spot of The Aizle, just off the main road, and dined on some wonderful seafood. She hadn't expected such incredible food in a simple gift shop and café, in what felt like the middle of nowhere. Now she realised it was *here* that was the middle of nowhere, and what a breathtaking middle of nowhere it was. Arshia thought of how she would describe this later to friends. The only thing she could say was it felt as if someone had pulled a dramatic backdrop down on a film set; it was so perfect, so peaceful, so still. Then something caught her eye and drew her vision towards a little white cottage on the side of the loch, adjacent to a shingle beach. It appeared to be a small boy on the water's edge, bent over, picking things up. She smiled. What a place to grow up and live! Why would anyone want to leave such an idyllic and picturesque spot? Arshia scrambled back down to her car parked on the viewing platform and was glad to find she still had a signal on her phone. She texted her thanks to Doctor Stuart Mooney, who had told her where to go for the best view.

Just hours later, in the bar of The Strathkin Inn, Marcie Grainger was nervously nursing her drink. 'I know, *I KNOW*, ripping the plaster off, blah, blah, blah.'

She drank down the rest of her large glass of red wine while Simon, standing with his palm on her back, said '*steady on,*' into her ear. The four friends were soon to be reunited after the most traumatic of circumstances. Marcie, who was the most anxious, waited nervously for Bella to make an appearance.

'That's him!' Heather gestured to the man sitting at the window in the bar lounge with a copy of the *Press and Journal*, slowly sipping on a pint of lager.

'Looks not bad. *Potential*?' asked Dina.

'Could be. No ring.'

Ruaridh, similarly sipping on a pint, leaned on the bar counter and held up his left hand, also ring free. Simon held his left hand up, again ring free.

'Okay! Okay! I get your point,' responded Heather.

'Want me to engage him in conversation?' asked Ruaridh, clearly in an attempt to be helpful.

'Nah, let me have my dreams for now.' Heather pointed to the table in the dining room. 'Let's go through.' They were about to pick up various coats and bags when they were disturbed by a quiet voice behind them.

'Hi, everyone,' said Bella softly.

Marcie was taken aback by her friend's new appearance. Bella was wearing a plain black fitted dress with a string of single pearls at her neckline. Her short hair seemed to be freshly washed and set in a spiky style that showed off long pearl drop earrings. Her frame was thinner, her face slightly drawn. Bella's long hair would normally be up in a messy bun, and she tended to live in casual riding clothes, fleeces, and gilets with high boots. Eyes flitted from side to side as the girls watched each other's reaction. It was Heather who gave in first and approached her friend with a long hug.

'Welcome home, Bells!' she said warmly and stood back. 'You look amazing.'

'Thanks, H.'

Ruaridh was next in the line with a bear hug and held her tight for what felt like an eternity, lifting her off the ground. He winked at her, his eyes smiling. Simon leapt forward and hugged her quickly.

'You're looking well,' was all he managed to say before he stepped back behind his wife, forcing her forward. Bella and Marcie eyed each other warily for a second. Then the ice melted, and they fell into each other's arms.

'There's only so many ways I can say I'm sorry, Mars,' she whispered in her friend's ear, and Marcie gave her an extra squeeze before letting her go. There would always be a tension between them, they both knew that, but for the time being, all animosity was put aside. Heather encouraged them into the dining room. When she glanced back, she noticed that Moran Maguire was straining to look at her friends, and she sighed as she noticed his eyes had followed Bella, and not her.

The dinner was relaxed and friendly. It appeared for a while as if the events from the past year had a veil drawn over them. But as the wine flowed, tensions appeared to lift. Laughter came easily as Bella was updated on life in Strathkin, and Marcie told them about life as a newlywed. Inevitably, conversation turned to what was happening at her former childhood home and the whereabouts of Uncle Callum.

'He is just *so* happy. He's relaxed, he's tanned, he's made loads of friends. He was even working in a bar for a while! A beach bar! Callum? Can you imagine?'

'Well, wasn't it only for a week when someone called in sick?' qualified Simon, and Marcie threw him a disapproving look.

'He's very personable,' said Dina. 'People would love him!'

'His medication is working, there's no need to be home just yet,' finished Marcie and crossed her fingers so that the girls could see. They all gave sighs and thanks, and then watched as Bella leaned around to see Swanfield across the water, quiet and stately in the sunshine.

'I'm pretty sure they're going to turn it into a hotel,' moaned Heather with an exaggerated pouting lip. 'Just when I'm turning some profit, and the coach parties are coming back.'

'I don't think they'd get permission, H, the planning just said refurbishment, modernisation,' reassured Ruaridh with a pat on his friend's hand as it rested next to her wine glass.

'We're just getting back on our feet. I couldn't take it.'

'The place looks great,' Bella agreed, glancing around and seeing the Inn properly for the first time since its remodelling.

'Understated Highland Chic,' continued Heather, with air quotes, and they raised a glass in Dina's honour. They all smiled. Afterwards, Bella announced a toilet break and left the table.

'I'm not sure she wants to talk about what has happened up at the trekking centre,' explained Heather. They all knew Marcie's investment and partial upgrade of the property previously owned by Bella, and now owned by Marcie, would be the one sticking point that could bring their genial dinner to an abrupt end.

'It would have gone bust if I hadn't stepped in. I wanted to help, though I'm sure Bells has other thoughts,' she concluded and took another large gulp of Malbec.

'Bloody knew it!' said Heather, and they all turned to where Bella was engaged in a deep conversation at the bar with Moran Maguire. 'She's only been out of the pokey five minutes.' They all watched as Bella threw her head back, exposing her long, elegant neck and the glistening pearls that enhanced it. Heather put her elbow on the table, rested her chin in her hand and shook her head.

They'd settled quickly into their past routine, but Marcie felt there was something of an undercurrent bubbling under the surface, other than the tension between her and Bella. But she put this feeling to one side and decided whatever it was could wait another day.


The woman in the corner table of the bar laid down her cutlery as she finished her supper. She drank down her glass of Pepsi and left a twenty-pound note on the table. She met the bar manager on the way out and stopped her.

'Can I just check that for Strathdon, I just head back along the road to the junction then take a sharp left up over the hill?' asked the visitor.

'Yup, there's a sign but it's a bit faded so you're straight along that road until you catch the sign for Strathdon and Strath Aullt.'

The woman explained she was visiting a friend from university, and Ally noticed her flawless dark skin, eyes perfectly kohl lined and dazzling white teeth. She was wearing a beautiful light perfume and Ally pondered, *what has happened to bring all these beautifully glamorous people to our sleepy Highland village?* The woman's long, thick, straight black hair was the opposite to her own mousy, home-dyed curls. 'Och well.' She collected the plates from the woman's table, noticing the large tip. She smiled to herself and caught the couple laughing at the bar. Her poor boss – unlucky in love again. She sighed and went to the kitchen to dispose of the crockery.

# TEN

'Peace. Shattered. Again.'

Marcie pulled the thick quilt over her head.

'Is that your hangover speaking?' asked Simon as he sat on the end of the bed and tied up the laces on his running shoes. 'Wine and water in equal parts, I've told you this before.'

'Aargh!' shouted Marcie from beneath the duck down as she heard helicopter rotors slow down and fade to a stop. 'I'm going to speak to Jamie!'

'And say what? Dear Mr Policeman, there are people landing their helicopter on their own land and it's disturbing *my* peace?'

Marcie pulled the quilt down sharply. 'Just go!' she ordered, and when she heard the door close, she slid out of bed. She pulled on a long silk dressing gown and made her way to the back of the house, where the helicopter was once again disgorging people at the end of next door's driveway. From behind her binoculars, she watched a group of about six or seven new guests stroll along the newly tarmacked road. Then she heard a bit of a commotion before a man in a wheelchair was pushed up the drive. Maureen Berman approached them with outstretched arms of welcome. They clearly knew each other, as long hugs and embraces were followed by air kisses and handshakes.

'It's like bloody King's Cross Station,' Marcie said aloud, shaking her head. She stepped back into the shadows as they neared the house until they disappeared inside. Her eyes were suddenly drawn to what was set up in the garden: a large gazebo, and a long table, groaning with fresh flowers, fruit and food. Bottles of champagne and a selection of breads and charcuterie plates were being arranged by a young Asian woman dressed casually in chinos and a polo shirt. *Wedding breakfast? Celebration brunch?* Marcie thought, her curiosity getting the better of her. She decided there was only one thing for it. After a quick shower, she'd call her best friend, who had only yesterday been released from prison, and invite her for morning coffee.


'She's done an amazing job!' enthused Bella as Marcie gave her a quick tour of Sweet Briar. 'Cannot believe it's the same place. It's so light. Wonder what Callum will think?'

'Oh, he's fully up to speed. He likes things fresh and bright, but I just don't think he wanted to change anything while Lisanne was alive. He's had the FaceTime tour. No complaints. But you should see next door.' Marcie poured strong coffee from a French press. 'It's like The Ritz. It's stunning. I don't think they've spared a single penny. I need to try and get in to see it all. Did the girls tell you, though, they're an odd bunch? Can't make out what they do, where they get their money from. There's so many comings and goings. It never stops. And don't start me on that helicopter.'

Bella took a cup from Marcie and walked to the front window. 'Why would they build a huge wall and a big gate?' she pondered and then turned sharply to Marcie. 'You don't think it's *him*?' she continued, wide-eyed with the horror of her incarceration fresh in her mind.

'No. I don't think so, I mean, why would he come back?' asked Marcie, a shiver running down her spine at the thought of a return visit from Brodie Nairn. 'I mean, he wouldn't, would he?'

'He's a *sleekit* bastard, I wouldn't put it past him,' spat out Bella.

Marcie pondered this and then decided it would be in no one's interest for the hustler to come back while he still had a number of outstanding criminal charges against him, all submitted *in absentia.*

'I've had an idea,' said Bella, putting her coffee down on a side table. 'That guy at the bar last night. I'm sure he said he knew the people who have moved in?'

'The new GP? Or at least, Heather thinks – wishes more than thinks – he's the new Stuart Mooney,' replied Marcie.

'No, I don't think so,' pondered Bella. 'Said something about visiting friends in the area before he goes back to Bally-some-thing-or-other in Ireland. He didn't say anything about moving to the thriving metropolis of Strathkin.' They stood for a moment, both now at the window, and gazed down to where a beech hedge used to split the two properties.

'You've got that look, Mars,' said Bella.

'What look?'

'The look that says, *Let's start a detective agency.*'

Marcie raised her brows at her friend and smiled.

'Not at all!' she responded, but they both knew they were each plotting and scheming in their minds.

# ELEVEN

On that beautiful warm morning, around the long, perfectly laid table, under the gazebo at the rear of The Retreat, people tucked into lavish amounts of food while corks popped. It could have been a wedding breakfast, Marcie thought. She was watching proceedings from her bedroom, through binoculars, until she heard an *'Ahem!'* behind her that made her turn around. Bella had changed and was now wearing Marcie's expensive riding gear with tan jodhpurs and tight leather boots showing off her tall slender frame. She wore a fitted hacking jacket and carried a riding crop which she was swinging seductively. Their hatched plot to gently question Doctor Moran Maguire was beginning to fall into place.

'Go get him, tiger!' Marcie laughed as Bella headed out the bedroom door just as Simon entered.

'What the...?' he began. 'Marcie, you're up to something.' Simon watched Bella swaying to the door.

'Moi?' Marcie turned back to the window as Simon peered over her shoulder, and she lifted her binoculars to her eyes.

.   .   .

Bella walked down from the back of Sweet Briar to the gate at the end that took her into previously shared ground. It now ran down the lane to a landing pad for the neighbour's helicopter. She and Marcie had been flitting from front to back rooms to see movement from the Inn across the water. As soon as they saw Doctor Moran Maguire, in the distance, head out to his car, she put their plan into action. Bella quickened her step past the parked helicopter and made her way down to the new road, hearing chatter and laughter drift across the wall from the party beyond. She was striding purposefully when she saw the doctor pull into the drive and park in front of the house. Leaving his car, whistling, he made his way up to the house, glancing up to see who was coming towards him at a speedy walk. It took him a moment to register, and then he pulled his sunglasses down off his nose before letting out a wolf whistle.

'I'd say *top of the morning* to you but it's a bit of a cliché.' Bella beamed as she closed in on him, still swinging her riding crop.

'Now, that could be classed as a dangerous weapon in the wrong hands.' He smiled with a hint of excitement in his voice. 'And where are you coming from this fine morning?'

'Lost my horse. Bolted.'

'Bolted, you say?'

'It's okay, I'm sure he'll find his way back home. I borrowed him from over there,' she said, gesturing to the stables across the loch and squinting in the sun. They were both distracted by laughter coming across the wall as a champagne cork popped.

'Someone's having a nice birthday, I'm sure.'

'You've forgotten your gift,' Bella said and waited for a response.

'Oh, I'm not here for the shindig. Someone in the party isn't well so I'm paying a wee house call.'

'Are you the new Doctor Mooney?'

'I'm sorry, the new *what*?'

'I was sure I was told you were the local doctor?'

'Oh, no, this is a wee bit of a private call, if you know what I mean. Doing a favour for a friend.'

'Ah, I see, well, I'd better be off, try to find that horse before he does a real runner.'

'Now, will you be heading back to the hotel yourself?'

'Probably. Just back in the area after a spot of bother,' she said with a touch of her nose. 'I was a wee bit naughty and *'just out'* if you know what I mean.'

He smiled at her, trying to figure out where she was leading with her chat.

'Prison,' she whispered.

'Ah! A woman like yourself put away, that's a bit wayward, is it not?' He flashed her a wide smile, and she returned it.

'Well, there's naughty and there's naughty.' She winked. 'So, I'm on the lookout for a job that's going to pay well and keep me out of trouble. If your friend needs a hand around this here place, I'm your gal.'

'Now, that's interesting and I'll be sure to mention to them that they can get a fine-Highland woman on the cheap.'

'Oh, I'm anything but cheap.'

With that, Bella turned and walked down the driveway, past the sensor that opened the large gate and headed out on to the single-track road that ran in front of both houses. She knew Marcie would bring her car around later so decided to walk back to the stables pretending to be on the lookout for an imaginary horse.

'And *she* was?' questioned Maureen Berman as she opened the door to the doctor, one eye on him, one eye on the CCTV cameras that sat in a panel behind the lintel.

'A beautiful woman simply searching for her lost horse.'

Moran breezed past her to head to the small sitting room-come-office at the rear of the property.

'Beautiful woman?' Maureen thought quietly to herself. 'Not seen one 'ere yet, have we, Bri?'

Maureen followed him to the back of the house where the office was bathed in morning sun. There the group sat around a small coffee table in large vintage tan leather chairs while Doctor Louis De Groot led an informal meeting.

'Well. Word of mouth. The best advertising one can get, I'm sure you'd agree,' he said.

'If anything,' added Angelina San, sitting directly opposite her husband, 'we're getting a little bit backed up. We have what you would call a *queue*.'

'Well, we can't have that, can we, Angelina? No, we can't. Options – that's what my Bri would say – we need options so that our clients don't decide they need to go elsewhere. I don't see why some people 'ave to stay for days 'n' days – I mean, I know they've paid for it an' all, but it's a business we're runnin' 'ere, not a fancy hotel. Well, it *is* a fancy hotel in their books, but it's all about cash flow at the end of the day. If my Brian were 'ere, I just know he'd—'

Louis held his hand up, and Maureen stopped talking abruptly. She sat back in her chair and glared at the small man.

'Doctor Maguire?' he asked of the doctor sitting next to him.

'Well, I'm only contracted for the certificate, but I can certainly speed up if you're ordering in more of the hard stuff.'

Louis sat back in his seat and pressed his fingers together to make a triangle shape with his hands. His small eyes behind his round spectacles darted back and forth. A young woman, yesterday dressed as a nurse, was today wearing beige chinos and a blue polo shirt. She delivered a tray of iced mango juice to the group on this warm morning and left the room as quickly and silently as she had entered, then returned to her job of serving the guests in the garden.

'Let me think carefully about this, but dealing with *everything* here may be a quicker, cleaner option as you have suggested,' stated Louis, and Maureen Berman gave a nod of *told you so* to the doctor sitting opposite, who winked an Irish eye at her.

Moments later, as they stood in the wide, bright vestibule Maureen sneered as the small man headed out to his car, while the tall, broad, bearded man who had come to collect him to take him to the airport, paced around on the driveway outside.

'You win again, Mrs B,' said Moran as they both watched the small Dutchman climb into the black Range Rover to make his connection for his quick flight to Amsterdam.

'I've told him time and time again, it's all about maximising his profits for minimum outlay but 'e seems to think I live on a different planet, me. It's all about money, we all know that it's 'ow the world turns, as my Bri would say.' Maureen opened the door wide for the Irishman to leave.

Before he could turn around to say what time he would be back later that day, she had unceremoniously shut the door behind him, and he found himself standing on the porch less than twenty minutes after he had arrived.

'And top of the mornin' to you, too, Mrs B,' he said aloud and walked down to his car, pondering how he could attract the services of a long-limbed equestrian into this operation.

# TWELVE

'Surely there must be something you can do?' asked Marcie of Constable Jamie MacKay while the police officer was looking around the large newly refurbished kitchen in astonishment.

'Can't believe this is the same place,' he repeated for the umpteenth time.

'The noise...'

'Firstly, Mars, you don't really live here so I'm not sure how it disturbs you. I mean, I'm sure the Balfour boys just love it!' he said. 'Plus, I did my homework. They *did* apply for planning, although there was no need. The landing site is within the curtilage of the property, it's not obstructed by any obstacle such as trees and more than thirty metres away from their property, and the noise is not excessive I'm told.'

'Who told you?'

'Well, Ruaridh.'

'He lives across the loch; it's directly behind me!'

'*Us*,' corrected Simon from his place leaning on the new heather-coloured Aga.

'I think,' Marcie began, then, '*we* think,' she corrected, 'it's less than five thousand feet over the house – that's against Civil

Aviation Authority rules. I did *my* homework, too.' Marcie crossed her arms in defiance.

'Look, if you're making a formal complaint, I can talk to them but I'm sure they'll just come in the other way over the bank. I'd have thought you'd have tried to get on with your new neighbours instead of raising a complaint before they've got their feet under the table, so to speak.'

'They're odd. There are all sorts going on.'

'Such as?' he enquired with a glance to Simon who was shaking his head.

'Well, I mean, I've only been in the hall so far.'

Jamie shook his head at her then he and Simon burst out laughing.

'Seriously, Mars? You want me to talk to your neighbours about their preferred mode of transport and the fact *they* haven't let *you* see into the house *they* bought?'

'Well, don't you think it's odd? And who has a helicopter pad in this part of the world?'

'You'd be surprised. But it's not a regular house, is it, Mars? It's a flipping great gigantic monstrosity of a house. They could be turning it into a luxurious holiday home like a lot of the old estates up here. I think you're just trying to find an excuse, but for what, I don't know.' He shrugged his shoulders.

Simon cocked his head at Marcie in a gesture of *I told you so* as Jamie drank down the rest of his coffee and picked his hat up off the table.

'But, *but*, just to put your mind at rest, I'll go in, introduce myself, and have a scout around. Even though I have no need to,' he said by way of compromise. He headed to the back door with Marcie following close behind. Once outside in the back yard, however, he was forced to change his mind.

'Ah,' he said as he was confronted with a newly constructed high drystone wall. He turned around to Marcie.

'Barrier, much?' she asked and then followed him back into

Sweet Briar, where he made his way to the front of the house and his 4x4 parked next to her hire car.

'I'll report back, ma'am.' He smiled in resignation, took off his chequered hat and slipped in behind the wheel.

The large gate opened slowly as Maureen Berman reapplied her lipstick, one eye on her mirror and one eye on the CCTV. She watched as the police vehicle snaked up the drive to park in the newly constructed parking spaces at the front of the house.

'Good morning, officer,' Maureen said with a wide smile, 'I've not been up to anything!'

'Good morning, ma'am,' said Jamie with a nod. He took his hat off, tucking it under his arm. 'Nothing to worry about. It's just a courtesy call. There's no main office in the village now so I pop up once a week or so and do my rounds. Just here to introduce myself.' He outstretched his hand, and she took it, shaking it firmly.

'Constable MacKay,' he said in introduction.

'Mrs Berman, Maureen, I'm the housekeeper.' She smiled endearingly. 'Do come in.'

Like others before him, he was taken aback by the changes to the house that used to be dark and dreary and was now light and bright and modern. She took him immediately into the front room, and he glanced up the broad stairs as he stepped in.

'Well, it's a bit of a transformation since my last visit,' he said, his expression of astonishment not lost on his guide.

'Yes, quite. We've spent a lot of money and made some changes.'

'Not half,' was all he managed to say.

'I'd show you around, but we have some friends staying. One of them is a bit poorly so I'd better not give you the grand tour.'

'Oh, absolutely, I understand. A bit of a party in the garden, I heard.'

*Nothing gets past that one next door*, thought Maureen and tucked that thought away for later.

'Well, we've got to enjoy this weather when we get it, 'aven't we? My late husband always said make 'ay when the sun shines, so we thought we'd cheer everyone up with a little garden party. Put a smile on everyone's faces, eh? Know what I mean?'

'Absolutely,' agreed Jamie and fished in his body armour for a calling card. While he was searching, another woman entered the room and approached him.

'Good morning, officer, my name is Angelina San. I'm the owner. It's a pleasure to have you pay a visit.'

'Jamie MacKay,' he responded with a handshake and a smile. 'I was saying to your housekeeper, it's just a courtesy call, nothing to worry about. I go round the villages once a week.'

'How pleasant,' said Angelina with her immovable face.

'Well, I'd better be off then. I'll get the grand tour next time!'

Both women looked at him without responding. He made towards the door to the hall and turned right before Maureen uttered the words, 'Ah, ah, ah!'

'So sorry, force of habit from when it was Swanfield. I noticed you changed the name?'

'Yes, indeed. One must make it one's own and it is our blessed retreat, so it was only natural,' responded the owner.

'Aye, true,' agreed Jamie and headed for the door.

The noise of people chattering drifted down from the top hall, and a small woman in a nurse's uniform quickly came down the stairs, smiled briefly and headed to the rear of the property. His eyes darted around the hallway as he made his way to the door, taking in the newly installed CCTV unit.

'So, ladies, you have my card if you need me for anything –

happy to call back in for a chat or a cuppa, offer security advice or whatever.'

They watched silently as he placed his hat back on his head.

'I'll be sure to keep all of that in mind,' Angelina San said and smiled.

'Likewise,' replied pink-clad Maureen with the matching lipstick. As he made his way to his vehicle, parked haphazardly in the middle of two parking spaces, Angelina turned to Maureen.

'We'll need to keep an eye on him,' she whispered.

'Oh, he'll be fine,' Maureen responded with an exaggerated wave to the policeman as he pulled out and on to the driveway. 'I think it's 'er next door we need to keep our eyes on.'

She closed the door slowly, taking in the CCTV cameras, and particularly the one trained on the back door of Sweet Briar.

# THIRTEEN

GIRLIES ASSEMBLE!

The text pinged simultaneously around Strathkin. Arrangements were quickly made, and afternoon tea agreed to at the stables, well out of the way of prying eyes that may surface at the hotel. Although Isabella was delighted to be back in her own tied house, she knew she was forever indebted to her friend Marcie for keeping the stables and livery going while she served out her custodial sentence. Mismatched mugs of tea and coffee were handed out around the small office and Dina, who still seemed very tired, was encouraged to take the one spare seat. Heather and Marcie took to leaning on the filing cabinets.

'Well?' encouraged Heather.

'Firstly, you've lost your licence in the Strathkin Detective Agency,' stated Bella.

'Eh?' said Heather, seemingly oblivious to what her friend meant.

'He's not the new doctor over at Strathdon. Mr Potential,' stated Bella to the annoyance of Heather.

Heather crossed her arms in disgust. 'Knew it was too good to be true.'

'He appears to be the visiting physician to the new owners at the big house,' said Bella with a flourish.

'Ah, right,' Marcie said, intrigued. 'Interesting.'

'So, could be one of them is ill and he's their personal doctor? I mean, it looks like they've got the money for it?' said Dina, joining in.

'Precisely.' Marcie leaned her elbow on the filing cabinet, resting her chin in the heel of her hand.

'I spoke to Jamie about the helicopter,' she said.

'Not to complain, I hope? The boys love it! I mean, how exciting to have a helicopter flying into your garden. Think of how quick it is to get to the airport now. I think it's amazing.' Dina had a wistful look in her eyes, clearly thinking of the excitement in her house every time the helicopter was heard above them.

'Well, you don't have it flying back and forth over *your* house,' complained Marcie.

'Aw, come on, Mars, what's it been? Three or four times? Join in the fun, eh?' Heather leaned over to give her friend a nudge, but Marcie continued in her sulk.

'Oh, if we're sharing gossip,' Heather went on, 'one of my guests was visiting Stuart Mooney, according to Ally, so maybe she's the new GP?'

'She?' repeated Dina.

'Yaaaas,' Heather replied. 'She, totally gorgeous of course. Young.'

'So, no potential there, then?'

'Well, Moran Maguire is still potential.' Bella winked.

Heather folded her arms. 'Can't believe I saw him first!'

'Ladies!' cut in Dina. 'There's plenty of fish in the sea!'

'Says the woman who bagged Strathkin's most eligible bachelor,' stated Heather. 'Besides, I've been on that dating site. Know who I was matched with? Jamie!'

They all giggled until Bella joined in, and said, 'Me too,' in an almost embarrassed tone, and they all drifted into hysterical laughter.

Peace had most definitely broken out between the four friends after the last few years of trauma. They were settling back into the easy rapport of long known familiarity. But something was still haunting Marcie. Despite the laughter, there was something unsaid in her circle of friends, she sensed it. She eyed them all closely. Bella with her newly cut short hair, her sparkle now returned, welcomed back into the fold with grace. Heather, still searching for her elusive *Mr Potential*, but happy for now as a hotelier with both a growing clientele and bank balance. And Dina. Never changing. Still thinking the best of everyone and still glowing, but now with the ever-tired look of a new mother and a distant expression. Marcie dismissed her concerns and went back to the conversation, which now focused once again on Strathkin's newest trio.

# FOURTEEN

A discussion was taking place in the elegant front drawing room of The Retreat between Angelina San and Maureen Berman.

'You're going to have to speak with them. We can't have that. Arrangements are all in place, Maureen, so people changing their minds at the last minute – it's not on. Once papers are signed there is no going back,' said Angelina, staring outside and not making eye contact with the self-proclaimed housekeeper.

'Oh, we can't 'ave that at all, Angelina, I totally agree. My Brian would always say once you've made your mind up, you've got to stick with it, *and* the consequences, and my Bri was never wrong, as you well know. Never wrong. Leave it with me.'

Maureen turned and marched out of the room, straight up the stairs to where two young women clad in nurse's uniforms, Sissy and Sylvia, were speaking in hushed tones outside the largest room in the house where the door was slightly ajar. Maureen knocked softly, and the group gathered around the bed turned their eyes to the door. The man, who had been celebrating joyously in the garden earlier in the day, was sitting up in bed looking pale and wan. He held the hand of his wife, who seemed strained and worn. The other couple, on the opposite side of the bed, were fatigued. As Maureen walked to the bed, a chink of bottles made her turn around sharply, and as Sissy wheeled in a drinks trolley, she waved her out without breaking her stride.

'And how are we all doing, my darlings?' she asked in a gentle voice, full of care and concern as she took hold of the wife's hand and stroked it gently. Her husband's breathing was rasping as he sat propped up on expensive pillows.

'Oh, Maureen,' the wife began with a glance to her husband.

'Oh, I know, my dear. And how are you, dear? Could you do with a little bit of oxygen there?' asked Maureen reassuringly, while deftly leaning around the woeful wife to press a buzzer situated on the bedside table. Immediately a gentle knock on the door was heard and Sylvia peered in from the hall.

'Be a dear and call Doctor Maguire, would you, nurse? See if we can get our lovely guest here a bit more comfortable, and bring in the oxygen,' she said.

The man's wife smiled at her with grateful eyes and then leaned in. 'Maybe we could have a minute?'

Her sister-in-law and husband left, clinging to each other, tearful and slow moving. A small Filipino nurse wheeled an oxygen tank from behind the patterned screen in the corner of the room and began to place it beside the bed, smiling at the gasping man, with fluttering eyes. His wife kissed the back of his hand and moved towards the window with Maureen following closely behind.

'We've been thinking...' began the woman.

'*We?* Yes, dear?' offered Maureen with a look of concern and slight worry.

'He thinks he's changed his mind. He thinks he'd rather be at home,' began the woman.

'Oh, I see, and who's put that thought into his mind?' asked

Maureen, still with a look of concern but her words betraying a slight air of menace.

'Well, I just think he's beginning to regret not talking this over with the children.'

'Oh, 'as 'e now?' Behind her steely eyes, Maureen's mind was racing.

'Yes, I think he made his mind up in rather a hurry when he was told his, well, final diagnosis, but he's kind of regretting it. It's the children, you see.'

'Oh, darlin', I understand,' said Maureen, taking the woman's hand and gently stroking it in a comforting gesture.

'It's nothing to do with the money, we've got plenty of that. It's just the children.'

'Oh, I *fully* understand, my love, but I think we're getting to the point of no return, you see, and the decision may be out of your lovely man's hands by now. I mean, I've called for our wonderful Doctor Maguire, and it might be up to the physician to say whether he's too ill to be moved. I can really, *really* understand if you want to head back to Gloucester but I think the good doctor might say 'e's now too ill to be transported, so to speak. I mean, we wouldn't want anything to happen to your lovely darling when 'e's up there, would we?' said Maureen, with a thumb facing up towards the sky.

The woman opposite appeared worried at the very thought of her husband breathing his last in a helicopter at ten thousand feet. She bit her lip and turned to see her husband with his oxygen feed now in place.

'I suppose you know best,' the woman said, anxiously glancing over to the bed.

'Oh, no, no, no, my lovely. It's up to our wonderful doctor to decide what's best for you both. I mean, he tended to *my Brian* and what a lovely bedside manner 'e 'as. So gentle, so caring. Let's see what Doctor Maguire 'as to say and we can do whatever 'e decides, how about that? We do want your lovely man to 'ave the best send-off. I'll make sure of it.'

As if on cue, music drifted faintly into the room.

'Oh, Maureen, you do know what's best,' agreed the now less distressed woman, and Maureen led her back to her husband's side.

'All right, lovely?' Maureen asked, patting the man's hand with a reassuring smile before she headed out the door, opening it wide so that the family members outside could return.

She headed down to see the tall Irishman enter the hallway, swinging his black medical bag. He stopped whistling immediately as he caught her admonishing eye.

'What's doing, Mrs B?' he asked in greeting as the nurse closed the door behind him.

'Tip him over. Time for him to leave,' Maureen ordered as she breezed past him. Moran, hands in pockets, raised his eyes. He knew what he was getting into. He was more unscrupulous than most, but even he thought the suggestion from his friend, and possibly accomplice was, as he was prone to say, a little above his pay grade. He knew why people would want to come to The Retreat, and the money that was exchanging hands. But Moran Maguire, as ever, had one eye on his bank balance and another on his personal freedom. While he was willing to play very close to the edge, anything that may make *him* tip over the edge was most definitely out of the question. He made his way up the stairs slowly, down the corridor and he gently knocked the door of the terminally ill man.

# FIFTEEN

Another day, another pick-up at the airport, and from the moment Doctor Louis De Groot inched his way into the car, Ruaridh sensed some tension.

'All okay up at Swanfield, sorry, The Retreat?' Ruaridh apologised.

'It wasn't always called Swanfield, you know,' began De Groot. 'It was Strathkin Lodge in the past. Only changed in the sixties.'

This was news to Ruaridh, and he gave a little sound of surprise. He was intrigued by the way the man spoke, the 's' sounding more like a 'sh', and he mulled this new detail about Swanfield over in his head as they swept through the dappled tree shadows that guided them along the road towards their destination.

'Who owns all this land?' asked De Groot.

'Oh, that's a deep question. Some is owned by landowners who have been here for centuries, some Crown Estate, some by Middle Eastern millionaires, some by the nouveau riche... a *mescla*.' He gave a smug smile, using a word from his son's Spanish homework the night before.

'We own a lot of the land around our new property, but we could do with a bit more. Do you think the previous owner would be amenable to a private sale?'

'Oh, now, if you knew Marcella Mosse, she'd be the only one to answer that question, but as they always say – money talks!' Ruaridh turned to the man whose face did not reveal anything he was thinking. He merely rounded off the conversation with, 'Hmmm.'

Normally music would fill the void but now, a man whose life was surrounded by noise, Ruaridh had taken to switching off the radio. He had been caught unawares on a trip back from the airport on his own by the 'Ashokan Farewell'. The haunting lament had taken him by surprise, and he had switched off the radio, tears almost drowning him as he pulled the car over, resting his head on the steering wheel. Music he and Dina had shared would never escape him. And now, silence descended on the vehicle once more; the rest of the journey contained nothing but dead air.

When Ruaridh pulled the car into Swanfield's driveway, a sensor newly attached to his car automatically opened the gate. They were confronted by what could only be described as a commotion past the garden where a helicopter sat quietly in the distance. Despite Doctor De Groot saying, 'Wait here', as Ruaridh took the car up the drive, he put his foot down to take him closer. When they stopped, the doctor slid out of the car with a look of disdain. Ruaridh remained inside with all the windows open to ensure he caught as much of the conversation as possible.

'I fully understand,' Maureen was saying reassuringly to a very tearful woman who was now quite distraught. 'Why don't we go back inside, and we can all have a nice cup of tea?'

'I need some fresh air!' the woman demanded and pulled herself away.

'Tension always runs high at this time, so it does,' said a tall man Ruaridh recognised from the hotel as Moran Maguire, the doctor Heather and Bella were both interested in. 'I agree with Mrs B, let's all go in and have a nice cuppa, and she might even offer us something a wee bit stronger to get us through the rest of the day. What do you say?'

'I don't want anything. I just want the children to come up and see their father,' cried the woman, now unceremoniously dissolving into Maureen's arms.

'There, there,' reassured the comforter. 'Why don't we have a chat about that, because it wasn't in the original plan. You're staying tonight to be with your lovely husband, are you not? And you're all leaving tomorrow because we have other guests arriving, hmm?'

As soon as Maureen said the words she was on the receiving end of a scowl from De Groot. She hoped Moran would step in.

'I know it was quicker than you expected but it was what he would have wanted now, wasn't it? No pain, no fear, no distress. I think your lovely husband looks peaceful, so I do.'

Ruaridh listened intently to the man's reassuring tone, which sounded like soft butter melting into hot toast. The way he took the woman's hand in his, settled her into something akin to a trance. 'Why don't we all go inside, and you can go and sit with your lovely husband, and I'll come up and see you both in a wee while? We'll get transport organised for ye's all and your children can see their dad tomorrow like it was decided. Now how does that sound to you?'

'Oh, thank you, doctor. Yes, that will be fine,' agreed the woman, now calmed, as she was led back into the house by Maureen.

'Well, that was a close one,' said Moran as he watched the women leave. Doctor De Groot nodded towards the car, where

Ruaridh was busying himself pretending to look for something in the interior, with the visor down on both his and the passenger's side.

Moran strolled casually up to the car, whistling.

'And how are things in Mr Balfour's world?' asked the Irishman through the window as Ruaridh was frantically searching for imaginary items to bluff himself out of the situation.

'Oh, hiya, can't find my keys!'

'Aye, that's always the way, isn't it?' The doctor smiled as he investigated the car, expecting to see the keys hidden in plain sight.

'Are you still at the hotel? We must grab a pint.'

'Ach, I'm not really a mixer.' The doctor tapped on the roof of the car a couple of times. 'Safe trip home now.'

He strolled back to speak to the small Dutch man, who waved a theatrical wave of goodbye. Ruaridh held up his now 'found' keys and switched on the engine to drive back to Lochside Croft.


Marcie stood at her window as the helicopter blades whirred into action and the machine lifted off and drifted over the hills to the back of the house, before disappearing into low wispy cloud. With the windows of Sweet Briar closed there was minimal noise, but it didn't stop Marcie's annoyance at the disturbance of her peace and quiet. That, and some new building work she could hear in the distance, deep in the woods that lay behind both her house and the big house next door. She heard Simon talking and went downstairs where she saw him on the phone. When she entered the lounge, he switched to *speaker*, and Marcie realised it was Ruaridh on the other end of the line.

'Free tonight?' Ruaridh asked, a disembodied voice, as Simon held the phone between them.

'Sure, it is barbecue weather after all,' Marcie hinted.

'Nah, we'll be keeping it inside away from the prying eyes of your neighbours across the water. I think you're right. Something odd about that crowd.'

Marcie flashed her eyes to Simon with a definite look of 'I told you so'.


The Balfour house was its usual controlled chaos. The four boys were delighted at their visitors' appearance and the abundance of food that was on offer, laid out temptingly along the centre of the table. They all had healthy appetites, and nothing would be going to waste. Dina was a firm believer in leftovers being used up for several days afterwards – if, in fact, it hadn't been demolished at its first outing by at least five hungry mouths. Laughter was easy and fun was always at the top of the agenda. Ruaridh and Dina were generous and kind, and that stretched to the four young boys who were all eager to help either set a table or move the used dishes in a conveyer belt to the well-used dishwasher. But on this early summer evening, Marcie noticed a difference in the couple, and she presumed it was simply exhaustion from a lengthy, and difficult, delivery some months ago: Ruaridh's longed-for girl had been eagerly awaited, but Marcie saw a weariness in her friends' young faces that she'd not noticed before. Ruaridh ordered the two women to sit out the clearing up of dirty pots and trays and they gladly left the mess behind.

They made their way out to the blue garden bench seat, the warm sun beating down on the beautiful evening. The sky had taken on a golden hue of pinks and oranges which cast a warm glow over the mountainous landscape. The water in front of them was still and silent and reflective like glass. The brutal dark days of winter now long in the past, the summer was ready to invite in days of never-ending sunshine and warmth. Spring flowers were dying off and buds of azalea and football sized hydrangea that bordered each side of the house were going to burst into life in the coming months. Marcie swilled light pale pink wine around in her glass. She noticed Dina had resorted to the tonic water and lemon she had had early on in her pregnancy to disguise her condition.

'It's lovely wine, you should try some,' Marcie said, explaining that it came direct from a supplier in Provence. 'It's such a beautiful colour. When you open your first bottle then you know summer is truly bedding in.'

'You know we've always talked about ripping the plaster off,' said Dina suddenly, and she turned to look square on at Marcie.

'Please don't tell me you're pregnant again!' joked Marcie and grabbed her friend's hand, squeezing it tight.

'I have cancer,' said Dina firmly.

The statement hit Marcie like a punch straight to the solar plexus. She sat back in the seat and waited for Dina's words to sink in. She gazed down at the hand she held, at the red friend-ship bracelet that wrapped around both women's wrists. They were homemade bands they had worn since their teens. Never one to be short of a word or a quip, Marcie was struck dumb. She felt as if an actual chill had run through her as she looked at this woman opposite her; a new mother and wife of her first love.

'I...' Marcie began before realising she had no words to fit what she wanted to say. They sat for what felt like a century of silence.

'I've told the other girls, but they're all in denial. I asked them not to say. I wanted to tell you myself,' said Dina, so quietly it sounded like a whisper.

The furtive glances, the whispers between them now made sense. She knew there was something bubbling under the surface – and this revelation chilled her to the core. Marcie felt herself nodding, words of comfort swilling around her head, but nothing came out. She was trying to escape the maze in her brain to reassure her friend that, whatever it was, they would get through it together. But still the words didn't come. She felt herself well up with tears of shock, of disbelief, entirely dumb-founded. Pain was written on her face, her finger tracing along her lip line, her comfort tic.

'If we didn't have Mari, I'm not sure they would have found it. I'm waiting for my latest test results from my consultant,' she began, and immediately Marcie felt her face crumple. Tears that had welled up, started to spill from her eyes as they clutched at each other. 'But,' continued Dina, 'unless there has been a dramatic change from my last appointment, it's not good news.'

'What do you mean?'

'It means' – Dina took a deep breath and swallowed hard – 'I was ignoring my symptoms. Thought it was just problems after Mari. She was a difficult birth and, well, I was bleeding a lot. A lot of back pain. Didn't bother going to see Doctor Mooney. Thought it would all settle down. What it means is—'

'I can't believe what I'm hearing. I can't take this in, Dina. I just...' Marcie knew her friend couldn't bring herself to say the words that she dreaded to hear. She covered her mouth with her hand.

'They call ovarian cancer the quiet killer. It's just there lurking in the background pretending to be something else.' Dina sat back on the bench, her other hand covering Marcie's as they clung to each other. 'I was bloated so I cut down on bread. I was bleeding so I thought I had maybe a little tear. Sore back – thought it was lifting Mari and the rest of them. I'm so fatigued but I blamed the birth and the fact, well.' She waved a hand around indicating toys and bikes on the lawn. 'Ruaridh's in denial, too. I've told him we need to speak. We need to talk. To *really* talk. We need to plan.'

Marcie smiled at her friend as she searched for the right words.

'I have money, Dina. I'll go and get the laptop. We can do it together. We can find somewhere we can go. They're discovering new treatments all the time. Didn't they just find out that Viagra can slow down Alzheimer's? That new drug for Multiple Sclerosis that stops people going into hospitals for infusions – it's an oral medicine that was used to treat leukaemia or something. It stabilises people. I read about this stuff all the time since Callum's diagnosis. There's so much available now. There will be something out there for you. I'll find it. I'll research it. We'll go there. I don't care where it is. Germany – aren't the best cancer doctors there? Look at Callum – he's in remission. We'll go. We'll go anywhere. I'll find it, Dina. We'll find it together,' said Marcie, almost pleading with her friend not to give up, talking fast to get all the words out.

Dina gave a weak smile. 'I've spoken with the new doctor. I've spoken with my oncologist. I've investigated all my options. There are none. I have months at best, Mars. Maybe weeks. I don't want to go to a hospice. I want to stay here. I want to take my last breath in Strathkin. The treatment is punishing. I can't do it anymore.'

Marcie gazed at her friend and her perfect face, her ice blue eyes and her thick blonde hair. *How can you have cancer?* she thought to herself. Dina was tired – who wouldn't be with a young family of five to look after? But here, right now, she also appeared as if she was the healthiest woman in the world. For the next few moments, they sat in silence, hands held, as a stillness came over them. The warm breeze encircled both women and calmness descended before the boys made an appearance and noisily headed down to the shore. Ruaridh and Simon came out laughing and joking, with bottles of beer in hand, and strolled down to join the boys on the shingle beach at the end of their lawn.

Marcie wiped her tears away and sniffed as quietly as she could as she released herself from Dina's grip. She sat back on the bench, drinking down her wine in one last gulp. The two friends exchanged a nod of recognition, and Dina stood up and shouted down to her youngest.

'Douglas! Can you help me get the ice cream?'

Both women watched as the youngest of the four boys beat a path to be at her side, with a smiling glance to Marcie, as he headed into the house with his mother, hand in hand.

Marcie bit her lip and walked down to join the group wading in the water at the edge of the shingle beach. She slipped her hand into Simon's, and he gave her fingers a gentle squeeze. She returned the gesture as she turned and caught Ruaridh's eyes. They exchanged a knowing glance until his eyes left hers and he looked away and over the loch. She stared over at Swanfield and for the first time in a long time she felt a real longing to *come home*. To *really* come home.

# SIXTEEN

While things were settling down at The Retreat, everyday problems were still cropping up as the team settled into new working practices, and today was not going well.

'I'd like this not to happen again,' said Angelina to the small group in front of her that composed of the visiting doctor, her housekeeper-come-fixer and Sylvia, one of two women who floated quietly and unseen around the house and who today was in a pristine nurse's uniform.

'Circumstances, Angelina, circumstances. People change their minds, dear. They come here for a bit of a... rest... then things move on. Maybe it's us who need to do a bit more due diligence, know what I mean?'

'Hmm, I don't want it to happen again,' Angelina said firmly as if to emphasise her point, and she watched as the doctor opposite her scrolled on his phone. 'Doctor Maguire? Are you with us?'

'I'm with you, yes, Angelina, I was just checking flights. I'm listening to you for sure, yes,' he said with only a brief glance in her direction. 'I didn't book a return, you see. Wasn't sure how long you needed me or if I was still on probation, so I can either drive back down the road or I can stay over the road a few days now that Louis is back.'

'Doctor De Groot would rather you dealt with the... I don't want to say *messier* side of things.'

'Oh, I wouldn't say *messier*, either, dear,' interjected Maureen. 'Sounds a bit, well, my Brian would say that means *untidy*. And there is *nothing* untidy about *that* side of things. I believe everyone has been delighted. I mean, I'd say we've had some teething problems, and that might continue until we all settle into our routine, wouldn't you say so, doctor?' She turned to look at Moran, who had put down his phone and was gazing over to The Strathkin Inn from the wide windows of the front room of The Retreat.

'I agree, Mrs B. I think we all need a wee bit of time to settle down, so we do. I'm more than happy to stay on until we iron out any of our teething problems, no, *minor issues*, we'll call them. As I say, I'm happy to hang about.'

Moran was more than happy to hang about in Strathkin a bit longer. He had a gambling debt still to be settled back home, and an eye for women – two women in particular, for a start – and he could easily double his money in a week or so at The Retreat, with each *short-term resident* paying a premium to stay in this Scottish paradise. Moran also knew he could do a deal with the owner of the delightful hotel at a reduced rate for the pleasure of his company.

'What are you finding so funny?' asked Maureen suspiciously as a smile graced Moran's lips.

'Oh, just happy with my lot, Mrs B!' Moran responded with a theatrical wink.

Doctor De Groot slipped into the room almost unnoticed. He handed his wife a paper spreadsheet, and both Maureen and Moran exchanged a quick glance as they watched a smile sneak joyfully across her face.

'If you can stay for another week, Doctor Maguire, we will obviously pay you a slight enhancement to your fee.'

'Whatever you desire, Angelina.'

'Maureen, what experience do we have of the ladies in the village?'

'In what way, my lovely?'

'Do you think we could, well, trust any of them for a short-term contract until we are, say, bedded in, or would you rather we bring in one of our own?'

'Oh, definitely our own, Angelina, I wouldn't trust any—'

'Oh, now, wait a minute, Mrs B. Don't write off any of these lovely ladies. I certainly have one in mind,' started Doctor Maguire.

Maureen raised her eyebrows. 'I bet you 'ave.'

'Now, now, Mrs B, I'd say to you to get your mind above your navel but I'm a gentleman, so I am!'

Angelina let out a little laugh until she immediately composed herself.

'Not 'er from the other day?' asked Maureen.

'Well, you see there, Mrs B, she let it slip that she might have been a wee bit of a naughty girl and spent some time at His Majesty's Pleasure, so I'm pretty sure she'd want to keep her nose clean. I'm thinking that she would be an ideal fit.' He observed the two women exchange a look and smiled content-edly. There was plenty of down time in this job and he had already identified several areas outside of camera range where a little assignation could go undetected.

'Let us discuss it later. Meantime, Doctor De Groot would like to discuss the next consignment that he needs a double signature to sign off,' finished Angelina, and Moran saw this as his cue to leave the women to talk in more general terms about the benefits (*or not*) of having a local person on their small, secretive and perfectly vetted team.

Moran left the room with Louis, and they headed to the

office at the back of the property, where he opened a large file to peruse.

'Sometimes the old ways are the best. More easily destroyed. I prefer burning records myself. No trace,' said Louis.

Moran examined the papers with names, addresses, bank details, payments and next of kin notices. He took a mental note to look more closely at these sheets to ensure his name appeared nowhere on them for fear of possible reprisals from upset relatives or family (or worse, law enforcement officials). He watched carefully as Louis put them inside a large envelope and then into his desk on the left-hand side, locking it securely. Moran glanced around briefly, saw a small safe, a set of numbers casually sellotaped to the side, and thought – *easy*.

'I've asked the Balfour chap to take the relatives to the airport and pick up our next guests. The relatives don't want to travel with the body of our guest,' said Louis as he glanced at the ledger in front of him. 'I have no issue with that. No point in asking him to come all the way back here when he can pick up the...' He scanned the diary on his desk, flicking the pages back and forth searching for a name. *How old-fashioned this man is*, thought Moran, who kept everything, including his little black book, on his phone. 'Macintyres,' said Louis finally, 'and then next week we have Mr Lightbody. What a strange name. I understand Mr Bartlett is flying in.'

Maureen Berman came into the room. 'You still 'ere?' she asked the taller of the two doctors.

Moran grinned. 'Just leaving, Mrs B.'

'Did you call Balfour?' asked Louis and Maureen gave a nod.


Ruaridh saw Moran strolling out of the house as he navigated the driveway in the newly washed Range Rover and pulled in just in front of the main door.

He noticed how Moran stared at his clothes. He almost always wore cargo shorts, no matter the season. Ruaridh felt that the man now standing in front of him was about to comment on his casual attire.

'I'm not wearing a uniform, if that's what you're thinking, and that's a hill I'll die on. I'm a loose kinda guy.'

'Here, not at all. I'm just wondering what the widow might think,' said the Irishman then realised he may have said a bit too much.

'Widow?'

'Aye, one of our guests passed away unexpectedly last night.'

'Aw, sorry to hear that. I saw Stuart Mooney earlier. He never said he was over at the big house?'

'Och, I just happened to be here, you know, so everything was tidied up and all. We're all sorted, Ruaridh. Here, this is a nice car, so it is.'

'Am I taking her...?' Ruaridh began.

'Oh no, she and her poor husband are flying back home, but his sister and her husband, they found it a wee bit creepy now, being so close to his body. Hope I'm not speaking out of turn there?'

'No, not at all,' replied Ruaridh, thinking that travelling on *any* long journey in close quarters with the body of a relative would be taboo in his world.

'They're still a wee bit in shock, the sister and her husband, so maybe keep the chat in the car down to the minimum, if you know what I mean? Some people take a wee while to process such a thing, you know?'

'Oh, absolutely. Fully understand,' agreed Ruaridh. It occurred to him that it was strange that a visiting physician just happened to be in the area when someone had died so suddenly. And even stranger that the local GP wasn't involved. Odd things were happening in Strathkin more frequently nowadays, but there was plenty going on in his own life to keep his mind occupied. He would no doubt drop it into the conversation the next time he got together with his gang but was he just being suspicious because Marcie was back in town, and wasn't she always full of questions and sceptical about people's motives for moving to the area? And who would blame her after what they had all gone through.

Ruaridh heard a noise like a clatter and wheels. He realised this must be the removal of the recently deceased guest to the helicopter at the rear of the property. He wondered why they hadn't called Ramsay MacPhee, the local undertakers from Strath Aullt, but was distracted as a couple, clearly in the raw shock of grief, made their way out of the front door, and Moran waved for them to come over to the waiting car.

'I'm sorry for your loss,' Ruaridh said as the couple reached the car, and he extended a hand to the sister of the deceased. She turned to her husband and he enveloped her in his arms and guided her into the rear passenger seat of the car as Ruaridh held the door open, head bowed.

'Sometimes, it's better to say nothing than remind them of their circumstances,' reminded Moran, leaning in close as Ruaridh waited for the couple to climb securely inside.

'Thanks, chief,' Ruaridh replied, and he made his way into the driver's seat to prepare for the journey ahead.


When he reached the airport, with hardly a word exchanged, Ruaridh guided his passengers into Departures. The man passed him two large notes as they made their way, luggage free, straight to the small executive lounge. He didn't check the cash until he went to the coffee concession and was pleasantly surprised at their gesture of goodwill. He didn't particularly enjoy the trips up and down the road that took him away from home, but he was very grateful for this addition to his income, an income which had been more than erratic in the previous months. With Dina's diagnosis, they had taken the hard decision to cut down on guests to the room rental attached to their house, and to their two glamping pods, despite the fact the income was substantial. Even with the able assistance of Ruthie Gillespie, the ex-postmistress, Ruaridh did not want to put extra pressure on his wife as she came to terms with her future. And *their family's* future without her in it. Any extra cash was a welcome addition. It went straight into a ceramic pot in the kitchen that said, *Saving for better days.*

The next flight was early, and Ruaridh was grateful that he would at least be home in daylight. He took the sign that said, 'Macintyre Sisters', and waited at Arrivals for the new guests.

When he returned to Lochside Croft later, dinner had been made and served and the boys were all in the garden, lying on the grass with colouring books, model aircraft and magazines.

'What age, do you think?' asked Dina as she put away dishes and plates that the boys had taken from the dishwasher and piled neatly on the counter.

'Late twenties, early thirties, not far from our age or thereabouts,' replied Ruaridh, taking a lone piece of celery and munching on it as he watched his wife. 'Are you sure I can't...'

'No, I want everything to be exactly the same,' responded Dina as she bent and then reached high to cupboards and units. It was only when she stopped and turned to him that he saw her face was strained and drawn. They looked at each other for a brief second before he scooped her up in his arms, embracing her tightly. He could feel the change in her body and her bones beneath the thin shirt. They hugged for some moments and tears welled up in Ruaridh's eyes as he tried to contain them. They had spent many nights in deep and intense discussions about the future of their children, and their business, and the days they had left, but Ruaridh was still in a mood of denial. He wanted to take Dina away somewhere warm with white sand beaches and swaying palms and gently make love to her under dark skies lit only by bright stars. They had lain in bed night after night discussing their favourite places and what they could do and where they could go. It was, they knew, no more than a fantasy, one that would never be realised. Ruaridh leaned on the counter, his hands holding hers, his fingers entwining her long, elegant artist's fingers. Then he raised them to his mouth, kissing each one in turn.

'What do you think has brought those sisters so far north? Do you think they're here to visit family or do touristy stuff?'

'Dunno,' replied Ruaridh, caught up in his wife's scent, gently running his fingers over her painted but chipped nails.

'What were they wearing? Expensive clothes, no doubt. Everyone who goes there must have money to burn.'

'One of the guests passed away,' said Ruaridh quietly. 'I spoke to the Irish guy, the doctor. They were taking him down the road by helicopter. I took the family to the airport.'

'Imagine dying this far away from home,' Dina sighed and turned to Ruaridh. 'We need to discuss it, darling,' she began until she felt his index finger cover her lips to silence her. She opened her mouth and took his finger in, biting the end playfully. They smiled at each other. 'Just because we push it out of our minds isn't going to make it go away. It's inevitable.'

Ruaridh didn't want to discuss anything that reminded him of his wife's limited time left. He firmly believed that if he didn't bring it up, it was unlikely to happen. He was trying to convince himself that it would just drift off and they would continue to live out their simple, glorious lives in Strathkin. It was a dream that he had long shared with his wife that they would grow old and grey sitting on their blue bench surrounded by grandchildren and dogs.

'What were they called?' Dina asked, bringing him back to her.

'The Macintyre sisters.'

'First names?'

'Dunno, I never really get a first name. I think they like to keep it formal, but they were identical twins, like our two.'

'How marvellous.' Dina smiled. She released herself from him and slowly made for their door and the handmade bench outside that faced across the loch. Ruaridh followed, sitting down and draping his arm over her shoulders, once again feeling her paper-thin skin.

'I wonder what they're doing over there?' asked Dina as they gazed, hands entwined, at Swanfield and the scenery beyond. 'I'd love to meet them. I *love* twins.' Her eyes rested on the two boys lying a few metres from her near the shore. Donald and David had been inseparable from birth, mostly entertaining themselves. She clutched her husband's hand a little tighter and, as she did so, tears began to slip out of his eyes once again. Instead of wiping them away, he simply let them roll down his face until they disappeared into his heavy stubble.

Like Marcie, Bella was astounded at the transformation of Swanfield, a place she had visited almost daily growing up. It now appeared like it had been designed for the pages of *Archi-tectural Digest*. The rooms at the front appeared twice the size after their light and bright refurbishment. The public rooms, as well as the bedrooms, were certainly glossy magazine material, Bella thought as she was guided around the tour by Maureen Berman.

'So, how do people book to stay here? Is it through one of

the accommodation apps?' she inquired of the woman who might soon be her new boss.

Maureen gave her a sideways glance. 'Not exactly, no, dear.'

'I'm quite familiar with the booking systems from when I worked at the stables, plus when I was away in the, well...'

'It's not a hotel. It's a *Retreat*, we call it, dear,' said Maureen.

'We did some online courses so that some of us could get *real* jobs as, well, hairdressers or beauticians, or online travel consultants, or the like when we got released from—'

'Your further education centre, dear,' said the older woman firmly, and she made her way down the broad staircase. A small Filipino woman in chinos and a pale blue polo shirt hurried up the stairs, closely followed by another woman dressed in a pristine white nurse's uniform.

'I'd love to work here, Maureen,' said Bella.

'Mrs Berman,' Maureen corrected.

'It's just so peaceful and lovely and tranquil like a holiday of...'

'Last resort?'

'Excuse me?'

Maureen peered at her watch. 'I've only got till four o'clock, you know. Got people just arrived. Couple of twin sisters visitin' for a look see.'

'Do you want me to sign anything today, that is, if you're happy to take me on? You mentioned an NDA? Is that because it's famous people, or that, who come here?'

'Oh, we get all sorts, dear. A Non-Disclosure Agreement is a very standard piece of paper nowadays. It's not about celebrity or any of that nonsense, although we did have our fair share when we were based somewhere else but, you know 'ow it is, paparazzi and all that palaver. Got no time for that, me.'

Maureen looked at her watch again, then motioned with a nod of the head indicating that Bella should follow her in to the exquisitely furnished front room. She pointed at the large blue sofa facing her. Bella sat down with a smile on her face that displayed her eagerness to join this small team. In the meantime, her eyes surreptitiously darted around to glean whatever information she could about the kind of operation that was being run in the sedate surroundings of this new palatial residence.

'Ever been married, love?' asked Maureen as she sat down opposite Bella. But before she could answer, Maureen had continued the conversation. 'I met my *first* husband, Ronnie, in my local pub. Blond 'air, blue eyes, angelic looking, though my mum always told me about 'is sort. Keep away, she warned me. Saw him watching me, and me best friend Rita, dancing. Of course, in them days it wasn't any of this modern datin' stuff. 'E asked me out, I said yes. We were married within six months.'

Bella felt herself staring at this elegant woman sitting in front of her, legs crossed at the ankles. It was clear she took great care of herself, with an enviable figure for an older lady, and Bella wondered what age she was. Late seventies, early eighties?

'Then it started,' Maureen went on, and Bella leaned in.

'Sorry? What started?'

'What is it they call it nowadays? Some fancy schmancy name they didn't invent when it was 'appening to me and my girls. It was happening to all of us in them days. Told me I embarrassed him in front of his friends for something. I was jokin' but he never forgave me for it.'

The ball suddenly dropped for Bella. 'Coercive control?' she suggested.

'That's the fella!' said Maureen, with a slap of her hands together. 'Well, in them days it was just called beating your wife into submission, weren't it?'

Bella sat back.

'So, one night, I'm coming back from work – I worked at the card factory up Leytonstone – and it's foggy, a real peasouper, and Rita's brother, Lance, he worked the buses, you see, he decided to walk me home for safety's sake. Saw me to my door, a gentleman 'e was, and then he's off. Well, what I got when I got in; he'd got back from work early, 'adn't he? Got it all ways, I did. Had to call in sick, and Rita's on the phone like, *what's wrong with you, girl?* Well, I blurted it out, didn't I? I mean, she never knew up till then 'cause he never hit me on my face, you see. I was very pretty in them days and he wanted to show me off, but my body was just like a blackcurrant jelly, know what I mean?'

Bella listened intently, strangely drawn into a life alien to her own in the western Highlands. She shuffled further forward and, with a nod, encouraged Maureen to continue.

'Next thing I know, Rita's at my door, Lance has been beaten up and 'e's in hospital. What a state 'e was in. Well. It wouldn't take bloody Sherlock Holmes to discover who did it, would it? Rita was distraught. I couldn't believe it; lovely gentleman like that, just doing a girl a favour, seeing her all right.'

Bella noticed the tears welling up in Maureen's eyes and she, too, felt a cloud of emotion settling in the still room. Maureen suddenly stood up, wiped her watery eyes and walked over to the drinks trolley. She took two crystal glasses that were sitting on a silver tray and upturned them. Bella noticed her pressing on a buzzer that was situated on the side table next to the expensive glass trolley.

'I requested this special, you know.' Maureen made an open hand gesture to show Bella the discreet buzzer. 'I said to Angelina, we need something unobtrusive, you know, something discreet. Something to call our staff for a bit of assistance or help and, oh, hello... that were quick.' The door was knocked twice and one of the nurses that Bella had noticed earlier peered around the door.

'Could you get us some ice, and some of the good tonic,

dear?' asked Maureen, and the woman disappeared. 'I think we need a large gin and tonic. Well, I certainly do.'

This time it was Bella who peered at her watch. Though she was keen to get on, she knew that what she was listening to was gold to her best friends; listening to Maureen was akin to listening to an audiobook. The woman who had been summoned by buzzer returned with a tray, refreshed with ice and lemon. She offered the tray firstly to Maureen and then to Bella, who took a sip of the heady concoction of more gin than tonic, and considerably less ice than lemon.

'Sorry, darlin' – where was I? Oh yes! So, next thing, Rita's on the blower inviting me to her parents' anniversary *do* at their 'ouse. Ronnie, well, he was so jealous, so he agrees I can go only if I'm picked up and dropped off by me mum 'n' dad.'

Bella nodded, intrigued by where this lengthy story was going from the woman who had seemingly forgotten to breathe.

'So, we get to Rita's parents', Winston and Elizabeth.' Bella waited while Maureen took a large gulp of gin. 'Turns out, it wasn't an anniversary party, but a wake for Lance. My mum and dad, well, they was beside themselves. They thought Lance was, what did my dad say about him? He thought he was mustard.' Maureen took another large gulp from her crystal glass, and Bella sat waiting in anticipation.

'I had this feeling, you know, in me bones, you ever get that? Like a shiver runs down your spine? I knew there was something up. I asked my dad to not only take me 'ome, but come to the front door with me, and 'e did. Thank gawd.' Another large swallow, and the glass was empty. 'Bottom of the stairs, he was. Two-up two-down we had and there he was – sprawled out. Spreadeagled. Naked as the day he was born. And that would have really got to 'im, you know, 'cause he wasn't exactly well endowed, if you know what I mean? So, he would 'ave been embarrassed for people to see 'im like that. Talk about it in the pub. I mean, I was shocked by what had 'appened but I knew 'e 'ad it coming.'

'What *did* happen?' asked Bella, both horrified and intrigued.

'"Injuries consistent with a fall",' stated Maureen in air quotes. 'That's what was on the coroner's report. A push more like. Rita told me later, that Winston junior, Lance's twin brother, was "seen in the area", but I knew they wouldn't catch 'im. My Ronnie was up to all sorts, 'e was always on the make and I'm sure the Old Bill knew what was what and just wanted 'im out the way.'

'So, he died?'

'Killed,' Maureen said, draining her glass and giving a little hiccup to complete the story.

'That's awful,' said Bella, genuinely horrified at the tale.

'Was it hell-as-like,' stated Maureen with a final nod. 'Deserved everything that 'e 'ad coming to him.'

Bella sat back and thought, no matter what is happening here, this woman deserves to live a better life than she had started with.

'Then I met my Brian,' she started, and Bella sat back with a sigh and waited for the next part of the fascinating life of Maureen Berman. But they were interrupted by a knock on the door, and the tall frame of Moran Maguire leaned in with a beaming smile and a twinkle in his eye.

'Well, there you are, Mrs B! Been searching all around for you, and Sissy tells me you're in here having a wee drink to yourself, so she does!' he laughed.

Bella sank into the sofa and sucked in her stomach as he strode purposefully into the room.

'And who's this? Oh, Isabella, if it's not yourself.'

Bella smiled, slightly embarrassed that he had found her wiping a tear from her eye and with nothing but a full gin in her empty stomach.

'A wee party going on, is it?' he enquired of the two women.

'Just catching up,' said Maureen, and Bella saw her check her watch.

Moran was also glancing at his wrist. Bella was keen to not intrude further. She needed some air and an escape from hearing about what had sounded like a living nightmare for her new employer.

'I was just going.' Bella made to stand up only to feel Moran's hand on her shoulder. With a slight push, he sent her back to her sitting position.

'No need to rush on my account, darlin'.' He gave a theatrical wink and a nod to the woman across from her. 'So, Mrs B... what have we got here with Bella? Is she in with the in-crowd as it were? Baptism of fire? What do you think yourself?'

'What do *you* think, Bella? I know you haven't signed up for anything, but I really think you'd be an asset to our—' Maureen hiccupped rather loudly and excused herself with an embarrassed giggle, then pulled herself together. 'And since you've got previous, you'll be fine in our little group.'

They were interrupted once again, this time by the low drone of rotor blades above as a helicopter began its descent near the back of the house. Bella caught a knowing glance between Maureen and Moran. Maureen then stood up with the slight waviness of someone trying to appear completely sober.

'Bella, get yourself together. We're off to meet a millionaire. Whassisname?'

'Jonathan Bartlett,' said Moran in a stately manner, and he pulled himself up to his over six-foot frame. 'We'd better jump to it, ladies. He's on the clock.'


At the Inn across the water, Heather was on the phone in her office, negotiating with the person on the other end, and becoming increasingly frustrated. She made faces of exasperation to Marcie sitting opposite her. Marcie was playing, unsuccessfully, with a Rubik's cube. Also frustrated at her lack of progress and ability to join the colours up, she tossed the object unceremoniously on the table of piled papers that Heather was leaning her elbows on. She had come to talk about Dina, but Heather's office phone was ringing non-stop.

'It's impossible, I have bookings,' she was saying for the umpteenth time to a caller on the other end of the phone, who was not taking no for an answer. Heather shrugged her shoulders in a gesture of *what else can I do?* when the person said they would speak to someone and call back. Heather insisted there was no point as she couldn't fulfil the request. The call ended abruptly.

'What was *that* all about?' queried Marcie. Heather was engaging in controlled breathing.

'It's the people at Swanfield. They want to borrow Adam for the night.'

'Adam? Why would they want your chef?'

'There's some big shot arriving who wants a seafood feast like we do here, 'cept it's a last-minute request and "they have neither the ingredients nor the wherewithal to accede to his request"!' responded Heather, mimicking the voice of the person who had just called. Both raised their eyes to the ceiling when the phone rang again. Heather stared at the landline and made a face before Marcie reached over and picked it up.

'Good evening, this is The Strathkin Inn,' she said in a fake sultry voice into the handset. 'I see, I see, ah, yes, I understand. Hmm. Ah, uh-huh. Indeed. Well, that seems like it's something we can help you out with. What time?' Marcie gesticulated to Heather to find a pen and paper and started frantically writing on the back of a printed bill when it was placed in front of her.

'Absolutely. Yes, if you email the full, ah, I see, over the phone only, no paper trail, yes, I understand. Cash only. Thank you, no, thank *you*. I'll make sure everything is delivered in a timely fashion. Thank you again. Where's Adam?' asked Marcie as she put the phone down.

'Upstairs, I imagine, having a snoozette, why?'

'He's going to Swanfield to cook for some guy.'

'What?' asked a shocked Heather. 'He can't! We have bookings tonight, not many granted, but...'

'No buts. I've just pimped him out and it'll pay your heating bills for the next couple of months. Get your apron on.'

'What?'

'Hmm, this could be a nice little money earner,' said Marcie as she sat back in the chair and briefly ran the pen around the outline of her lips.

'What have you done?'

'I've just put four figures in your bank account.'

'*Four?*' Heather was astonished. She was still open-mouthed when the door flew open, and a harassed Bella flew in.

'Have you sorted out a chef for tonight?'

'I have done just that!' replied a smug Marcie, and then she asked sharply, 'How did you know?'

'I've just come from the big house. Oh, my gosh. They've offered me a job! And I've got a uniform.' She held up a fabric tote bag, eyes wide with excitement.

'Seriously?' asked Heather.

'What's going on?' asked Marcie.

'Some big shot from London is up and has requested a special meal tonight before leaving tomorrow, or the next day or whatever. I don't know where but because it's a last-minute thing they were completely stumped. They were talking about flying stuff up from his favourite restaurant in London, but I suggested trying here. Apparently, he's minted. I hope you got a deal?'

'I got a five grand deal by pimping out Adam,' said Marcie, biting the end of her pen.

'Seriously? You could have charged ten times that much – I

heard them talking – he would have paid anything! I'm going back shortly so they can show me the ropes or something.'

'You've got a job though, back at the stables?' stated Marcie, thinking of her own new venture as stable owner, with Bella as the manager of the trekking centre in a change of operation.

'You wanted me to find out what was going on, didn't you? Plus, I mean, I'll still be able to do that and when we get down to talking money, if they offer me enough, I might be able to buy you out in a year or so,' said Bella, breathlessly, and with that she left.

'A year or so?' Marcie called after her. 'I don't think it's up for discussion, Bells.'

Alone once more, Marcie and Heather exchanged a glance. 'What the heck was that all about?' asked Marcie.

'I have really no idea what just happened,' said Heather with a stunned look on her face.

'I know we asked her to find out what was going on, but I didn't think she'd jump ship,' Marcie sighed, sinking into the chair.

'I'm going to wake Adam. He's not going to be happy about this, but I'll soften it with a bonus.' Heather patted Marcie's shoulder as she passed. Marcie was about to leave when Isabella reappeared wearing a pair of beige chinos and a blue polo shirt.

'Ta dah! I've been told this is "unobtrusive work wear". Something that blends us into the background according to Mrs B.'

'Mrs B? You've got your foot under the table. I call her the old crone. She's up to something and I'm going to find out what! *You're* going to find out what!' stated Marcie, pointing the pen she had been holding at Bella with a clear determination in her voice.

'Oh now, she's amazing! What a life! I must tell you all about her!' responded Bella enthusiastically and with a broad smile.

'She feels to me like a witch who has infiltrated our village!'

'Mars, I hate to break this to you, but you don't live here. If she's bringing employment back, then that's good enough for me and probably everybody.'

'You've got a job, Bells, you run the stables! I thought you were just going to find out a bit about what was going on – not jump ship.'

'I'm not jumping ship. It's not just you – we *all* want to know what's been happening in the big house since you sold it, so this is ideal as far as I'm concerned. I don't think from what I can see that I'll be working all hours. I'm kind of taking on logistics and operations and stuff, so I'll still be able to pick up my shifts at the livery.'

'Kind of *logistics and operations*? What are they doing over there? I thought it was some sort of exclusive hotel?'

'Well, a kind of luxury resort, I'd say. A respite home for the wealthy as far as I've found out. This guy that's just checked in, he's some sort of millionaire, I think I heard them say. He's away tomorrow morning but back next week, although now they think he might stay on. I don't know if he's up viewing property or catching up with friends or whatnot, but I'll find out all this intel and report back. Then a set of twins turned up. Around our age.' Marcie was perplexed. Bella appeared as high as a kite, speaking faster than a bullet.

'A millionaire? Are they famous, the people going to this respite place?'

'Dunno, Mars, why?'

'All the security cameras and stuff, big gates, it's like trying to get into MI6.'

'I think they're just careful. I mean, after all the things that happened before,' began Bella then stopped, clearly not wanting to bring up what ended with her spending her own time away at His Majesty's pleasure.

'There's something going on,' said Marcie again, pen still

outlining her lips, 'plus we need to talk about Dina. I can't believe you never told me!'

'I know, I know! She swore us to secrecy,' replied a harassed Bella. 'I'll get us together on my next day off. Plan a picnic or something?'

'Yes, but don't put it off! Seriously.'

'I won't. Promise. And if there's something going on I'll find out! Trust me,' she said, and she gave Marcie a brief kiss on the cheek before turning tail and heading for the door.


Marcie walked through the front of the hotel to the main entrance and out into the car park to see her old home across the still water. The new wall was visible even from this distance, but the old house was still standing like a stately old lady, red sandstone glistening in the summer sun. *I'm definitely going to find out what's going on over there, and put a stop to it if it's dodgy*, she thought to herself. Marcie was aware of a feeling that had begun to sweep over her. She knew deep down she probably shouldn't have given in so easily and sold the property to the highest bidder quite as quickly as she did.

# SEVENTEEN

Doctor Stuart Mooney was sitting in Lochside Croft with Doctor Arshia Brahmins. He was preparing to hand over the reins to this young and vibrant woman who had taken up the lease on his long-held but remote GP practice, to enjoy his retirement, spending a year on his forty-seven-foot sailboat, *The Rannoch Rose* in the smooth, warm waters of the Mediterranean. He had paid a crew to sail it from its moorings in the western Highlands all the way to the Portuguese coast. The next scheduled stop was the Atlantic Ocean to the edge of Europe, and through the Straits of Gibraltar to the small port of La Duquesa on the Iberian coast. Now, when he closed his eyes, he could already feel the warm sun soaking into his bones and absorbing as much vitamin D as his body could take. He was lost in his reverie when his colleague asked him the question he was dreading: 'And what do you think, doctor?' He realised he hadn't been listening to a thing she had been saying, in her soft English accent, that he found so soporific.

'Well, now, that depends,' was all he could say in response and cocked his head to one side, a clear invitation for her to speak.

'Well, of course there are some options about end-of-life care...' began Doctor Brahmins.

Dina Balfour stared wide-eyed as she prepared to hear what her options were in what was to be the remaining part of her short life. Ruaridh puffed his cheeks as he let out a long sigh, sitting on the edge of the coffee table, running his wife's fingers through his own. The new doctor, while encouraging, wasn't coming up with any new treatment plan, no new opportunity to allow Dina to be whisked off for trials at a European hospital with experimental drugs to extend her life indefinitely and see her live out her life with children and grandchildren around her. Her cancer was inoperable. Spreading. Invasive. Life limiting. Quiet and deadly. Dina gazed at her husband, who was biting his lip and unusually silent. He'd told the doctors that he was finding it increasingly difficult to play hard with their five boisterous children, instead wanting to grasp them to him at every opportunity. He wanted to feel their young skin against his and never let go. He found himself standing staring into the sleeping face of his young daughter knowing she would never remember the loving face of her own mother as she grew into childhood and adolescence. It was hard to comprehend.

Doctor Mooney couldn't imagine how it must feel: being so enthralled one moment that you wanted to climb to the high ridge and shout to the sky that you were the happiest man in the world, only to have it snatched away. He was pleased to see that the new doctor was sympathetic, compassionate, even affection-ate. She spoke in soft, gentle tones, being open and honest. No point in pretending it wasn't happening – it was. And it would, unfortunately, be sooner rather than later.

When both doctors left, Ruaridh led Dina to their bedroom upstairs in Lochside Croft. There, they clung to each other until tears began drowning them. They tried to speak, to plan out what time they had left, as waves of emotion rolled over them again and they fell into a silence where they communicated by their eyes only. Eyes locked on each other, sharing their deepest thoughts through an almost telepathic bond. Mari slept soundly that afternoon at her grandmother's house and when the boys tumbled in from school, the eldest, Dax, aware but not yet in full knowledge of what was happening, encouraged the boys to dump their schoolbags and help make tea. He took what had been prepared out to a blanket on the lawn by the shore where they were intending to spend their entire summer. He stared up at his parents' open window when he heard a moan and what sounded like a little scream and then ignored it, running to the water's edge. His three younger brothers followed him at pace. He was a deep thinker, like his mother, and he knew it was only a matter of time before he would be taken into his parents' confidence.

Across the water, just two hours later, Bella was helping Adam Logue, the new chef at The Strathkin Inn, set out a spectacular seafood table at The Retreat. Maureen appeared at their side. The buffet table in the dining room was groaning with fresh langoustines, homemade rum-rubbed hot smoked salmon, prawns and local lobster. There was a display of octopus that impressed even Bella.

'What can I say!' Maureen enthused. 'I've never seen the like!' She greedily eyed the expanse of shellfish and licked her lips, the alcohol she had consumed earlier clearly sparking her appetite.

'Best in the world!' said Bella as she watched her new boss's eyes move from platter to platter hungrily.

'Oh, I've no doubt 'e'll be pleased,' Maureen enthused.

They were interrupted by the sudden arrival of Angelina San. She inspected the table like a sergeant major, looked Bella up and down with suspicion, then left the room, clearly indicating to Maureen that she wanted her to follow. Maureen raised her eyes to the ceiling in fake despair and traipsed out after her. Bella heard words being exchanged in the hallway before Maureen walked back into the dining room.

'Okay, it's time for you to skedaddle 'cause none of this is coming back,' she ordered to a bemused Adam.

The chef, who would normally stay to discuss allergies or issues with guests, took one look at Maureen's face and clearly sensed no discussion would be forthcoming. She escorted him to the back of the house and out into the small Strathkin Inn delivery van.

'You're staying,' Maureen said once she'd returned, with a sideways glance to Bella. 'I've got something better for you. But you'll need a little makeover. Follow me.'

Bella found herself quickly trailing after Maureen and around to where the kitchen led off to a newly constructed extension that held a walk-in wardrobe and luxurious shower-room beyond. By the time she caught up with Maureen, the older woman was flicking through the rows of clothes of various colours and sizes. Bella observed outfits that appeared to be like uniforms resembling those worn by nurses and doctors.

Bella eyed Maureen suspiciously as she pulled out a beautiful silver gown that shimmered in the light. She held it up to the younger woman who made a face. 'Nah,' said Maureen. 'That's not going to work.'

'What is it you're trying to do? I'm not really a clothes horse,' Bella said, attempting to make a joke. She presumed she was going to be attending the party that evening, though she would feel more comfortable attending in her own clothes.

'I can see that,' said Maureen and went back to her search. Bella had a sense of nervousness creep over her. While she needed the money of this job, since her release after serving half of her sentence, in the back of her mind she had convinced herself that any misdemeanour could see her back in the line of sight of law enforcement. Until she really knew what was going on in this huge house, and had made sure it was all above board, she was reluctant to get too involved in any of Maureen's schemes.

'I'm really not sure if...' began Bella before Maureen pulled out an iridescent blue jumpsuit.

'Now, that colour with your hair—'

Bella gave an audible gasp as Maureen held the outfit up to her as she faced the mirror. As someone used to living in jodhpurs and dressing down, suddenly seeing herself in something bright and, clearly, extremely expensive almost took her breath away. When Maureen held up a pair of long drop diamante earrings, she decided – no matter what – she was putting this dazzling outfit on and started taking off her polo shirt.

'Oh no, no,' began Maureen as she pulled the outfit away from her new protégé. 'I need you bathed and sparkling clean, then we'll get some make-up on you.' She pointed to a door that Bella remembered as an old cupboard which contained brooms, brushes and buckets.

When she opened the door, she saw that it now held a small but beautifully decorated bathroom with a long mirror, and expensive wallpaper. She quickly stripped out of her working clothes and leapt into the shower where expensive Floris toiletries were attached to the wall in glass bottles. Bella luxuriated for a few moments as the warm water dripped over her shoulders. She drenched her body in liquid extravagance and smoothed out her skin with a rough Japanese washcloth. She briefly thought of her recent communal showering arrangements, and she allowed a small, contented smile to drift across her lips as she absorbed the smell of the exclusive toiletries. She was awakened from her reverie when Maureen knocked on the shower-room door.

'Get a move on, love, 'aven't got all day. We've got a tight schedule here, you know.'

Bella took a huge, fluffy white towel from the cabinet. She closed her eyes briefly to absorb the moment that she might never experience again and stepped out onto the thick mat.

'Out here in five,' Maureen ordered.

Bella stepped out of the shower-room and glanced around. The wardrobe had been pushed aside to reveal a dressing table with showbiz-style bulb lighting surrounding a large mirror. The table in front was scattered with make-up and brushes. She quickly slipped into the jumpsuit and revelled in how it enhanced her figure; Maureen was without doubt correct in her choice of outfit. Within moments, Maureen had also worked her magic on her auburn hair, along with carefully applied make-up, and Bella was astonished at her transformation from ugly duckling to swan in one fell swoop. A pair of strappy silver sandals completed the look.

When Bella stood up, she towered over Maureen who was smiling like a Cheshire cat at the metamorphosis of this local country woman into a red-haired beauty. Bella reached into the pocket of her chinos that she had discarded on the floor and pulled out her mobile phone.

'I'd love a selfie, Maureen. I can't believe what you've done to me,' she said as she fiddled with the password on her phone, unsure that the face ID would recognise her.

'Oh no, no, dear. We don't do photographs here. You must have read that in your contract. My mistake, we usually collect staff mobiles at the door.' Bella watched as the woman's fingers reached out and pushed her hand firmly down then deftly released the phone from her grip. 'Let's put that aside for the moment and remember in the future, we don't do phones here for *any* reason.'

'I don't remember seeing that in the contract. You sort of got me to sign and whisked it away.'

'All in good time, dear. I'll give you a copy at some point. I'm a one-woman HR department, if you don't mind.'

Maureen's voice had changed from genial to steely and hard-shelled, and Bella gave up her phone with a slight gulp. Outside there was noise from the vestibule, and Maureen swiftly turned and left. Bella followed her out and immediately locked eyes with the Irish doctor, Moran, who, even from some feet away, gave her a nod of approval. Bella felt herself blush at this male attention, after such a long time, and made her way to stand next to Maureen, who was now with a group of people, one of whom – a tall, thin blonde – Bella presumed was the new guest's wife.

'Well, it's just a pleasure to be beside such beautiful women, is it not?' stated Moran, whose eyes were firmly fixed on the shimmering blue of Isabella's jumpsuit which enhanced her firm figure.

Bella felt Moran lean towards her and, in her ear, he whispered, 'Will we be seeing each other later?' She felt herself blush and caught Maureen glaring at both her and Moran, which felt like a warning.

'So, what brings you this far north?' Bella asked the pale man to her left side, who was leaning on a very ornate and expensive walking stick. She was aware of glances between Maureen, Angelina and Moran and realised immediately she had put her foot in whatever unknown pact had taken place. She suddenly felt a sharp nip on the skin on her back: another warning from Maureen to not speak until spoken to. Bella forced her lips together, catching Moran's eye as he gave her a slight smile, as if to say, 'I'll explain later.'

Moments later, Bella found herself standing next to the hugely extravagant buffet and it was her turn now to survey the seafood with the eyes of the ever hungry. She found herself next to the man with the stick and she held out her hand.

'I'm so sorry if I've offended you.' She smiled a dazzling

smile. 'I'm new here.' The man took her hand and shook it weakly.

'Absolutely no problem, it's my first time at this, too!' He smiled, and she was curious, unsure of what he meant. 'I noticed you earlier, but can I say, you're as spectacular as Maureen said you'd be. I'm Jonathan Bartlett.'

Bella smiled, cocked her head, and tried to catch Maureen's eye as she flitted around the room showing off her chatty cocktail party conversation.

'Maureen said you're local?'

'Yes, a local. Born and bred here.' She tried again to catch Maureen's eye for a quick chat before she put her foot in it again.

'First time I've been this far north again for a long time. I now wish I'd come by car instead of helicopter. The scenery looks spectacular.'

'I'm sure I can take you out if you wish. I know some lovely secret little coves and bays on the other side of Strath Aullt. Not sure how long you're staying.'

The man looked at her strangely. 'Hmmm, let me think about it. We can discuss later. I'm staying in The Osprey Suite – best in the house, I'm told,' he said with a small smile.

Bella was scooped up by a passing Moran Maguire.

'Can I steal this lovely woman away from you, sir?' said the doctor as Bella found herself spun around and forced to the far end of the buffet table. Moran handed her a plate and surveyed the bountiful, groaning table in front of them.

'I'm not sure the fragrant Maureen has fully briefed you on our mission statement here at The Retreat, Bella, love.'

'Well, I know she took my phone away,' moaned Bella.

'We like to think of The Retreat as the perfect last resort for the wealthy elite who don't want the ignominy of spending their final days hooked up to a machine in an anonymous hospital with staff too busy to call you by your right name.'

'Uh?' Bella was unsure of where the conversation was going or indeed what exactly he meant.

'We like to help people *on their way* – pain free. Give them a good death, you could say. Grant them any last requests. Assist them in fulfilling their desires – if they have any, of course. A bit like that 'Hotel California song' – you can check in, but you never leave... well, you do, but...'

'I thought the song said you can check *out*...'

'It's a play on words, Bella. I'm trying my best to make it sound a bit more appealing, so I am.'

'I'm still really not sure what it's all about.' Bella responded, slightly perplexed. She had to admit he was extremely hand-some, and his well-honed bedside manner was something she was keen to try after her incarceration.

'We help people along. A little cocktail of something special, if you will.'

Bella stood back as suddenly she realised what he was saying, albeit in a roundabout way. 'What? Like Dignitas?' she asked, eyes wide.

'Aye, that'll be the place, so it will. But this is a bit more glamorous, I'd say, a bit more upmarket than a wee room in a nineteen seventies block of flats in Switzerland. This is where the great and the good pay us rather a lot of money to live out their fantasies, you could say, before they shuffle off their mortal coil. I am a *real* doctor, as is Doctor De Groot.'

Bella gazed around slowly and saw the man she had spoken with earlier talking to Maureen and Angelina. His wife had appeared and was speaking to the small nurse she had been introduced to as Sylvia and who was wearing an equally glamorous dress in sparkling silver lurex, the folds clinging close to her petite frame.

'Now,' began Moran, before being interrupted by Bella.

'Is he really that ill?' she asked, catching sight of the man in the mirror in front of her as he joked with her two new bosses.

'Very ill,' said Moran as he, too, followed Bella's gaze to the chatting threesome.

'And he's come here to die?'

'Correct.'

'When?'

'Well, he's hoping in the next day or so. He was coming for a quick look then heading south again but he's had a wee change of heart, so he has,' he said, not taking his eyes off the mirror. 'And it would appear he's taken a bit of a shine to a highland lass.'

Bella turned and stared at him sharply.

'What?'

'He'd like you as his companion before he makes his, let's say, retiral plans,' Moran finished.

Bella watched, eyes wide, as he speared a large piece of hot smoked salmon on his well-filled plate and ate it slowly, savouring every bite.

'I'm not sure I like where this is going.'

'I did a wee bit of digging into you, so I did. We don't just employ anyone here, you know.' He glanced again at the mirror. 'Now, I know the woman who used to live here bought out your trekking centre business across the way there. I'm kinda thinking you'd like it back, would you not?'

'Uh-huh?'

'If you think you can spend a few hours in the company of our Jonathan here, well, that's not entirely out of the question.'

Bella stared up at the handsome doctor, hardly able to believe what he was suggesting.

'*Absolutely* not. That's not my scene, no way,' she said firmly and glanced around at the man they were discussing, who was still talking animatedly with the two women.

'Here, now, don't let's get the wrong impression here, Bella. I'm not asking you to be free and easy with your favours, darlin'.

He's just looking for a bit of company. He'd pay very generously.'

'Let me get this straight. You want me to be his companion? A bit of conversation. Nothing else?' Bella folded her arms indignantly.

'That's not a very ladylike look now, is it? He's after a bit of intelligent company, he's interested in you and I'm thinking you'll both get out of it what you need.'

'Let's get this straight. I will not... I'm not a pros—' she began before Moran's finger covered her lips. She removed it firmly. 'I might have made a big mistake coming here.'

Bella turned to leave before she was grabbed firmly on the wrist by the doctor.

'As I said, I did my research, Bella. Two hundred and eighty-three thousand pounds. That's what your pal Marcella Mosse paid to buy that place across the water, after all your hard work to make it viable before your wee stay in the big playhouse down the road, wasn't it? Our guest is seriously minted and that's a drop in the ocean to a man of his means. You could have your life's work back in your own hands within months, maybe weeks. Days even.'

Bella watched as he forked another piece of salmon into his mouth. To get her stables back from Marcie would be a dream she never thought she could realise. Bella queried the man in question through the mirror opposite her. A bit of gentle companionship over his last days, to offer kindness and compassion, she would clearly consider. *But that was an awful lot of money just for companionship, and she was absolutely* **not** *inclined to let it be anything else.* Her mind began to work overtime. She gazed up directly into Moran's pale blue eyes.

'Let me think about it,' she found herself saying, and even as the words were coming out of her mouth, the good devil on her shoulder was warning her to shut up and make a bid for freedom from this hotel of last resort. The last thing she needed was to get mixed up in illegal activities again. But the thought of owning her stables once more was tempting.

'Don't take too long, eh? There's a good girl,' said Moran to Bella, as, he smiled across the room at Maureen.


Bella stood in front of the mirror, out of her glamorous party clothes and back in her polo shirt and chinos. Thinking how dowdy she appeared now she had returned to workwear, she examined herself closely. *What would it take? Was it only companionship and nothing more? What if he made a proposition to her?* The door opened behind her.

'What kind of operation are you running here, Maureen?'

'Oh, hello, love. That was a nice get-together, wasn't it? Everyone had a lovely time, and I must congratulate you on the marvellous food. Just tremendous—' She was about to continue when Bella cut in.

'I'm not sure what I'm doing here.'

'That's a bit philosophical, Bella, dear.'

'You know what I mean.'

'We all want the perfect life, dear. Only very few of us are blessed with the perfect death.' The two women looked at each other through the mirror before Bella turned and hurriedly left the small dressing room. She made her way to the front door where she pulled forcefully on the long handle. It didn't move the door an inch, and she suddenly felt a rising panic at the thought of being trapped in the house she had known intimately since childhood. Bella pulled and heaved at the handle and the door refused to budge. She stood back, breathing fast and heavy, and was ready to let out a scream in frustration and horror when she heard a loud click. When she turned around, Doctor De Groot was standing with Maureen, who was holding a black remote control, an enigmatic smile gracing her normally pursed lips. Bella heaved the door open wide and rushed to her car. She threw herself into the vehicle she had parked in the front driveway and turned the car so fast, she churned up gravel as the car spun round. At the gate, she waited impatiently, tapping on the steering wheel until it slid silently open to allow her to leave the house that had once emitted openness and warmth and now had a sinister edge.

'Do we have anything to worry about?' asked Louis De Groot of the woman standing next to him, still pointing the remote control at the door.

'Wouldn't have thought so,' responded Maureen. 'She signed so quickly she didn't read the contract, so I'm not worried in the slightest. Nightcap?'

'Don't mind if I do.'


Bella drove to her stables and sat in the car in the courtyard for what felt like hours. Her mind was racing. She knew in her heart of hearts that Marcie had done the right thing in taking over her business during her incarceration. But she wanted it back so much it actually felt like a physical yearning. *How far was she willing to go?* Blindly walking into The Retreat. How foolish was she to think they hadn't done any research? It was like someone had fed them all the information beforehand. *Who would have done that?* Bella turned the car around and drove back into the car park at the front of The Strathkin Inn with such speed that two guests leaving must have expected a Formula 1 driver to slip from the front seat claiming victory. She rushed in and was caught in a melee of patrons leaving the dining room. Eyes scanning, she could see into the lounge bar where she managed to catch a glimpse of Moran leaning over the bar counter and chatting animatedly to Heather. Her friend was throwing her head back and laughing in what Bella recognised as full flirting mode. Bella pushed her way into the busy room, past the milling visitors and guests with several '*excuse mes'* in a raised voice. This caught the attention of the two at the bar, and Moran started to make his way over to her through the throng.

'Can I rescue you?' Moran shouted with an outstretched hand which she batted away.

'I was just chatting with your pal there,' he began. 'We need to have a chat, Bella. I mean, you don't have to do anything you don't want to do. He's a genuine guy, so he is. We need a little talk...'

'I don't want to talk,' Bella said, her mind suddenly a whirl of confusion about her future. She wasn't even aware that he had taken her hand, and she found herself in the long corridor that led off the main building to the rear of the Inn. New luxurious rooms had been built at the back of the Inn, and suddenly Bella was filled with fury about her best friend. *Another injection of cash from Marcie Mosse*, she thought to herself, *wanting to buy up Strathkin bit by bit*. Her own life's work signed away to Marcie. She was outside Bluebell, one of the newly built rooms in the hotel's extension and, hearing a click, she realised it was the proximity card opening the door behind her.

'Let's have a little chat in here, darlin',' said Moran, and Bella found herself stepping into the room.

# EIGHTEEN

The Aizle was a well-known stop-off point on the road to Strathkin, a road that changed from verdant green forest to desolate landscape on the drive from the biggest nearby city of Inverness. It was a welcome break for the weary traveller or a meeting point of choice for those who wanted to get away from village gossip. Marcie was waiting at a window table for Jamie MacKay of the local constabulary while he chatted with the owner about poachers, incomers, and the best way to cook a freshly caught brown trout. He made his way over to Marcie, weaving through the busy café. She smiled as Jamie, tongue skimming his lips, concentrated on not spilling a drop of his freshly made cappuccino. A slice of homemade lemon drizzle cake sat on a plate, resting on top of the wide cup, carried with care.

'I could have helped you with that?' suggested Marcie to her schoolfriend. Jamie steadily put down the cup and saucer, and Marcie watched as he deftly removed the plate with the cake on top. He sighed with a smile at this incredible achievement.

'Made it!' He grinned.

'The rest of your day will go well. Can I suggest you buy a

lottery ticket after that incredible success?' Marcie suggested as he savoured his first bite of the light citrus-scented cake, and he closed his eyes in satisfaction.

'You know this is my mum's recipe?' he offered.

Marcie waited.

'I've nothing for you. Checked them out. All legit.'

'I'm not convinced.'

'I knew you wouldn't be but what else do you want me to do? You sold the house, people bought it, you don't like what they're doing to it. May I suggest... move on.'

'But I...'

'You don't live here, Mars. We have a very delicate balance of happiness and tragedy here. When you appear, you turn that on its head and, well, I for one prefer the fact that I'm the one looking after the good residents of Strathkin. Not you. No offence.'

'None taken.'

'So, you're going to leave us all in peace and allow us to live our new lives out of the shadow of Swanfield?'

'Hmm.'

'I'm not taking that as tacit agreement. They seem okay. I don't know why you can't just let go?'

'Women's intuition,' she stated.

'Women's intuition? Marcie Mosse's intuition or plain jealousy that they've turned that mausoleum into an amazing place, and you sold up before you had the chance to?'

'They bought it for a million over the asking price.'

'And?'

'Don't you think that's a little strange? It's dodgy.'

'Mars, good God! You are the only person that would complain when someone pays over the odds for something. You got a million pounds more than you expected and you're moaning about it? *A million pounds*! That's a lottery win to the rest of us.'

'I'm not moaning, I just find it... intriguing.'

'You're inherently nosy.' He finished his cake, picking up the crumbs.

'Comes with the territory. I'm a lawyer. I have an inbuilt curiosity that's constantly asking questions.'

'You're a nosy besom!' stated Jamie. 'Maybe they wanted to pay that sort of money for remoteness, peace, quiet, solitude. You can't deny them that – who wouldn't want to live here?'

Marcie was unconvinced. 'They've called it The Retreat,' she scoffed with air quotes.

'Well, it is, it's a perfect retreat. Good for them.'

Marcie harrumphed and they began packing up their table, putting their used plates back on to a tray, when her eyes were caught by the couple that were waiting in the queue at the counter.

'Look, it's Bella!' she said to Jamie, who was already making his way over to them.

'Hey, Bells!' called Jamie as he approached the couple.

When the man with Bella turned around, he gave a startled look at the uniformed Jamie.

'Oh, I didn't know you'd be here,' said Bella, shocked at seeing two of her best friends in front of her, with Jamie clearly waiting for an introduction or an explanation.

'Doctor Moran Maguire,' said the tall Irishman, extending his hand to Jamie for a firm handshake, then offering the same hand to Marcie.

'Marcella Mosse,' said Marcie and noticed his tight grip from very soft hands.

'Grainger,' corrected Jamie.

She nudged him. 'Not long married.'

'And is this a meeting or are you being arrested for some misdemeanour, Mrs Grainger?'

'Just a catch up. I live in London, so I make a point of trying to see everyone when I come back up to Swanfield.'

'*Swanfield?*' asked Bella with raised brows.

'Strathkin,' she corrected and shook her head slightly.

'Doctor Maguire works at The Retreat,' stated Bella, clearly trying to move the conversation on.

'Ah, Heather told me *you'd* taken a job there?' asked Jamie.

'News travels fast,' said Bella, and Jamie noticed the quick glance between her two friends.

'And how's that going? Must be strange seeing it all so different?'

'Aye, it's a grand place to work,' interjected Moran and turned to place two cups of coffee on their tray. 'Catch up later, officer? I'm doing a wee bit of showing Bella here the ropes. Not so much a coffee morning as a business meeting.'

'Why would they need a doctor at Swanfield? I mean, The Retreat?' queried Marcie.

'Every grand hotel needs a doctor on call, don't you think?' he replied.

'I didn't think it was a hotel?' asked Marcie.

'Don't go all *lawyerly* on us, Mars,' interjected Bella and, as she turned, she noticed Moran and the tray had moved away, leaving her to pay the cashier. Marcie watched as Bella took her receipt and walked out to the courtyard where most patrons were sitting on this bright and sunny day.

Jamie pointed to his nose. 'Keep out of it, Mrs Grainger,' he said, knowing that it would annoy her. But Marcie was already plotting and planning as they made their way out to the car park and to their respective vehicles, one heading west, one heading south.

Marcie found herself half an hour later sitting in the hotel bar with Heather, who was looking less than cheerful.

'Surely not?' Marcie said.

'Seriously. I think she went with him last night.'

'Surely not,' Marcie repeated.

'We were getting on great, full-on flirting. I was getting all the vibes, then Bella turns up – what a face she had on her – and next thing I see them on CCTV heading to his room. I tell you; I'm not having it.'

Marcie let out a little laugh. 'Heather, what can you do?'

'He's the potential I've been waiting for! She's back five minutes and they're at it in my hotel. MY hotel. MY new rooms. I ought to tell him to move out,' said a very aggrieved hotel owner.

'You can't do that! Be sensible. You said he'd changed to a long-term booking. Could be they were just, er, chatting about her new job.'

'She had bed head when she came out.'

'Ah.' Marcie conceded that her friend was right.

'See?' concluded Heather and she sat back, angrily folding her arms. They were interrupted by the sound of heels on the flagstone floor of the entrance from the car park and both turned to see Maureen tottering into the hotel, large, wide sunglasses affixed to her face. Her head was turning from side to side like an owl searching for prey.

''Allo!' she enquired loudly.

Heather slid off the banquette. 'Hello there!' she greeted Maureen with a fake smile and a tilted head.

'Oh, there you are. Trying to find your friend Isabella. I've been up at that horsey place and she's not around.'

'The trekking centre,' corrected Heather. 'She's not still over the road?'

'No, not supposed to be working today but I need her to do a little job.'

Heather reached into the back pocket of her jeans and deftly pressed some keys and then heard a phone ringing in echo. Maureen held up her large black patent leather handbag.

'I've got 'er phone 'ere, you see,' she said and held the bag to her ear for a second while it rang out, 'or I'd 'ave phoned her meself.'

'I saw her earlier,' said Marcie, joining them. 'She was having coffee up at The Aizle.'

'What's that then?'

'The Aizle – it's a rest stop. A coffee shop type place off the main road. She was with that doctor.'

'What doctor?' both women asked in unison.

'The Irish one.'

'You never told me that!' hissed Heather.

'I never got a minute!' Marcie replied.

'So, when was this then?' asked a clearly aggrieved Maureen.

'Say, about, half an hour ago?'

Maureen left and made her way out to a new Mercedes SUV that had barely any miles on the clock, sliding behind the wheel, then slowly guiding the large vehicle out onto the road. Both women watched in silence as the car disappeared and turned right at the end of the road that led her back to the house across the loch.

'Why has she got Bella's phone?' asked Marcie curiously.

'What is Bella doing up at The Aizle with *my* potential,' sulked Heather.

# NINETEEN

At The Retreat, planning was taking place. Upstairs, a bedroom door opened after a brief knock and Angelina San walked into the large room with a notebook and smiled at the two women who were sitting on the plush window seat gazing out to the loch.

'I've never seen two people so alike.' She smiled, and for the first time in a long time, it was a genuine warm smile. Angelina looked at the twins in front of her, Lucinda and Gemma Macintyre.

'We're identical!' they exclaimed at exactly the same time and in exactly the same tone, their youthful exuberance coming as a bit of a shock to Angelina.

'Which one is...?' she began, and one of the women raised her hand.

'Lucinda!' she said with a large wide-toothed grin.

'You look remarkably...'

'Well,' said both women together and then dissolved into giggles.

'You've got me on a good day,' said Lucinda and cocked her head to one side; suddenly, on closer inspection, Angelina saw the sadness in her eyes, her pale face, and her bony frame.

'I've just come back from India; *we've* just come back from India. I needed some cultural and spiritual wellbeing and some tests, and it hasn't changed my mind. I still want to go.'

'Me, too,' added Gemma with a warm smile towards her sister, and Angelina watched as the two sisters reached out and clasped hands and then turned towards her.

'Erm, hold on,' began Angelina and opened her notebook, flicking through to the marked page that had 'Macintyre, L' listed. 'We have you, Lucinda, but we were only planning on one, er, departure.'

'I'd like to,' began Gemma, 'go at the same time,' said both women together.

Angelina walked over to the wall and picked up a chair, taking it to where the two women were sitting at the window and placing it between them.

'I've watched my sister become more ill and, I mean, you're seeing her on a—'

'Good day,' they both said simultaneously, with a glance to each other, 'and I know I can't carry on without her, so we'd like to go together,' they said in unison.

'But you have nothing wrong with you?' Angelina queried, her eyes turning to Gemma Macintyre.

'No.'

'What age are you?'

'Twenty-nine,' they said together.

Angelina sat back. 'I'm not really sure about this. I mean, you are perfectly healthy, and you have a life-limiting disease?' she asked, her eyes flitting from one then the other.

'Duchenne's Muscular Dystrophy,' they replied together.

'I really do think I have to talk to my husband, Doctor De Groot.'

'Oh, he was here not that long ago,' began Lucinda. 'He said it's... not a problem,' they concluded together, and both sat back, releasing their grip on each other and smiling at the woman opposite them.

'It's not the money. We were left plenty by our parents. We just don't have... anyone else,' they finished and smiled at each other.

'Maybe we should talk over dinner?' suggested Angelina, and both women nodded at her before exchanging glances with each other.

'We'd rather not leave the room,' they said at the same time, 'we love the view.' And with that they both turned in unison and gazed out over the driveway and to the loch beyond. With the windows open, the distant sound of children playing on the shore on the other side of the water could be heard.

'I can certainly have more food sent up,' began Angelina, and then Lucinda pointed to the Inn across the loch.

'Actually, do they do bar meals and stuff?' she enquired.

'Yes, it's not a bad hotel, seasonal food and local ingredients, all the rage I'm told.'

'Should we...?' began Lucinda.

'Venture out?' They smiled at each other. 'Can you call the man who brought us here?'

'Oh, I'm not sure he's available at the moment, but we'll get you over to the Inn if you want to go out?'

'Yes! Please!'

'Now?' asked Angelina.

They both smiled as Angelina stood up and replaced the chair against the wall.

She closed the door quietly behind her and leaned on it with a sigh. She had absolutely no issue whatsoever with helping a terminally ill person over the bridge, but she had severe reservations about killing a fit young woman like Gemma, even if Louis was willing to double his money.

· · ·

Bella stood in the driveway with the keys to the Mercedes purchased by her new employer. She had one simple job to do: take two women for something to eat and bring them back. She was worried about her upcoming decision. Worried about organising a get-together with her girlfriends. Worried about the fact she could easily fall for her Irish doctor, despite her misgivings. She was pacing and tapping the keys against her palm when the two young women, younger than her, stepped out into the bright sunshine.

'Ladies, good afternoon.' Bella smiled broadly at them. 'I understand you want a little trip around the water to sample the delights of our fabulous Inn?'

'Oh yes!' they said in unison, and she opened one door then skipped around the car to the other side and opened the offside door. One of the young women assisted the other to climb into the back of the SUV, and Bella took in the fact that she was, on closer look, quite painfully thin and, despite being identical to her sister, her eyes appeared almost hollow compared to the one who slid into the back seat to be with her. Bella closed the door after the women were settled and climbed into the driver's seat.

'I didn't catch your names?'

'Gemma.'

'Lucinda,' said the weaker one of the two, and Bella suddenly had a feeling of dread in her stomach and a shiver ran over her.

'Isabella – Bella.' She smiled through the rear-view mirror, but the girls were locked in a silent conversation. Bella swallowed hard as she pulled the car through the open gates and out on to the single-track road.

Bella had called ahead to make sure there was a table waiting and that a full menu would be available, but she wasn't expecting an invite to join the women for a meal. She tried to protest but they insisted she take a seat at their table. She felt uncomfortable at this arrangement and felt even more awkward when, after Ally showed them to their extended table for three, it was Heather who came out with the menus. She smiled at the two guests and then tossed the third menu on to the table setting in front of her.

'Drinks?'

'Water,' said the girls in tandem, and Heather left to get their order.

'Excuse me a second.' Bella smiled at the twins and headed off after Heather to meet her at the bar.

'Listen,' she began.

'I can't have anything of my own, can I?' asked Heather while pressing the water button on the water fountain.

'I know you saw us, and...'

'I don't want to talk about it,' replied Heather firmly, placing all three glasses, and a jug, on a tray.

'It was just a thing, nothing really happened.'

Heather pointed to the CCTV at the back of the bar and specifically to the camera that watched the corridor on the next extension.

'Ah.' Bella sighed guiltily.

'You're only back five minutes and you've bagged the only decent thing I've seen in years, new pals, new job.'

'Heather,' Bella said and reached her hand out to pat the top of her friend's hand in a conciliatory manner, but Heather snatched it away. She looked towards the table where the twin sisters were animatedly talking. Bella took this as her cue to return to the restaurant.

'If it's not Marcie coming up here and turning our lives upside down, it's Isabella muscling in on my life. I can't catch a break.' When Heather came out from behind the bar, she stepped right into the path of Doctor Moran Maguire who had appeared from the rear car park.

'Now, are you talking to anyone in particular, Heather, or just having a wee moan to yourself about life in general?' Moran smiled with a casual wink, in effect blocking her way as he leaned on the bar over the hatch.

'Maybe you and I should have a drink tonight, get to know each other a bit better,' she suggested, the words out before she could stop herself.

'Now, that sounds like a wee plan I could talk myself into, Heather, so I could.' He smiled at her and she thought to herself, 'I'll sort you out, Forrester,' and brushed past him, swaying her way into the restaurant, glasses and jug carefully balancing on the tray and on an ever so slightly shaking hand.


In the restaurant, the twins were talking animatedly, giggling and finishing each other's sentences. Bella was intrigued and completely drawn in by them. Their skin was a pale white, almost translucent, and their eyes were wide. She did, however, notice a marked difference in the two women, despite being identical twins. Lucinda was ever so slightly bent over as if being pushed from behind, and every so often she took such a large breath that Bella thought she was struggling to inhale the air around her. Although the two women were chatting and laughing with Bella about fashion and holidays and houses over-seas, there was an overarching sense that they were in such a buoyant mood because something was hanging over them that they didn't want to confront. It was as if they were using well-honed diversion tactics. They had demolished their early supper and were pondering a pudding when Bella decided to break the ice.

'So,' she began, 'do you two girls know Maureen? I'm wondering what brought you both this far north. I mean, you're staying over the road and not here at the Inn?'

They looked at Bella and then at each other.

'What do you mean?' asked Gemma, who came across as the much more animated of the two. 'Don't you work at The Retreat?'

'Yes, I've only just started,' Bella started to explain, 'so I'm not fully up to speed!' She smiled, and the two women examined her curiously.

'Lucy has Muscular Dystrophy,' stated Gemma, with a loving look to her sister. It was something Bella had heard of but had no idea of what it really meant.

'There's no cure,' the girls said in unison, and Bella felt as if she had intruded on some private time the girls had organised together. Lucinda gave a look to her sister and Gemma stood up.

'We're just going to the bathroom,' she said, and Bella watched as she helped her sister to her feet and then assisted her out the door to the hotel's toilets.

Gemma returned quickly and sat down opposite Bella and smiled.

'Do you know why we're here?' she asked with a cocked head to one side. Bella nodded at the young woman and wondered how to broach the subject.

'I know what happens there, yes, if that's what you mean,' she responded.

'She's gone downhill very fast. We took a little holiday to India last month, but it was awful. I mean, the place was lovely and everything but the heat, the noise. We managed one tour out and that was it. It was when we were there, we made up our minds that this was the best course of action in the circumstances,' said Gemma, and Bella noticed the happy demeanour that the women shared had dried up now that only one sister sat opposite her.

'She's struggling to breathe a lot more, she's not eating, and her heart is beginning to fail,' said Gemma.

'I'm so, so sorry. You're both so young and beautiful.'

'Well, we're lucky that we're going to stay this young and beautiful.'

'I thought it was only Lucinda who was ill?' Bella queried as it began to sink in what this woman, younger than she, was saying.

'I can't live without my sister. We're twins. Our parents are dead, we were brought up by an aunt in Dorset. We have no living relatives now that our auntie has passed away. Why would I want to live the next fifty years alone?' stated Gemma, who appeared resigned to the fact that she was about to give her life up at the same time as her desperately ill sister.

'But you can't!' stated Bella, in shock at what this woman had decided. 'What you're saying is that you'll take your own life after your sister dies?'

'Oh no, not after. At the same time. We've discussed it with Doctor De Groot. He doesn't have a problem with it,' said the young woman, and she smiled beatifically to Bella whose mouth was open in consternation.

'That's murder,' she found herself saying aloud.

'Not if we've signed the papers,' said Gemma firmly.

'It doesn't matter what papers you've signed. You've asked someone to kill you,' said Bella, the full horror of the proposal sinking in.

Gemma stood up and Bella noticed that Lucinda was coming back from the toilets, although she had no idea how Gemma could have known this other than by the bond that twins have. Bella then stood to greet the woman as she returned to their table. She watched as Gemma gently assisted her sister back to her chair, and they all sat down.

'Sticky toffee pudding all round?' Gemma smiled, and both sisters clapped their hands in delight.

·  ·  ·

An hour later, Bella was searching for Maureen and moving from room to room on the ground floor of The Retreat. She was about to venture into the back rooms which she had been told were forbidden when she heard her name being called. She looked up the stairs to where Jonathan Bartlett was leaning over the balustrade.

'Isabella! I was looking for you earlier!' shouted the man and waved for her to come up the stairs. She closed her eyes and sighed. She was trying to find Maureen so that she could tender her resignation from a job she had only started a day before and one which she was quickly realising was not for her. In fact, Bella was very aware she should report her employers to the police. However, as she did not want any kind of spotlight back on her, this was something she was loath to do. There was no doubt she was torn, and her mind was working overtime.

'Um,' she began, while her eyes darted around.

'Isabella!' he shouted again, this time more sharply, and she began to make her way up the stairs only to see him disappear into The Osprey Suite. With a deep breath, she followed him into the room and saw that he had taken one of the two seats in the bay of the window with spectacular views over the loch and the mountains. Today they were bathed in sunshine and the distant call of birds could be heard through the open casement windows, each one unlatched to precisely the same height.

'I tried to catch you last night, Isabella, but you disappeared so quickly after dinner.' He motioned for her to sit opposite him in the spare chair. Today in the daylight, he didn't look as old as she remembered from the night before, and he didn't look as pained in his expression either. She imagined he would have been a very handsome man in his youth and now, in his late fifties or early sixties, he still had a strong jaw and grey expressive eyes. She was unsure of whether to sit, as she could imagine Maureen's face if she came in to see her, in her chinos and polo shirt, holding court with this millionaire businessman. She opted to stand at the side of the chair.

'I'm sorry that I was so full of questions the other day,' she began with an apology as she took her place opposite him. 'I'm just new, you see.'

'I thought so, but *we* all know why we're here.'

'What's...?' she began.

'Pancreatic cancer.'

'Oh.' She gasped slightly. 'I'm sorry.'

'It's okay. I've tried to fight but I no longer have the energy. There are some battles that simply can't be won so sometimes it's the sensible thing to lay down your arms. Not to give up but to resign yourself to the fact that this will see you out.'

She watched him as he turned his gaze from her to look at the spectacular view from the window and silence fell upon them.

'How did you find out about this place?' she asked as he turned to face her.

'I'm a banker. Used to live in Switzerland with my first wife. I'm not saying it was all the rage there, but we knew why a lot of people came to Zurich. Rich people, poor people, *all* people at the end of their life. It was a stressful life we led, and I watched my wife die a long and painful death with nurses and palliative care health professionals swarming around.' He turned away for a moment. 'I'm not condemning them; they were so attentive that I could barely get near to her in her final days. She was begging to die before her drugs sent her into unconsciousness. It's my opinion that in this day and age, it's inhumane. I swore if anything happened to me, I'd be the first to sign up, but I just didn't think a dingy flat in a suburb of a major city was the way I wanted to go. I knew I wanted to control the *end* of my life the way I'd controlled my *entire* life.'

She watched as he took a deep breath, and as she glanced around the room, Bella noticed an ornamental tray on the bedside table with a selection of drugs lined up in small glasses and knew this was an intelligent man who had decided that he was very much in control of both his life *and* his death.

'I was at a conference. One of the *secret* get-togethers for the wealthy in the USA. At that point I was trying to find anything to extend my life. Being cryogenically frozen seems to be the *in thing* but I met Doctor De Groot and he and I seemed to talk the same language. By that time, I had run out of options. He was involved in this sort of thing in Holland, and I knew from speaking with him that he was hoping to extend his business empire.'

'Oh,' was all that Bella managed to say in response.

'I'm of sound mind now but who knows in the months to come, so I made my decision some time ago to contact him, still had his card. And it was just lucky that I'd also get the chance to come back to where I'd spent long happy days as a child in Scotland. I was educated here, on the east coast, and I've always loved the bare ruggedness of the mountains and the barren landscapes. It toughens you up – it certainly prepared me for my career in finance. I have absolutely no regrets about what I'm about to do. I made the decision. And I shall stick by it.'

It was now Bella's turn to look out to the landscape beyond the room they found themselves sitting in.

'I've signed an affidavit. It's been countersigned. I know exactly what is going to happen. I'm a planner, you see. Under my instruction, it's all been planned out by Louis and Angelina so, as I've said, I've absolutely no regrets. I'm not *weary* of life, Isabella, I'm *wary* of what's ahead in what's *left* of my life.'

'But surely you have the money to try new treatments or go somewhere they're working on a cure?'

'What I have? There is no cure. I've accepted what's ahead of me and I've decided it's not for me. I'm checking out on my terms.'

Bella's eyes rested on the white cottage across the water,

where her friend, too, was waiting for her life to end. Not in the luxurious surroundings of a millionaire's paradise but in a little croft wrapped up in her family, waiting and watching as she slipped away. Bella felt a tear escape from the corner of her eye, and she wiped it away slowly.

'Here they can grant you any wish you want. You can have the best meal money can buy, the most delicious wine, as you know; you can have your favourite singer flown in from anywhere in the world if you have the money. This is dignity in dying, Isabella. This is the way we would all want to end our life if we could. With *us* making the final decision, *us*, not some doctor with a clipboard we've met for five minutes.'

Leaving Jonathan to rest, Bella closed the door quietly behind her. Her mind raced. Bella decided this was not the time to confront Louis De Groot about the awful situation with the Macintyre twins, but it was time to visit one of her oldest friends and make a suggestion to her. She might not be able to buy her stables back, but she could ensure her friend died the most dignified and pain-free death that she could.

Moments later, Bella was in Lochside Croft. Dina stared at her in disbelief.

'I don't believe you, it's impossible. Not across there!' she exclaimed in shock, surprise, and horror in equal measure.

'Listen, whatever happens, we can't tell Mars. You know it'll just descend into chaos and nonsense and, probably, I'll end up back inside,' pleaded Bella. 'Much as I love her, she can't keep her nose out of anything. Just come with me to look. It's beautiful. Please.'

'Just for a look? We can't tell Ruaridh. We can't tell him anything at all.'

'Absolutely,' she agreed, and they hugged each other. Bella felt the thin skin and bones through her soft wool sweater.

'How much would it cost?' she heard Dina whisper in her ear.

'Nothing, nothing at all,' she said in return and felt a weak tear from her friend's eye splash against her cheek, and in that moment, Bella knew she was doing the right thing. She could certainly offer Jonathan Bartlett companionship in his final days. But not only that. She could offer to share with him the strength of character she never knew she had. Courage she felt in her dark days when she first stepped inside the prison, courage that she used to embolden herself. She would do anything to help her most wonderful friend, Dina, in return for the love and support she had shown to her in what had been *her* darkest of times. She would do all this just to give Dina an option of a different way out. This secret they needed to keep to themselves, though.

'You told me about Granny Gabs and the trauma you had watching her die. We can plan this for *you*. Please come over with me,' Bella urged.

'At least I can look. There's no harm in that, is there?'

'No harm at all. Leave it with me. I have a plan to get us in. But let's keep it a secret for the moment, hmm? I said I'd organise a get-together just for us four. How does tomorrow morning suit?'

'Perfect,' agreed Dina.

The old and abandoned jetty was the ideal place for a picnic. On this late spring morning, blankets and outdoor cushions were thrown down on to the fading concrete reminding the participants of picnics long ago. The three best friends had set out early to miss the strength of the noonday sun and had organised a trestle table with a borrowed red and white cloth on it. Heather had taken her time over seating positions, and a giant parasol that they had all struggled to move was shifted with every movement of the sun until they believed it was in the best position. Each had brought a favourite dish and a mocktail and when Heather stood back to admire their work she knew, as a hostess, she couldn't have made it look more inviting. She had raided the store and the freezer, and ensured Dina's favourite treats were centre stage. Jugs of homemade lemonade with ice were sitting in the shade alongside cake stands with sandwiches stuffed with hot smoked salmon and spiced beef piled high.

'Those Balfour boys will eat well tonight!' joked Bella, knowing that despite the huge array of delicious offerings, they would hardly make a dent in the savoury and sweet delights. Heather's arm relaxed over Marcie's shoulder.

'Okay, what are you not happy with?' she suggested.

'Oh nothing, nothing, nothing really.' She knew her two friends would exchange a look and imagined Bella's eyes reaching skywards.

'I just can't...' she began.

'None of us can, Mars,' said Bella quickly before walking to the edge of the jetty to look into the still water on this glorious day. Their friend's diagnosis had hit them all like a bomb. Marcie was relishing and dreading their upcoming conversation in equal measure. The sound of a car in the distance made them all look up.

'I still can't believe you pair didn't tell me.'

'She swore us to secrecy.'

'I know, Heather, but I can keep a secret, too!' Marcie's hands were on her hips, annoyed and frustrated at being kept out of the loop on this momentous news.

'I have a secret, too,' she continued huffily.

'Pray tell,' suggested Bella.

'I think I've made a mistake,' Marcie began before being distracted by the car coming along the low road. Bella and Heather exchanged a glance, not knowing what their friend meant, and they all turned to see the Range Rover making its way to them along the long path that led to the picnic spot.

'Selling Swanfield?' suggested Bella.

'Yes, and...'

Heather ran to greet the car as it reached its stopping point, and Marcie and Bella exchanged a brief look. Marcie's eye was caught by the swirling motion above her of a red kite circling its prey near to the wood that led up to the Drovers' Road.

'Can't believe I'm not invited to this shindig,' said Ruaridh, suddenly in front of his friends.

'Last minute,' offered Bella.

'You arrange *this* at the last minute?' he asked in astonishment, his eyes greedily studying the table groaning with food.

'Well, when I say *we* organised it, I mean H!' confessed Bella as Dina arrived arm in arm with Heather.

'Never knowingly under-catered,' she joked as Ruaridh helped his wife into the only comfortable seat, an old rattan armchair that had been carefully set under the parasol. Folding festival chairs were placed around the table, but it was clear the most enviable chair had been strategically set to one side for the most important guest.

'So, who am I pouring back into the car at six p.m.?' asked Ruaridh, leaning forward to steal a mini quiche from the display.

'Oh, I'm working at one, so I'll be long gone by then!' stated Bella.

'Jeez, that's a busy place, Bells. I'm like a full-time driver there at the minute!'

Bella smiled and offered nothing more.

'It's mocktails so there will be no pouring of anyone, anywhere,' joked Heather.

Ruaridh nudged Marcie. 'Cat got your tongue?' he asked, and she smiled back at him while placing sunglasses on her nose.

'Well, it's clear that this is a guy-free zone so I'm off to take some guy from your place to meet up with a ghillie at the river,' finished Ruaridh, and he leaned down to kiss his wife and whisper something in her ear, which Marcie caught the end of. *'Call me if it gets too much,'* he had suggested as he tapped the mobile in her pocket and she touched his cheek before he whistled his way back to the car.

'I'm very lucky,' said Dina with a sigh, 'he's so attentive.'

Marcie stood behind Dina and pressed her palm on her shoulder. Dina patted it as Heather carefully placed a huge hat on her head.

'I am actually feeling quite well today, thanks. I'm not on my last legs yet!' she joked at this caring gesture, and the others laughed as they sat down.

'I chastised them, you know,' began Marcie.

'Because I told them first? I knew you'd just jump on a plane and start fussing. You've enough on your plate! Your house, new husband. I'd just be an interference.'

'Don't ever think that D! We're all here for each other. We always said we'd share everything, good and bad.'

Marcie leaned over to squeeze Dina's knee gently. Bella handed Dina a linen napkin and the sandwich platter, which she waved away. Bella ignored it and placed a sandwich on the white square and watched as Dina picked at it. Marcie, Bella and Heather swarmed around the groaning table and filled their own plates and then sat down as the serene silence embraced them. There wasn't a bird call or a wave lapping on the shore. Just peace.

'You need to keep doing this,' Dina finally said.

'What?' asked Heather.

'Having these picnics when I'm not here.'

'Stop it!' insisted Bella.

'You're pragmatic, Mars. You know what I mean.'

'Do we have to talk about it?'

'Yes.'

'Let's change the subject.'

'Is there another subject? Would we be doing this on a weekday morning in June if I wasn't ill?'

Heather shoved her fingers in her ears, closed her eyes. She made a face and started singing. Dina let out a little laugh.

'Let's talk as if we're here for a catch up,' suggested Dina, and they all agreed.

'Okay. Change of subject. I think I've made a mistake.'

They all sat forward.

'Breaking news!' said Bella, making her hands into a megaphone. 'Marcie Mosse admits failure! Tectonic plates shift!'

Marcie shook her head. 'This is why I wasn't going to say anything! You lot...'

'What is it, darling?'

Marcie waited, playing several things over in her mind. She wanted to say what she had been dreading telling her girls but there was too much grief already in their lives.

'I think I was too hasty in selling Swanfield.'

'Is that it? Well, we all know that!' Bella sat back in her chair.

'But it wasn't just your decision. You made the decision with Callum, so don't blame yourself,' suggested Dina.

'I know but...'

'Admit it, you're just miffed at the fact they've turned it into a wee gem, and you didn't get the chance to.' Bella now folded her arms.

'It's the noise, it's a racket, that helicopter.'

'My boys love it.' Dina smiled.

'I'm clearly in the minority here.'

'You got an inheritance, then made a fortune and you're still not happy!'

'Who said I wasn't happy?' Marcie was about to blurt out

what she was really meaning to say but was interrupted by Dina.

'Can't we all just accept where we are?'

'I don't want you to be here!' cried out Marcie. 'I want you to be in a clinic or a hospital where they can fix you and we can all go back to where we were before any of this stuff happened!' Marcie's emotions burst open, and she gave a little sob.

They all sat looking at each other, then glancing away. Dina was the first to speak.

'You've offered me all this help, Mars. I really, really appreciate it. But, if you hadn't sold Swanfield, you wouldn't be in a position to offer it to me, so every cloud, eh?'

She pulled herself up from her chair and took the two small steps to where Marcie launched herself up from her seat and the one-time rivals embraced. Dina soothed her like she would her children while Marcie's emotions bubbled out into floods of tears. Bella and Heather exchanged a look before they, too, wiped away a tear as one gazed up to the mountains and the other took in the forest that led to the Drovers' Road on the opposite side and the wild, crashing Atlantic Ocean beyond. Neither wanted to intrude on this intimate scene, fighting their own emotions. They were all strong-minded, fierce, independent women who were also emotionally blunted by the news that had rocked them to their very core.

'Right, you two, have you taken root?' Dina asked over Marcie's shoulder to the two who had remained seated. They eagerly got up, formed a huddle and with quivering lips broke into a smile. Dina cleared her throat a little and then began to sing in her delicate sweet voice, almost quiet at first.

'Oh, the summertime is coming, And the trees are sweetly blooming...'

Marcie joined in the verse, 'And the wild mountain thyme...'

'Grows around the blooming heather,' sang Heather, breaking into a smile.

'Will ye go, lassie, go.'

Unexpectedly they all began to sing 'Wild Mountain Thyme', the last song that cleared a busy night at The Strathkin Inn, and the first dance at Dina and Ruaridh's wedding. A song that they had learned at the feet of their parents, grandparents, elders. It meant so much to each of them. Within moments they were standing, eyes closed, tears staining their faces, singing it out loud. Four women swayed to the music, and peace finally broke out on the edge of the glistening loch, each one knowing it would be the last time these four friends would sing in perfect harmony.

# TWENTY

As a stillness set around the women on the jetty, Moran Maguire was closely watching the two women opposite him at The Retreat. The only thing distinguishing them from each other was the increasingly pale and wan features of the thinner twin.

'I can understand what you're saying, Gemma, but you're a beautiful and very healthy young woman, so you are.'

'Doctor, I don't want to be here without my sister. You must understand. We want to do it, together.' The twins nodded at each other as the word 'together' came out in unison.

The doctor was torn. It wasn't his moral compass that was causing a problem – that had spun out of control years previously. The money, for once, was a side issue. As a doctor, his job was *normally* to keep people alive unless they had an illness or condition incompatible with life, like Lucinda Macintyre. But the beautiful Gemma said she simply could not go on without the twin sister who'd been beside her since birth, just twenty-nine years ago.

'Have you spoken to anyone else about this, ladies?'

'Well, Doctor De Groot, and he agreed – with us,' said

Gemma, with the last two words being completed together as they gazed at each other.

The agreement from Louis De Groot didn't surprise Moran, but he imagined it was Angelina who would have the final say. All three were driven by money for vastly different reasons, but even he thought this might be a step too far, causing the untimely death of a perfectly healthy person. Moran sat quietly for several moments contemplating the scene before him.

'What are your plans for later, ladies, tonight, tomorrow?' he asked, to break the silence.

'We're having a self-care day!' they said in unison, with Lucinda clapping her hands in excitement like a small, excited child.

'Massages and face packs, manis and pedis to make ourselves look amazing!' said the thinner and gaunter of the two, and he shook his head slightly as he stood up.

'I'll catch you later, then, girls,' he said and patted the back of the chair and turned to leave.

He had just reached the door when he heard Gemma call out after him.

'*You* said we could have our most innermost dreams realised here. *You* said we could have exactly what *we* wanted and leave exactly how *and when we* want. This is what *we* want, Doctor Maguire, this is what we want as our final wish.'

He didn't turn around but opened the door and left quietly. Moran had never been overly sentimental and was not one to dwell on the maudlin side of life. This, however, had made him think about what the next few days would bring.


He made his way slowly down the stairs to the back office, where he knew Louis De Groot would be knee-deep in paperwork.

'I'm not that sure about it, Louis, I'm really not sure about the moral dilemma we have here, you know,' suggested one doctor to another.

'We are here to grant them what they wish. That's what they signed up for. You were quite happy for the transaction to take place, were you not?'

'Aye, I was that. However, that was before I realised it wasn't as simple as a single despatch, so to speak.'

Moran was leaning on the windowsill, half sitting against the deep shelf, arms folded and with an occasional bite of the lip. Louis De Groot was sitting at his desk, hands pressed together, fingertips resting on his lips as if he was praying silently, but not really saying very much.

'I'm not comfortable with it, either, Louis,' said Angelina, finally.

'What are our options?' he asked, and the two people in front of him shrugged their shoulders while exchanging looks.

Outside the door that was slightly ajar, both Maureen and Bella were listening. Bella had updated Maureen on the conversation she had had with the Macintyre twins, and she was not best pleased. It appeared then that the only person happy at all about the emerging situation was Louis De Groot.

'I have the paperwork here, all signed,' he said with a nod to the folder on his desk, 'and it is not an inconsiderable sum at the end of the day.' He passed a piece of paper to Angelina who quickly glanced at it and turned it over before she passed it back to her husband.

'I can't quite believe I'm going to say this,' said the Irishman, 'but sometimes money has to take a back seat.'

Both Angelina and Louis looked at each other with a shared knowledge of his gambling habit.

'I think it's entirely up to the girls,' De Groot began as Moran held up his hands.

'I'm out,' he said, and was at the door so quickly that, when he opened it, Maureen fell in with a stumble. Her heels almost gave way, before she stepped aside to let the tall Irishman out at speed.

'Was just comin' in, me! What's up with ol' whassisname?'

'Were you being nosy, Maureen?' asked Angelina of the older woman.

'Just keeping abreast of the situation,' replied Maureen with a haughty air. 'We need to be careful. You wanted me as your eyes and ears, and that's what I'm 'ere doing – watching your backs. We're all in this together, remember? One person disagrees, we all disagree, wasn't that the arrangement?' Maureen stepped back, the last words being emphasised with a wagged finger and an indignant fold of the arms.

Silent looks danced around the room. Louis De Groot stood up from behind his desk to his full five-foot-two-inches, and left. The conversation was over.


Moran Maguire was leaning on the new Mercedes SUV, one arm behind him.

'The twins told me,' Bella blurted out as Moran took a pair of sunglasses out of his top pocket and placed them over his eyes on this bright day.

'And?'

'I can see why they want to do it,' she responded. 'I don't agree with it, but I can understand it. They're two halves of the one person when you see them together. When you love someone that much you can't imagine a life without them in it.'

He didn't respond, and she knew he was playing the scenario out in his mind. 'I've asked my friend Dina to speak to Gemma.'

'Why?'

'She has terminal cancer. She'd pay anything to extend her life and here is a perfectly healthy woman willing to cut hers short. It makes no sense to us, but it does to them.'

'I don't think the good doctor would be happy with you bringing someone else into the house,' he stated.

'They were supposed to be going back to the hotel to have a spa day, but I've persuaded them to stay in,' she explained.

'Can't understand that at all,' responded the Irishman with a shake of his head and a bite of his lip.

Bella didn't notice prying eyes following her from the side window of Sweet Briar.

# TWENTY-ONE

It took a lot of persuasion from Bella, and a discussion about money from Gemma with Maureen, who then had a long chat with Angelina. It was finally agreed to let Dina and Heather into the *therapy room* at The Retreat rather than for the girls to have their so-called spa day at the Inn across the water. The decision was made, away from Doctor De Groot. It was agreed that if Dina and Heather came in and out quickly, quietly and up in the back elevator, then they could both attend to the Macintyre sisters and try to persuade Gemma to not end her life along with her only relative.

Dina was aghast when she entered the girls' room, hand in hand with Heather more for support than assistance. Her keen designer's eye flitted from wall to wall, corner to corner as she took in the décor, the furniture, the ambience and the delicate fragrance that permeated the entire property.

'This is my friend Heather who'll be carrying out your treatments.' Bella smiled, extending a welcoming hand to Dina to assist her to the extra seat that had been placed opposite the sisters. 'And Dina is here to help!'

'You look quite surprised?' asked the more ill of the sisters of the new person who had appeared in front of them.

'Oh, I live across there,' replied Dina, pointing out the window to Lochside Croft directly opposite them. It was glowing silently with the sun on its white walls, reflecting in the loch. 'I used to visit here all the time when my friend lived here. It was stuck in time back then, now I can't quite believe what I'm seeing.' She continued to look around in awe.

'Are those boys yours?' asked Gemma excitedly.

'Yes, oh, I'm sorry if they're noisy. It carries in the wind,' apologised Dina with a blush.

'Oh no!' responded the twins in unison with a quick glance to each other, which Dina recognised in her own twins. The gestures continually surprised both Bella and Heather.

How two people could be in tune so much that they finished each other's sentences utterly confused them. The Macintyre twins seemed to telepathically transfer thoughts between each other, nodding in unison at unspoken words.

'We *love* them!' they responded together. 'We love hearing them shout and scream and enjoying themselves. We love the little one that's always in the water.'

'Douglas,' Bella and Heather mouthed to each other, then both sniggered as if they were copying the two sisters who sat in front of them.

'Oh, he would live in a swamp if he could. He's half boy, half fish,' said Dina, and the five women spent a minute or two laughing, and then they all turned towards the window as, on cue, the four Balfour boys came home from school and spilled out onto the front lawn of Lochside Croft. The smallest one broke away and headed straight to the shore.

For a moment Dina was absorbed in the scene. With the window open and the day quiet, the sound travelled naturally over the water, and she felt herself smiling at their antics. It was the same she witnessed most days, from a different angle from the bench in the garden, from her kitchen window or occasionally from her bedroom, its window always open.

'So, I'll be leaving you in a minute. Leave you ladies to it,' began Bella.

'Aw,' sighed the twins in unison, both cocking their heads to one side.

'But Heather here will be doing your massage and facials, and Dina will be doing your manicures.'

Dina suddenly and unexpectedly took a sharp intake of breath, and her hand moved to her stomach. The smile that had graced her face just minutes before was replaced with a look of sharp pain and her face crumpled, its fine features disappearing momentarily.

'Are you okay?' asked Lucinda, quickly pulling herself up from her seat, aware of her own pain, and moving to Dina, grasping her hand in hers.

'I'm okay, thank you.' Dina smiled through her agony and squeezed the woman's hand in response.

'Bella told me you're not well,' said Lucinda quietly into Dina's ear.

Dina caught her friend's eye who mouthed 'sorry' and gave a quiet shrug of the shoulders.

'No, not really.' Dina looked beyond Lucinda to her boys at the edge of Loch Strathkin.

'I'm not well either. I've never been well. I've lived a lot longer than people thought I would but sometimes you know when it's time to go.'

She glanced across to her sister who nodded slightly then followed Dina's gaze to the boys playing at the water's edge. Dina took another sharp intake of breath, and Lucinda, the weaker of the two, found herself guiding this new woman in their small friendship circle across to the window seat. Dina leaned on the cross of the casement window and her hand swept across her cheek, wiping away a tear that had escaped from her watering eyes. The women all remained silent. The only noise drifted through the window from across the loch; high-pitched screams of delight and whoops of laughter from young boys who were completely oblivious to the fact that the next few weeks would see a blanket of darkness thrown across them, their lives upturned like never before. When Dina turned around, Bella had silently left the room, and the four women exchanged knowing nods and glances.

'Who's first?' asked Dina with a broad smile, her composure returned, her infectious smile still captivating. 'I say you!' She pointed to Gemma who clapped her hands together and stood up.

She supported her sister in navigating past the chairs and table and headed to the therapy room, where she helped Lucinda undress and on to the massage table. Gemma returned to sit with Dina who had manoeuvred a table with a small bowl of warm water and various manicurist materials from her bag to the window where the light was brightest. She plunged Gemma's hand into the bowl to soften her nails. They picked a vibrant deep red colour together and giggled like schoolchildren at the various names of the varnish designed to entice the wearer. Dina took a deep breath and decided to play it cool but deep down wished she had swapped places with Heather. Her friend had suggested laughingly it was she who should oversee the massage and body treatments despite the fact both knew Dina was now unable to handle the power and strength that would be needed for the holistic treatment.

'I should be asking you if you're going anywhere nice!' joked Dina and both women laughed.

'I am actually,' responded Gemma.

'Oh?'

'The afterlife,' said Gemma firmly.

It took Dina aback for a moment and she glanced up at the

woman whose hand she was holding and could only respond with startled eyes. 'I-I, um, can't, er, quite...'

'Understand it?' asked Gemma.

'Well, yes.'

'It's simple. My sister is the only person I've ever loved. We're never apart. Never *have* been apart. Why should I leave her now?'

'But there's nothing wrong with you. Your sister is ill, not you,' began Dina.

'I'm very much aware of that!' responded Gemma, half laughing. 'What would I do? I have plenty of money, I could do anything, but I've never really *done* anything so why start now?'

'Start a charity?' suggested Dina, which brought a scoff from Gemma. 'There are a lot of ways to use your money for good.'

Dina realised that the twins were so obsessed with death and dying that they had probably forgotten how to live. There was a time when Dina thought if she had that kind of money, she would travel to every corner of the globe to find a place that could give her a cure. A month more, a year more, a lifetime more with her husband and her precious children, but instead she had a death sentence hanging over her and every night she went to bed, the fear would sometimes overtake her. She would stare, eyes wide in the darkness, fearful of her next breath and that it could be her last. But she was too far gone in her illness and every clinician she had spoken to had done so with sadness and resignation and said there was nothing, simply nothing, that could be done to extend her life.

The woman in front of her was speaking and she felt her hand being squeezed, as if bringing her back into the real world.

'I'm sorry,' Gemma was apologising. 'I didn't expect that to come out the way it did.' She squeezed Dina's hand tighter until she pulled it away. 'We made the decision together. We make *every* decision together. It's only ever been us. If I had a family like you, I would feel different.'

'Oh, you'd feel *very* different,' said Dina. A silence fell upon them for a moment and Dina found herself plunging the woman's left hand into the water a bit harsher than she intended, and they both stared into the scented lemon-lavender water.

'Have you thought about it?' asked Gemma. 'The end?'

'I think of nothing else.'

'That's why we're here, you see. We wanted to go at a date and time of our choosing. Luce is only going to get more sick, more unwell and we don't know what's ahead of us. She didn't want to die hooked up in a hospital bed, so impersonal. Here we can do what we like, eat what we like, stay in bed all day watching movies with champagne on tap – even though we're not really drinkers to be honest.' She made a face, and Dina smiled.

'Not everyone is in the same circumstances as you. This is your choice, not something available to most people. People like me. I'm *most people* and we always end up in a hospital or a hospice.'

'You?' asked Gemma.

'I'd like to die at home, then I don't. I think. Oh, I'm not sure,' Dina said firmly with a nod of agreement in an effort to convince herself it was the right thing to do. But already she was being tempted by the perfect scene Gemma spoke about. She remembered her grandmother's last breath, the trauma of it all; a family huddled round the bedside of a dying woman for days on end, watching the slow demise of a human being who had once been a vibrant and large guiding presence in everyone's life. The entire ordeal had so shocked her twelve-year-old self that she took to her room for days. She never entered the bedroom again and it was a jolt into adulthood that she had never forgotten, and now she was about to inflict the same on her sons. She didn't want them standing round her deathbed, watching the most disturbing scene of their young life unfold before them. She didn't want to impose on them the severe shock she had experienced, and the very thought sent a shiver all over her. It was a rite of passage for them, she knew that, a parent dying before a child, but she didn't want her young boys to experience what she had. She had discussed it, *or tried to,* with Ruaridh who dismissed it as he did each time she brought up the end of her life. For a long time, both had been in denial about her diagnosis, but while she had finally come to accept her fate, the same could not be said for her bear of a husband who faced everything head on except the limited life of his beautiful young wife. She could still hear the boys outside across the loch, and her eyes drifted from the woman in front of her to the window.

'Excuse me,' she said and stood up slowly, walked over to the large bay window and watched as her children ran around the garden, arms outstretched. Her own twins played 'air-planes', and her youngest, Douglas, was knee-deep in the shingle and sand at the water's edge, his hands and pockets full of shells and pebbles. She watched the scene silently for some moments, absorbing the vision in front of her, and let her mind process it. Dina sighed heavily and returned to her seat opposite Gemma.

'Is it expensive here?' she asked.

Gemma smiled. 'Eye-wateringly,' she said and rolled her eyes to the ceiling, 'but since you know Bella, you might get a discount.'

Dina eyed Gemma squarely. 'Do you think they'd let me look around?' she asked in a quiet whisper, not really believing the words that were coming out of her mouth.

# TWENTY-TWO

'Determined.' Dina responded to Bella's question between tiny mouthfuls of Cullen Skink in the restaurant of The Strathkin Inn.

'Can't be persuaded otherwise?' asked Bella, carefully removing capers from her hot smoked salmon salad.

Dina shook her head firmly.

'Forgot to tell Chef Adam,' apologised Heather.

Bella had an abject hatred of capers. She carefully dissected the food in front of her.

'She loves her sister so much that she can't see a life in the future without her in it. But she's so young and has so much to give; all that money, she could mentor children, set up a charity in her sister's name, travel, donate for research.'

'Poor Lucinda, she was just skin and bones. I had to be so gentle.'

'Have they decided on a date?' asked Dina but not really wanting to know the answer.

'Well, I'd still like to persuade her otherwise, plus there's the moral dilemma.'

'Hmmm,' both women agreed.

'God, you pair sound like the twins!' Bella laughed, and they all shared a chuckle.

'So, what's the deal? What really goes on there? And what *exactly* do *you* do? What's your role?'

'Well, I think you know what it is though none of you better squeal to you know who, you know what she's like.'

'Know what who's like?' said Marcie, suddenly appearing at their side. 'Honestly, that place next door is like King's Cross Station what with helicopters and vans and all sorts.' She threw herself on to the banquette next to Dina and put her hand over hers.

'How're you doing?' she asked of the friend who had turned into one of the best friends she could ever make. Marcie entwined her fingers in the red friendship bracelet around Dina's wrist. All four friends wore one, and it meant so much to them.

'Och, you know. Trying to stay normal for the kids,' answered Dina and put her spoon down, her substantial meal almost untouched, taut skin over bone now more visible in the daylight.

'So, what's everyone up to?'

Dina, Bella, and Heather looked at Marcie, looked at each other and in unison replied, 'Nothing much.'

'Same old, same old,' said Bella and continued her forensic examination of her food.

'You and next door's resident doctor seem quite friendly,' she began.

'Oh, just friends.' Heather smiled sheepishly then realised the question had been directed at Bella and simply said, 'Ah.'

Marcie sighed.

'What's goin' on?' she asked her three guilty-looking friends. 'Hmm?'

'I know you three. You're up to something. What is it?'

Marcie was trying to catch their eyes as they did their best to avoid eye contact with her.

'Och, the girls are trying to cheer me up,' said Dina with a glance at her two accomplices, which made Marcie even more suspicious.

'What's going on at Swanfield?'

'*The Retreat*,' corrected Bella as she started to individually count the capers she had gathered at the side of her large square plate.

'You told me it would always be Swanfield to you, so what's changed?'

'We all have to move on,' responded Bella, her head not shifting up to face her, 'so on that note, I've been thinking...'

Dina and Heather glanced at each other then the two women opposite as if they were about to commence a jousting match.

'I'm thinking of buying back the stables.'

The statement made Marcie lean forward.

'Pardon?'

'I'm so pleased you took care of it when I was away.'

'You were in prison.'

'As I was saying. When I was away *inside*, you very kindly took care of it for me and now I'd like to agree a price to buy it back.'

'What if it's not for sale?'

'You told me once everything is for sale.'

'Well, maybe I don't want to sell.' With arms folded as a signal that she felt the conversation was over, Marcie turned away as Bella pondered her next move. They had always bickered like family, Marcie acting as the overprotective sister in one breath and bemoaning her the next. But Bella felt there was something else lying beneath this apparent cold-hearted exterior. And Marcie was determined no one was going to find out. Not yet. Not now.

'You have no interest in it,' said Bella lightly in an effort to diffuse any potential fire.

'We have horses stabled there,' stated Marcie in an indignant tone. 'I'm taking one out later.'

'They can continue to be stabled there, that's not a problem. I'd love to have them stay. Just back in *my* trekking centre.'

'Where did you get the money?'

'That's not the issue. The issue is I *have* the money, or I *will* have the money, so I'd like to agree a price.'

Dina listened to them squaring off against each other like gladiators as it, too, crossed her mind: *where exactly did Bella get the money?*

'I didn't think you had any money?' she asked only to be on the severe end of a hard look from Bella.

'I *will* have the money!' she insisted. She stood up and headed purposefully out of the restaurant and through the back door, which would take her the short walk back to her home and the trekking centre she had so carefully built up over many long years and hard winters. She was furious with herself for giving her game away. She should have listened to Jonathan Bartlett who said not to arouse suspicion; for the benefit of her companionship (and they had agreed – only companionship) *he* could buy the stables back, following a conversation with Moran Maguire, and gift them to her in his will or she could simply buy through her lawyers as a silent buyer.

In the Inn, silence fell around the table.

'Why can't we all just live in peace?' sighed Dina, and Marcie glanced at Heather before taking Dina's hand.

'I'm sorry, we just get caught up. You know how things are now that she's back.'

'*She?* Now that *she's* back?' Dina raised her eyebrows at Marcie and the irony wasn't lost on her. 'Look, whatever went on between you two, just put it behind you. You can tell Bell's upset about what happened to her and to her precious stables,

Mars. We have enough on our plates here without listening to you pair bickering.'

Heather cast a glance to Dina which Marcie caught and she immediately regretted the outburst.

'I'm so, so sorry,' she said again, with a pleading look of forgiveness aimed at Dina, who simply smiled in a warm expression and patted Marcie's hand. She looked at her two best friends as they waited for either an explanation for her ire or for her to chase after Bella to offer her apology direct. Neither was forthcoming. Dina, as usual, was the voice of reason.

'Girls, there's so much going on, can't we just be kind to each other?' she said, and both girls noticed the sadness in her eyes.

'I forget sometimes. You just look so normal, Dina,' said Marcie by way of an excuse as she gazed at the woman in front of her who was fading away into a shadow.

Dina cocked her head and sighed, and they fiddled with their food and sat for the next half hour in silence, with Marcie realising her frustration at not being able to help Dina was manifesting itself in anger at Bella because deep down she was frightened.


Marcie had agreed to take two ponies out on a trek that afternoon, but Simon had decided at the last minute to renege. She was in no mood to argue, no mood to negotiate, no mood to cajole. As she built up pace with the gold-coloured Blaze, taking low hedges at speed, she realised she was acting recklessly and irresponsibly and slowed down to a canter before letting the horse trot to the bridle path that ran along the edge of the loch. Marcie was always in control and had to admit she was often controlling. But she had to be. Her job demanded high stan-dards, forensic investigation into minutiae and a determined steely focus. But it seemed to her that life was unravelling before her eyes. She hadn't been back in her beloved Highlands for long but already she could see the devastating effect that her friend's illness was having on both her and her family and she was dreading what lay ahead. But this time she wasn't thinking just of herself. Instead, she was thinking about this young family, such a mainstay in Strathkin, and the devastation that lay ahead. The family picnics, the ball games, the sleepovers, the bake sales, the shinty teas, the crafting circle. All of these events had Dina at their centre and Ruaridh as the overseer. It wasn't just her tight group of friends that would be impacted – it would be everyone in their orbit. She was finding it more and more difficult to hold it all together and instead of embracing her girlfriends, she was developing this uncanny knack of pushing everyone away in case they got too close. She was lashing out at people, the people she loved, because for once Marcie was in an uncontrollable situation and it wasn't in her gift to direct proceedings the way she liked.

She noticed someone ahead of her in the distance as she walked with Blaze to the shore. The horse took a sip of water then clearly indicated she wanted to go back to a tuft of delicious-looking grass at the side of the quiet single-track road near the bridle path. Marcie saw the person at the shore staring out across the water and then realised it was the unmistakable figure of Ruaridh. First making sure the horse was settled; she walked the few hundred metres to where she seemed to waken the man from a dream.

'Hey!'

Ruaridh peered at her before turning away.

'I know what you're about to say,' Marcie said as she neared him, 'I can't get a minute's peace!'

She stood near to the bench that she had never noticed before and followed his gaze out across the water. She glanced back at him, understanding she had obviously interrupted his moment of calm. He had clearly been crying and his eyes were red. Immediately Marcie felt embarrassed at intruding on his grief. As usual, when it came to dealing with Ruaridh Balfour, she wanted to say so much but her mouth could produce no words of comfort. She tried as casually as she could to walk over to him and it was then she saw the new brass plaque. It was dedicated to the Mountain Rescue Team members who had tragically lost their lives not so long ago. Ruaridh was one of the lucky ones. The bench stood in the shadow of the mountains which cast a jagged darkness onto the shore. She sat down, ran her fingers over the plaque and sighed. He continued to look out until he drew his eyes back, running his mobile phone through his hands. They sat in silence. Childhood friends. Former lovers. A soon to be widower in his thirties.

'I try to come here every day. Sometimes just for a few minutes. Sometimes for an hour. Dina needs quiet time, so I leave her with her thoughts.' His voice was quivering, and Marcie felt herself bite her lip.

'I can't deal with it,' he said as if to terminate any conversation she was desperate to start.

She reached out silently to take his hand, to cradle it in hers gently, but he motioned it away.

'I need to come to terms with this on my own, Mars.'

She turned to her left, down to where her horse was nuzzling the grass and let a tear escape from her eyes. She rested both hands on the bench on either side of her and heard him sniff loudly. A swan slowly drifted down from the sky above them and came to a smooth, gentle landing on the water. It raised itself up, shook water from its feathers before tucking its wings in and letting its head dive into the cool loch. Marcie searched for the partner, the other swan, but there seemed to be only one in front of them. It hit her hard that these birds that mate for life would at one point be left on their own. It was as if Ruaridh was saying, *I'll have comfort on my own terms.* They sat in silence until the swan drifted away on the water and at the same time a message pinged on his phone. She overheard the call from a ghillie to tell Ruaridh it was time to pick up a visitor and take him back to the hotel.

He got up and headed to the car that she now saw sitting further back in the shade of the trees. Marcie didn't watch him go but gazed out to the swan as it drifted down near to where some reed beds were situated on an inlet. And there she saw the partner, a female swim out to join him, and they went searching for food together. When she got back to Blaze, she was ready for a steady, calm and peaceful trek.

'Life is too short,' she felt herself say aloud as she let the horse meander back to the trekking centre. She stopped and turned to where her former home was bathed in a soft afternoon light. Selling Swanfield wasn't the only mistake she had made, she knew that now. Caught up in the excitement of a new life and with the money to live it well, she had been swept away in plans and enraptured about the future. Champagne weekend escapes with her girlfriends choosing dresses and favours. And then the gloss wore off quicker that she had expected. As she stared out across the shimmering water, she placed the blame firmly on her own shoulders but knew she couldn't admit this error of judgement to anyone, not now. It would seem contrived, maybe even to some manufactured, so she put it to the back of her mind and led the horse up on to the single-track road and back to the stables.


In The Retreat, Bella stood outside the door, her tongue sweeping her lips, as she let her hand hover over the handle. She was determined to put her plan into action. She had slammed her front door at home with such fury she could hear horses snickering and neighing loudly in their stables. She had driven, erratically, back to her place of work. Now, she knocked the door lightly twice and was about to walk away when she heard the disembodied voice from behind the door shout for her to enter. She walked in, the bottle of champagne that she'd opened in the rear lift secreted behind her, held tightly in her left hand.

'I was just thinking about you,' said the man seated at the window as he gazed out to the picture-perfect scene beyond, the light slowly fading over the loch. She smiled nervously then held up the bottle, its contents showing a good mouthful of liquid already gone.

'Started without me?' Jonathan Bartlett smiled back and leaned over to pat the plush seat opposite him, separated by a low table with a large ornate rim around it, the top which could be removed to make a tray. He made to get up, but she reached to his knee. 'What is it? I can get it?' she suggested, and he glanced over weakly to two crystal champagne flutes on the long dressing table that doubled up as a credenza. She collected them quickly and returned to the seat, an expert hand pouring the two tall glasses before she handed one to her companion.

'Slàinte Mhath,' she said in a mock-sounding Scottish greeting. The translation seemed inappropriate, toasting to someone's health suddenly feeling redundant in the circumstances.

'What will be, will be,' was his response, and before she realised it, she had once again downed the bubbly liquid in almost one gulp.

'You seem a little on edge, Isabella?'

She didn't reply. She had told both Maureen and Moran she was willing to offer him companionship. She was desperate to buy back her beloved stables. Desperate to return to a life that she craved, but she was more than annoyed with herself at having unfortunately given that game away to Marcie. It had, however, galvanised her into turning up at this moment with one thing on her mind.

'Just a bit nervous. I've been away from the, er, dating game for a while,' she said with a faint smile and a cocked head towards the man in front of her.

'Let me put you at ease,' he stated quietly and hauled himself up from the chair to make his way to the small sofa, where he collected his phone and returned to sit opposite her. 'I'm a man of some means, Isabella. A self-made man, if you will. What I miss is company, *female company*; the smile of a beautiful woman, the scent she leaves behind when she drifts past, the way people's faces light up when she enters a room. I find you interesting, intriguing, in fact. I don't have long, and I want to enjoy your company in what time I have left. I'm not trying to get you into bed which I imagine is what you were told. There is no doubt I find you attractive. However, I just want to spend time listening to your story and in return I will pay you handsomely. I have what you have seen, a so called *trophy wife*. She's not a talker, and she knows my money is mine to do with as I choose. This arrangement would be strictly between us; the others in this motley crew need not know of our private arrangement.'

'But...' Bella began.

He held his hand up, shook his head.

'It's cerebral company I crave, not physical intimacy.'

She took in his face, as intrigued by him as he was by her.

'I'm fully aware of what I'm doing here, Bella. I'm not doing this on a whim.'

'Well, if you can afford it.'

'That's what I'd like to see change. We need a debate. A healthy and honest debate in this country. Both sides. Scotland is thinking about it, no? Why should people have to leave their loved ones to travel abroad to end their last days somewhere unknown to them? It's too costly. It's too much of a worry. We just need to start a debate, not shy away from talking about something that is going to happen to each and every one of us. Yes – it needs to be strictly regulated; yes – it needs tight controls around it; yes – we need the clergy's input. But we need to start all of this now. It should be made available to the many not the few.

'I'm sure you've had your horses euthanised? Would I be wrong? Why can we not watch an animal in pain, but we're expected to watch our loved ones disappear in death in front of us?'

Bella agreed that she had, and they both fell into a thoughtful silence.


Maureen stood with her ear to the door and a smile on her face. She loved it when a plan came together.

'What about ye, Mrs B?' said a man's voice behind her.

'Oh, you startled me there, you minx!' said the woman covered in a cheetah print. 'I'm just getting a head start on planning for the rest of the week.'

'You have an organised mind like mine, so you do, Mrs B,' said the doctor, and he moved to lean on the wall in front of her, arms folded.

'So, about this business with the twins... do you think we can persuade De Groot otherwise?' he asked.

'Oh, I don't know, dear, he's a bit of a one.'

Moran stopped suddenly. 'What was that noise?'

'What, dear?'

He stood stock still, his head raised up like a meerkat sensing danger. He put his finger to his lips and made his way to the bathroom down the hall, where he gently opened the door and then gazed inside. It was empty, beautifully scented, and perfectly made up with fresh towels for the impending guests. He peered around the empty room and dismissed it as himself being a bit on edge. Maureen handed the younger man a tray she'd been holding.

'Make yerself useful. You can use that to bring me my tea into the drawing room. They should be setting it out in the kitchen,' she ordered, and he took it, following the woman out down the hall.

As the door to the bathroom banged shut, the draught caused the door of the large, ornate armoire to open and the man hiding inside it gave a deep sigh of relief at his sheer luck of remaining undiscovered.

# TWENTY-THREE

On the other side of the water, Lochside Croft was quiet and calm. 'Well, you can self-administer, but we do really suggest that your designated Macmillan nurse discusses your pain relief with you,' suggested Doctor Arshia Brahmins in the kitchen of the white cottage. Dina reached out to Ruaridh for support as he studied the syringe driver.

'I'm sure I could take care of it,' Ruaridh suggested.

The doctor stood up, letting go of Dina's hand that she had been holding lightly. She drank down the rest of the freshly made coffee, preferring to leave the homemade gingerbread on its plate. Recently she had noticed how her waistband was becoming tighter due to the generosity of her patients on home visits, more here than she'd carried out in her entire time as a GP in Birmingham. She went back to the kitchen table, where her laptop was open, and sat down for a few minutes, silently typing up her notes. She closed the lid and replaced it in her large black wheely case that she had adopted after her shoulders began to suffer from the weight of her handbag and doctor's case. They all remained silent for a moment.

'I wish there was something else I could say,' Doctor Brahmins said as she prepared to leave. Dina smiled and shook her head in acknowledgement.

'I'll see you out,' suggested Ruaridh and walked with her to the front door that took them out on to a beautiful lawn that stretched down to the water's edge, and where, shortly, a team of boys, fresh from school, would descend for afternoon play.

'Seriously, I wish there was something else to say,' repeated Doctor Brahmins. 'These things are painful for us, too.'

She smiled and took Ruaridh's hand in a gesture of support and then turned before stopping to briefly take in the view. Rather than drive back to the surgery at Strathdon, she decided to take her car up to the high ridge that majestically overlooked Strathkin Loch and the entire village and, on a good day, stretched out to the Glen of Strathpine. The day was still, the sun not yet ready to set behind the steep, jagged mountains, and she sat down on a bench set into a concrete plinth. The plaque on it simply said 'CALLUM' and she wondered who this person was who had a spot dedicated to him which took in one of the most spectacular vistas she had ever seen. She breathed in the clean air with her eyes closed and thought of her husband. They had been preparing for the rest of their lives when his shift in a Middle East hospital, for a charity he had dedicated all his spare time to, had cut his life tragically short in the blink of an eye. She was still in disbelief and had needed to escape her home city before it consumed her. She fled, rather than left, and moving to Strathkin had been the change she needed.

Arshia stood up, stretched, and pondered dinner. Suddenly, she caught sight of a figure in the distance at the back of the big house. He was tall and slim, dressed in black, and he disappeared into the forest at the rear. The silence was broken by the distant sound of a motorbike, and Arshia saw it speed away on what she knew they called the Drovers' Road. She really should do what Doctor Stuart Mooney had suggested at their last meeting and buy a pair of binoculars that would fit in her bag. He talked of sea eagles and red kites and stags rutting all within sight of the surgery. Arshia decided that the next time she was in Inverness she would find a place to buy them and keep them in the glove compartment for perfect moments such as these. She scrambled back to her car and made her way down the track to the main road. As she did so, the person she had seen on the bike sped past her. He was travelling at such a rate that she half expected to hear a skid and a thud as the driver came off on a tight corner that had caught her out previously.

Aside from this noisy biker, she found Strathkin peaceful. People had told her that the Scottish Highlands were magical, and she was beginning to believe that it was true. Arshia liked nothing better than to breathe in its clean air, the cleanest air she had ever felt. It was enabling her to sleep the most sound sleep she had managed in months. She'd found that since she had arrived, she had been able to wean herself off the sleeping tablets that her own doctor had prescribed in the days and weeks following her husband Krish's death. If her grief could be gradually lifted, then maybe, when the time came, she could help to heal this wonderful welcoming community.

While Doctor Arshia Brahmins was absorbing Strathkin's peace and tranquillity, that was not what could be said about what she had left at Lochside Croft.

'I don't believe it,' said Ruaridh incredulously. 'I don't think you know what you are saying.'

'I know what I'm saying,' repeated Dina, sat beside her husband on the sofa, although he had moved away a significant distance since her statement.

'I don't know why you would want to do such a thing,' he repeated, putting down his light beer.

'You know how traumatised I was after Granny Gabs died,'

she said. 'I want the boys to remember this as a loving family home, not one that has the ghost of me in it.'

'You will still be in it though. Your spirit will be everywhere,' said Ruaridh reassuringly.

'Yes, but not in that way. I don't want them sitting round my death bed. They're young boys, Ruaridh. Too young. They don't need this in their lives!' she pleaded.

'So, what about me? Don't I get a say in this?'

'Seriously?' she asked. 'No.'

Ruaridh sat back and folded his arms in a Balfour huff.

'This is my decision. I don't want to die here. I don't want to open my eyes and see my children in distress. What comes after will be bad enough. I need to remove myself from it.'

'To there?' said Ruaridh, pointing through the window to the big rambling house that sat opposite their small croft.

'I want to close my eyes and hear their laughter and their screams of joy and their fun. That's what *I* want.'

Ruaridh had his sulking face on. He rarely said no to his wife, a woman he was still desperately in love with despite five children and constant money worries. She was the foundation on which he had built up his entire life and the very thought of even one day without her made him weak at the knees. He picked up her hand, kissed the back of it, and made his way to the door and out into the fading day. He stood at the water's edge as his sunglasses slipped from the top of his head to cover his eyes, just as the sun was also beginning to set. He raised his hand and, in a fit of pique, threw the bottle he was holding high and long until he heard the splash in the water. He sighed. He remembered the first time he had set foot in the house across the water, when it was still called Swanfield, and remembered it as always being filled with laughter and joy and delicious smells coming from the kitchen. It was where he had had his first beer, his first kiss and experienced his first love. He wondered what Marcie would think when she learned that her one-time love rival now wanted to breathe her last breath at Swanfield. His own family tradition was to gather round a bedside, softly singing psalms or reading scripture until the moment of death. The suggestion of Dina doing otherwise was new to him, and Ruaridh did not appreciate change of any kind. The gloaming settled all around, and he made his way back into the house where his wife stood at the sink with her undrunk glass of Merlot sitting on the draining board. He scooped her up in his arms, kissing every inch of flesh on her neck until she gave a little moan.

'I'm sorry, I'm just so sore,' she said, and he gazed into her eyes as they almost pleaded with him to stop loving her. He held her gently as she buried her face into his shirt, and he could feel every minor change in her body. He tried to remain stoic, and she didn't see the tears flooding from him and disappearing into his trimmed beard as he bit his lip.

Dax Balfour watched this scene from the top of the stairs and knew, as the oldest of the four boys, he would be called upon soon to take extra care of his brothers and his little sister, who was gurgling in the room next door, completely unaware of their mother's fate.

# TWENTY-FOUR

'Oh, I don't know, dear,' said Maureen to Bella, 'you know what himself is like. Now where did I put whassisname?' Both women were in the main room on the first floor of Swanfield as Maureen sorted bottles and pills. She was perplexed.

'I'm sure I put it 'ere,' she said, talking mainly to herself.

'Could I speak to him?' asked Bella, a bit wary.

'To Doctor De Groot? Oh no, dear, that's not really on the cards now, is it? You know what he can be like, well, you don't really, but seriously, I'm not sure that's your best laid plan.'

'I was speaking to Moran and—'she began.

'Oh, yes, what's going on with you two? I see you 'aving your little chats and what not.'

'You see us? Are you spying on us?' Bella was only half joking.

'I spy on everyone, dear. Now where are you, you little bugger!' said Maureen dismissively while searching for names on bottles that matched her list. She left and returned quickly with another two brown glass bottles, checked the labels, and replaced them on the trays. 'I was sure I had done this. Are you sure you remember me doing it? I can't find me other sheet, you see. Should be on the back of the door and the pink copy downstairs. You seen it, love? I've only got this one.'

Bella was getting frustrated with Maureen and how easily she was distracted.

'What does that say 'ere?' asked Maureen, peering at the bottle.

'Analgesic.'

'Underneath that.'

'Morphine and Detro-propoxy-phene,' replied Bella, struggling with the length and spelling of the long name.

'And that?' she queried and lifted her large dark glasses up off her nose to peer at the paper. They slipped back down, and she peered over them, holding up a bottle while pointing to the sheet she had handed to her assistant.

'Digoxin and Prop-ran-olol, Propranolol. I'm not sure I can pronounce the rest.'

'It's okay, dear. Hmm. It's me macro, sometimes I just see a blur but I'm pretty sure there were no blurs last I checked them out meself.' Maureen had started to refer to her macular degeneration as if it were a long-lost friend.

Bella gave a deep sigh.

'Where were we?' asked the older woman as she took the sheet from Bella, scribbled over some numbers and replaced them with new symbols.

'Listen, Maureen, I was going to speak to Doctor De Groot. That thing we were talking about...'

'No, you wasn't. Leave it with me. I'll see what I can do. Unless your friend is loaded, he's not going to agree to anything, but I'm sure I can get round the little toad.'

'Thank you.'

'You make a nice couple, you do, you pair,' stated Maureen as she pushed the trolley back around the screen, and Bella saw a small jar of pills disappear into a pocket on the patterned dress coat. 'Moran is a one, but I suppose he's not bad, if it wasn't for his drinking and gambling and womanising. But I'm sure you'll try to change him into a decent human bein',' continued Maureen as they made their way to the door.

'Change him? Oh no,' said Bella and then put on a very convincing Irish accent, 'I'm not in the business of trying to change a man, Mrs B!' and both women let out a laugh as they left the room.

# TWENTY-FIVE

The front parlour at Sweet Briar was used to silence and stillness, save a ticking grandfather clock, when the house was owned by Callum McKenzie. Now the giggling foursome of Marcie, Dina, Isabella and Heather were making up for lost time and trying to pack in as many hours together as possible. A tension still hung in the air from Marcie and Bella's previous spat, but they had put their animosity aside for the moment after Dina suggested the get-together away from her own house across the water, away from her children's thirst for knowledge about what was going on in their lives. It was clearly noticeable to three of the group that Dina's drinks were being sipped very, very slowly and in fact she had taken no more than a mouthful from her first glass, the rest of the mocktails sitting untouched at her side on the floor. Heather rested her hand on Dina's, which in turn was resting on the top of her glass.

'Are you okay?' she asked with a look of concern.

'Sure, just tired. On reflection I should have suggested to Mars to have this during the day,' Dina replied.

'I know we're staying here tonight at Sweet Briar, but if you want to go at any time, I can stop and drive you back?'

'No, H, it's fine. It's nice just getting together. Before we know it, Marcie will be back down the road and we don't know when we'll see her again,' said Dina, and a thought drifted through her mind that they would be saying the same about her in the not-too-distant future. Dina had asked for the girls to get together so that she could tell them of her plans. A plan that involved her not dying in a hospice or at home at the end of her cancer journey, but to depart at a time of her choosing to a place that she knew well.

'Who wouldn't want to die in their *own bed and at home*?' Ruaridh had complained. Not Dina apparently. But she had always stood out from the crowd, and it was for this very reason that she had stolen Ruaridh's heart. He had been at Marcie's side all through school and it had almost seemed inevitable that they would marry: two of Strathkin's most notable families bound together like it was written in the stars. But when Marcie took off for university, Ruaridh had suddenly realised that his blonde-haired, blue-eyed friend had blossomed into an incredible and beautiful woman, and he was smitten. He always said he was in awe of her, at her natural way with people and animals. He saw how her demeanour was calm no matter the situation, so different to the determined, feisty and forthright Marcie, and it made him wonder how Dina had been in his orbit, unseen, for such a long time. When she sat, Ruaridh said it was like all around her was still.

Dina had accepted her prognosis after an internal battle with her own mortality. Though she wanted to live as long as she could with her young family, she knew that time was limited and her strength waning. She wanted to fall asleep to the sound of her children laughing; she wanted her husband to love again; but most importantly she wanted to die at a time and manner of her choosing. Her husband was battling his own inner demons about raising five children on his own when he hadn't yet reached the age of thirty-five. Sitting with her best friends, Dina opened her mouth several times to share her plan with the three girls she had known since they were all toddlers, but every time, nothing came out of her mouth. They were laughing, joking, and having a fun-filled catch up, and she didn't want to be the one to bring in a cloak of darkness and throw it over the evening. She couldn't enjoy a cocktail like she normally would: her self-administered drugs were incompatible with alcohol, just like her chemo was incompatible with breastfeeding. Instead, she sipped from the bottle of iron-enhanced water she had brought.

'Do you see ghosts here?' Dina suddenly found herself saying to Marcie, who was sitting propped up against the sofa opposite her and had just raised a large glass to her lips. 'The amount of people that must have been born and lived and died in this croft.' It was a strange statement, and the girls glanced at each other.

'I suppose I sometimes feel a presence,' Marcie replied as she placed her glass down at the side of her crossed knees, 'but isn't that the same of all old houses? I remember Callum saying he thought someone had come in when he was at the sink there this one time and he spoke to them only to turn around and realise there was no one there. We all live in old houses that are chained to the past, so I'm not saying I believe in ghosts but I'm not sure I don't believe either.' She shuffled up against the sofa. 'I love living here though. I mean, I know Callum will be coming back at some point, but for the time being, I wanted it to become my home, which is why it's so different from when he lived here.'

'Our home,' muttered Bella under her breath. Dina caught her eye in agreement.

Dina thought Marcie should remember that marriage was about two people, not one, but she had never been good at sharing.

'Well, yes, of course,' agreed Marcie. 'Mostly – it's strange, I know – I still want to nip next door to Swanfield.'

'The Retreat,' corrected Bella.

'*The Retreat* or whatever it's called. I still want to go out the back door and head over, but I'm faced with a brick wall.'

'Drystone dyke,' corrected her friend.

'Oh, for feck's sake, Bella! What is wrong with you?'

Bella remained silent and started fiddling with the phone she had by her side.

'Girls, please,' Dina sighed. Marcie hauled herself up from the floor and suggested a top-up. Dina eased herself up from the floor, too, deciding to choose a comfortable sofa when she returned, and followed her friend into the large kitchen.

Standing near the window, Simon was silently dispensing olives and large shards of cheese on to a platter, remaining as much as he could out of the way of the chattering friends.

'I know what you're going to say,' sighed Marcie without looking round, instead reaching for another bottle of wine and moving the detritus from their earlier cocktail making out of the way on the countertop. Simon held up his hand and Marcie moved away. 'Cut Bella some slack,' she said to herself while making a face and tearing the collar off the wine bottle on the table before piercing the cork with such force it was like it was an instrument of torture. She stopped suddenly, turning to Dina.

'I'm sorry, the last thing we should do is waste our time fighting.'

'You just have to let go and stop holding grudges.'

'I know. I can't help it.'

'Holding on to the stables is just childish.'

'Now, wait a minute,' began Marcie before stopping herself after Dina raised her eyebrows.

'You took care of the business when she was away.'

'In prison.'

'When she was *away*, and now she has paid for what she did, why can't you see reason? You don't live here, Marcie, you pay someone to look after them. Why can't that person be Bella?'

Marcie turned and continued to try to open the bottle of wine and found herself with a stuck cork and a face of fury. Dina took the bottle from her gently, and with a further twist of the corkscrew, the cork eased itself out of the bottle. She handed it back to her. 'Sometimes we just need a little help,' she said softly and smiled as her friend embraced her. 'I just want everything to be back the way it was, too.'

Dina looked up to see Simon standing with two filled platters of charcuterie and cheese, and he winked. Marcie started to speak but Dina lifted her finger to her lips in the hope of *ssshhing* her friend. It worked. Hand in hand they made their way back through to the front room, oblivious to the fact the entire scene had been watched by someone in the shadows outside the broad kitchen window, who slipped back into the darkness as soon as the women left the room.

Dina and Marcie settled into their places again, this time on the comfortable sofa, and conversation whipped around, no one wanting to talk about the inevitable until Dina brought it up. She spoke about her hopes for her children's future, and her lengthy discussions with Ruaridh about finding someone to share his life with. They all became teary, and then Dina told them all to snap out of it, turn up the music and change to *dancey music* as she called it, away from Marcie's cool background jazz. They needed no encouragement to get up and danced around Dina. Soon her eyes became heavy, and she drifted off to sleep.

# TWENTY-SIX

It was the early hours of the morning, almost light, and The Strathkin Inn was quiet.

'Well, that was a very pleasant surprise,' said Moran, sitting up against plump pillows.

Bella leaned over from where she was wrapped up in her duvet at the bottom of the bed, leaning against the baseboard. 'Thanks for picking me up.'

'Your text sounded like a plea for help, so it did.'

'I just couldn't take any more of Marcie and her high and mighty attitude. You think she'd be quite happy to shift the stables on but, oh no, now she's got her feet under the table she doesn't want to leave.'

'What's in it for her?' he queried.

Bella shrugged at the question. 'Marcie being Marcie. Still thinking she's queen of all she surveys.'

Moran gave a little laugh. 'You ladies always look as thick as thieves, so you do.'

'Well, we are in a way. We're like sisters.' Bella settled back on her own pillow at the bottom of the bed. 'Have you spoken to Maureen? She seemed a bit out of sorts yesterday.'

'Och, she has good days and bad days with her eyes, you know. Sometimes she says it's like peering through a tunnel and ye can't see the end of it. I'm surprised she's still wanting to work. I would think she's got a lot on her mind with the wee lassies. And the wee man has got some advisor on the go. He's getting special deals on stuff and our Maureen doesn't like it, you know. She likes to be in control and he's taking calls from some guy he met at an airport.'

'Hmmm.' Bella sighed. 'So, what's the deal with you and Maureen, how did that relationship come about?'

'Me and Mrs B? Oh, that's a wee while ago now, so it is. I was her GP in London. My surgery was next door to her salon, well, just along the road.'

'Really?'

'Used to go in to see her Brian to get my hair cut. A fine man he was, too. Then I was nearly struck off because of, let's say, irregularities in my drugs cabinets.'

'What were you doing, stealing prescription drugs?' asked Bella, more than surprised.

'I wouldn't say "stealing" as such. They would be, let's say, misplaced before turning up again. I was having a little dalliance with the practice nurse, and when my wife found out, well, she divorced me, didn't she?'

Bella sat upright with her eyes wide. The only word she could muster was, 'Oh.'

'It's my Irish charm.' Moran winked at her. He was certainly charming despite his *very* chequered past. 'I had to ease the pain somehow of the expensive divorce with a little bit of a helper in the form of some analgesics. Which I, of course, *borrowed*.' He leaned over. 'Mrs B's husband then got the dreaded *Big C*. She was devastated. Well, they decided early doors that he wasn't going to suffer, and Angelina offered them a way out. She had met the good Doctor De Groot in the Philippines when he was there on *humanitarian work*, as he called it.

I think he was involved in a wee bit of trafficking, too. I've never really met a more unscrupulous man. Could never prove anything, mind you. Anyway, Mrs B invited me round one night. She had a wee "do" with the good doctor and Angie, and let's just say, once we got talking, I realised they were offering me a way out of the wee situation I was in.'

'With your "indiscretions".'

'And the bit of bother I got in with a wee gambling debt.'

Bella inhaled deeply. *What am I getting into here?* 'And?' she encouraged, leaning back, eyes closed.

'To cut a short story long, Angie and Mrs B bonded and when it was Brian's turn, well, they helped him on his way. I know she was forever grateful. It was a good death, if you can have such a thing, and I thought to myself, well, here now, Moran, you could help people along and be paid handsomely for it... change your ways, my lad.'

'Isn't it illegal?'

'Well, yes,' he replied as he pushed himself up on the pillows. 'The fact of the matter is, as a doctor, you don't want people to suffer, and I've seen some horrendous suffering. We don't exactly advertise what we're doing, of course. It's all kept hush hush. If you're wealthy enough, the authorities turn a blind eye.'

'What if you don't have the money but you still want all that?' Bella said and found herself gesticulating at the phrase 'all that'.

'Well, that's where the good Doctor De Groot can come in. You can gift him your house, your car. My moral compass might be struggling to find its true north, but I can assure you, he has no moral compass whatsoever.'

'How much? How much does it cost?'

'Depends on your package, what you really want.'

'How much is Jonathan Bartlett paying? Or the twins?'

'Oh, now, Bella, that's way above my pay grade. That's

something you need to discuss with Mrs B or Angie if you're brave enough. She can be a wee bit cold and aloof but, underneath it all, she's really okay.'

'Maybe I can work out a deal for my friend.'

'I thought you had worked out a deal with yer man over the road to get your old place back?'

'Yes, well, now I think I need a little bit more.' She felt his hands on her ankles and could feel herself being pulled across the sheets from the bottom of the bed. 'I think we can discuss the package I'd like to offer you while we're still horizontal,' suggested the doctor as Bella felt his stubbled chin disappear into her neck.

And Bella had made up her mind that she was going to help Dina however she could *and* get her stables back, at whatever the cost.

# TWENTY-SEVEN

Early afternoon at Lochside Croft, Dina was drifting in and out of a restless sleep in her upright chair in the spare room she kept for overflow guests. She had a cashmere blanket over her knees and was curled up tight, even though she knew she would be stiff and sore when she got up. In the distance she heard her children playing outside, fresh in from football practice. Her chemo drugs were causing bizarre dreams in bright and psychedelic colours, and she was recalling her early days with Ruaridh; him teaching her to drive and bemoaning the fact he needed more self-control rather than dual control; his proposal after kite surfing on a deserted Uist beach, an Outer Hebrides favourite of theirs before family life took over just a year later. She felt herself smiling, remembering their secret engagement, their embrace, her legs wrapped around his waist tight as she leapt onto him with so much joy in her heart, she thought it was going to burst.

She was trying to tell herself that this was the right thing to do, but her husband was taking a lot of convincing. She knew she had to sit the boys down and tell them what the future held for them, a future without their mother in it, but she was putting it off repeatedly. Her close company of girls was so busy infighting that she was struggling to sit them down together and fully explain her decision, and she knew for a fact that Marcie would be the first to try and persuade her otherwise. Despite that, it was Marcie, Isabella, and Heather she wanted with her when the time came. And her husband. She knew people would question her decision, but she had thought long and hard and had now made up her mind. Her only concern was keeping her plan from her doctor who was trying to persuade her about palliative care in a hospice or hospital some miles away from the only home she had ever known.

'Mum's here!' she heard Ruaridh shouting from the kitchen, and she waited a moment before slipping out from under the blanket and stretching away her soreness, standing up slowly and with a deep sigh.

'Coming,' Dina tried to shout but it came out in a weak and quiet voice, her throat sore from her strong painkillers. Her own mother – what was she to say to her, too? How was Dina going to persuade her that she wanted *her* to look after her boys while she slipped away across the water? She could hear the arguments against her wishes being played out in her head.

Dina found herself glancing in the mirror, the mirror handmade by Ruaridh from driftwood found on the beach by her sons. Her face was pale, thin, thinning. She raised a fake smile and threw the blanket back onto the chair. She glanced at the dressing table and the expensive writing paper and envelopes she had bought, thought about the letters she had still to write. Slowly she walked into the kitchen and to her mother, who would fuss and bustle around her when the last thing she wanted was constant attention. She had asked Ruaridh to speak to the boys about constantly jumping on her in their own over-enthusiastic way, and they had listened intently and become more subdued and loving in her presence. Their eldest, Dax, had become increasingly attentive to her. The twins, Donald and David, were like sticking plasters, but it was the youngest of the four boys, Douglas, who curled around her like a vine, gazing up at her with huge blue eyes, silent and still. Little Mari was doted on by her father and oblivious to the chaos and confusion around her.

Dina stood at the table, which was groaning with an enormous post-football tea. The boys screamed their way in from the garden, until a look from their father silenced them into stillness.

Ruaridh leaned against the sink, his young daughter in one arm over his shoulder, fast asleep. Dina made her way over to them, tapping each one gently on the head as she passed before her arms encircled her husband's waist and he planted a soft kiss on her forehead. Her mother fussed around the table with plastic tumblers of juice, dishing them out with precision and the occasional glance to her daughter. She saw tears rise in her mother's eyes as she smiled, and then turned away.

*It's always difficult for those left behind*, Dina thought, remembering the words of her doctor as she clung to Ruaridh a little bit tighter. *What lies ahead?* drifted through her mind, and she closed her eyes, leaning against her husband's chest.

# TWENTY-EIGHT

The kitchen at The Strathkin Inn was in full swing as another huge buffet was being prepared for the residents of The Retreat. A list had been presented to Bella, who in turn checked it and handed it to Heather, who oversaw the work being done by Adam the chef. It was a 'special' dinner, Maureen advised Bella, who now knew that it was nearing departure time for several of the residents. The nearer that date came, the more anxious Bella was becoming. Despite knowing the Macintyre twins for no more than days, she had grown emotionally close to them, and to Jonathan Bartlett, too. Bella had tried long and hard to persuade Gemma not to die with her sister, but to no avail.

'Could we smuggle her out?' suggested Bella in a stage whisper.

'Smuggle her out, dear?' asked a bemused Maureen from behind large dark glasses with blue cat's eye tips. ''Ow on earth do you plan to do that if the girl doesn't want to go anywhere?'

Bella bit her lip as she tried to think of a new plan. They were interrupted by a severe rap on the back door, and they all looked at each other, eyes moving quickly from one face to another. Maureen went to the front door to check the CCTV in the office off the vestibule and hurried back.

'It's 'er from next door. Better see what the busybody wants,' said Maureen.

Bella realised that both Maureen and Doctor De Groot were looking at her, expecting her to see to the visitor. 'Oh, right,' she said, and she went to open the heavy door.

'Hi, Mars,' she greeted Marcie, still sensing a chill between them. 'Look, I'm sorry I had to leave early last night. Just such an early rise today—' she began but didn't get to finish her excuse.

'I think we need to talk,' said Marcie.

'Uh?'

'About Dina,' stated the woman, shuffling from foot to foot on the pathway at the back door of the house she used to own. Bella wanted to invite her in, but the distant voice of the man who now owned the property was drifting around the vast open hallway. The last thing she wanted was to get on the wrong side of the doctor. Silence enveloped them and Marcie bit her lip.

Bella sensed she was searching for a word that was almost alien to Marcie – that word being sorry – but nothing came.

'Why don't you come round to Sweet Briar? I'll text Heather and find out when she's available 'cause I have to start thinking about going home in the next few weeks,' said Marcie finally, trying not to catch her friend's eye.

It was a strange word: *home*. Swanfield had always been Marcie's home; Strathkin was both their homes from childhood. But while both had drifted away for a time, it was Marcie who had stayed away, and who had created a new and different life for herself in the bright lights of London.

'Sure, just text me the info,' agreed Bella.

'She still there?' came the dulcet tones of Maureen. 'You're lettin' in a draught!'

'I'd better go. Text H then let me know. Is Dina coming?

You know, it would be lovely to have something at Sweet Briar again, but you can also come to mine?' said Bella with a nod to the cottage next door.

'No, I think we need to chat through the next chapter, so to speak, just the three of us,' replied Marcie. 'Sweet Briar is bigger, more comfortable.'

Bella bit her lip at what she perceived to be a slight dig, then whispered, 'Gotta go' and gently closed the door on her friend. She leaned against the back of the door. *Why were they like this? Was the increased tension in the air about what was round the corner?*

'What was she after?' asked Maureen, who was standing so close to Bella when she turned round that she was startled.

'Jeez, Mrs B! I didn't realise you were so close!'

'I don't trust that one.'

'Oh, Marcie's okay.'

'What did she want?'

'Just to chat,' replied Bella.

'Go get changed. It's nearly cocktail hour,' said Maureen.

'You know what, I'm going to give it a miss,' replied Bella. 'In fact, I might just walk around the loch. I think I need some space.'

From Dina's illness to her romantic affair with the unscrupulous Moran, Bella had a lot to think about. She'd returned home from prison planning to steer clear of trouble, and somehow had found herself right in the centre.


The man standing at the high ridge wasn't interested in taking in the view. His binoculars were trained on the lone figure of Bella Forrester as she exited the house far down on the left at the head of the loch and made her way round the single-track road to where it joined the main road at the entrance to the village itself. Her pace had started swiftly as she walked with some determination, then slowed as she stopped and gazed out along the water, watching swans drifting towards a reed bed. Suddenly she turned and peered up, as if his movement had somehow been caught in the corner of her eye. She was looking directly at him, but Poytr Medvedev – the man whom Bella had known as Brodie Nairn – had changed his appearance so much that you would have to be standing extremely close to him to recognise him. He didn't flinch as she continued to look up, clearly thinking he was just another tourist on a motorbike admiring the spectacular view. He raised his hand to scratch his thick dark beard where once a blond stubble had covered his chin and ran his fingers through thick ebony hair. He slipped his sunglasses off his forehead to cover his eyes as a smile danced across his lips.

'Bella,' he whispered and began to head back to his motorbike. He shoved the binoculars into his jacket pocket. Poytr jumped on his motorbike and continued his journey until he reached his destination of Broomfield, a vacant tied cottage on the vast estate. It was sparsely but elegantly furnished and was not somewhere that the new or old owners of Swanfield were likely to venture to, not while they had their own issues to concern themselves with.

# TWENTY-NINE

Strathkin had been so welcoming, so open to Arshia Brahmins that it almost took her breath away. The neighbouring villages of Strathdon and Strath Aullt all seemed to have an open doors policy, too, and the friendliness of these sometimes-tough old Highlanders never failed to surprise her. Big ruddy-faced farmers with calloused hands and a gentle voice were always available for a chat and a discussion about their neighbours, whether good or bad. Arshia had laughed at the gossip, charmed them with her smile and bedside manner, and warmed to their bluntness. A chance meeting at the village store one afternoon led her to meet the man on his motorbike. When they came across each other the next day, she'd thought how fortuitous it had been. He invited her to a picnic which had gone down so well, Arshia had agreed to a 'light supper' at the home of the man she had come to know as Peter. He came across as charming, handsome and very attentive. He didn't make a move on her at the picnic, and this was one of the reasons she had agreed on this second date. She was intrigued by him.

With Doctor Mooney gone, she knew that she had to make

some friends other than the patients she was now seeing on a regular basis in this little gem of a place. She felt very at home, more than she thought she ever would have. Now, with a chance of romance on the cards, Arshia was beginning to think that moving to Strathkin was one of the best decisions she had ever made. A smile danced across her lips at the thought of meeting up with this mesmerising stranger, and she headed to her car.

When she arrived at Bloomfield, Peter was at the door, opening it wide in welcome. She was always surprised by these beautiful cottages and the subtle Highland decor that was featured inside. Whenever she visited the Balfour house, Arshia was always taken aback by the stunning design inside. Dina Balfour amazed her, with her strength of character and her zest for life that was to be cut so cruelly short. Such beautiful children and a husband so attentive.

She glanced at Peter as he fixed her a non-alcoholic gin.

'Where's that accent from?' Arshia asked as he sat down opposite her. The fire was lit on this lovely summer evening, casting a warm glow around the sparse but beautifully decorated room.

'I could ask you the same thing?'

'Well, I'm from Birmingham but my parents drilled the Black Country accent out of us!'

'Us?'

'Me and me brutha,' she replied with her Birmingham twang, and it made them both laugh. She slipped out of her shoes, tucked her feet under her bottom on the sofa and immediately felt relaxed.

'Is that definitely non-alcoholic gin?' asked Arshia as she stared at her empty glass.

Her host made his way to the open kitchen, held up the bottle of zero per cent Gordon's gin and examined the bottle with exaggerated effort.

'Unless it slipped through the net!'

Arshia's lids closed slowly over her sleepy eyes.

When she awoke in a panic some hours later, she found Peter at the kitchen table with his laptop.

'Oh, I'm so sorry! I don't know what happened!' she apologised, stifling a yawn.

'You were completely out for the count!' he said with a look of concern.

'I'd better get home.'

He kissed her briefly on the cheek and wished her goodnight as she left. Arshia was growing fond of Peter and his old-fashioned, gentlemanly ways.


In the workshop next to Broomfield, Poytr Medvedev studied the wax imprint of the keys he had taken from Arshia Brahmins's bag the night before as she slept. He thought back to the training he had received from first his father, then from officers in his platoon; so long ago, it felt now. He moved around the items on the work bench until he found the top of a beer bottle that he had put to one side. With a set of pliers, he pulled the edges out of the bottle top so that it resembled a flat badge. Next, he hammered it flat so that it now appeared to look like a coin. He pulled open a drawer and took out a roll of clear tape and cut a piece off. He warmed it in his hands slightly then laid it across the wax that had an imprint of the key from the workshop padlock on it, one he had made earlier. Using a matchstick, he carefully and deliberately eased it into the wax so that it imprinted the key on it. Once he peeled the paper back out of the wax, and cut it out, he was left with an exact copy of the key.

Poytr had a plan. And it was slowly being put together like a jigsaw.

Revenge. It was that pure and simple. Marcie Mosse was so

busy fighting battles on so many fronts that she hadn't even noticed that he was back in her beloved Strathkin. Back to where he, Poytr Medvedev, should be Lord of the Manor. Marcie had destroyed that with her meddling, so now he wanted to put an end to her once and for all.

# THIRTY

All hell had broken loose when Bella returned to The Retreat. She had come in the rear entrance that led into what was now a smart chrome and steel catering kitchen, far removed from the country kitchen of old, and found Maureen, Moran and the handyman gardener, Niall, in a heated discussion in a corner.

'Oh, there she is!' snapped Maureen.

'What is it? What's going on?' Bella's eyes were flitting between the three, searching for an answer.

'Old curtain twitcher next door, your so-called friend Marcella Whatsherface, calling our neighbourhood bobby.'

Bella glanced at Moran who raised his eyes to the ceiling in desperation.

'We've had a call from the local copper. Seems your nosy friend next door has asked him to pay us a visit again.'

'And?'

'We don't want him poking his nose around. He's your friend. Think of something to get rid of him,' replied Maureen and disappeared in a whiff of aromatic perfume.

'You heard the woman,' said Moran and took off after her, leaving Bella, eyes wide.

'Shit,' was the only word that came out of her mouth.

She noticed the two trays of freshly made brownies cooling on a double rack, quickly grabbed a plastic tub from the shelf, and filled it with six still-warm, squidgy cakes and ran to the front door, opening it as Jamie slid from the driver's seat of the police marked 4x4.

'Aye, aye, Bells!' he greeted her, and Bella went to stand at the side of the car in silence for a few seconds.

'Everything okay with you now?' he asked, shoving his hands into ill-fitting police regulation cargo pants.

'Yes, keeping my head low, under the radar.' She smiled. 'This is some beast!' Bella walked around the car, holding the box of brownies behind her back as she examined the wheel casings closely. 'Do they know your background, giving you a car like this?' She laughed as she returned to join him, with a clear reference to his pre-police life as a boy racer.

'Had to jump through a couple of hoops and suck up to the sergeant to get my hands on it.' He laughed and ran his hand over the still warm bonnet of the BMW X5. 'Listen, had a wee call from Marcie,' he began and turned to look at the house.

'Oh, what's Marple up to now?' said Bella with a half-hearted fake laugh.

'She's concerned about a vehicle she's seen in the grounds. It was blocking her access and egress points.'

'Oh, that's just the gardener's. It's an incinerator for leaves and stuff. Belongs to Niall MacPhail, you know Niall? Anyway, can't you lot just say *in and out*? *Access and egress,* tut.' She raised her eyes upwards.

'According to Mars, it's a bit bigger than a leaf blower.'

'How much do these cost?' asked Bella, and it was her turn to run her hand excitedly over the white painted curves of the elegant car.

'Hmm, sixty, seventy grand, thereabouts.'

'Is it true you get extra power put in them? Like a special police request type thing?'

'Myth,' replied Jamie.

'Would you let me drive it?'

'Not a hope! So, this car, truck, garden incinerator, whatever it is. Has he got a licence?'

'You know Niall, he's not going to do anything illegal. His *missus* would kill him!' They both laughed in agreement as Bella continued to caress the SUV. 'I mean, if you won't let me drive, you could always show me how she shifts. You know I'm a petrol head.'

'Can't really do that, Bells,' he said as she held up the brownies she had been concealing.

'Fair exchange is no robbery, as you lot would say. Freshly made,' she said and opened the lid, revealing the chocolatey aroma of warm baked goods. 'Have you opened her up down the runway?' The newly constructed road from Strath Aullt to Strathdon featured a long, straight stretch, similar in size and length to a runway and was so-called by the locals. Jamie took in the smell of the brownies and checked his watch. 'C'mon, you,' he said and pointed. She slid into the passenger seat and as he walked around the back of the vehicle, she let out a long sigh.


As Bella and Jamie sped away, inside The Retreat an argument was ensuing. Maureen was trying to hold court, but things were not going her way.

'It has to be tomorrow,' said the Macintyre twins in unison. Maureen was looking exasperated.

'I'm not sure if that suits *us*, dears,' she said, glancing at her clipboard.

The girls exchanged a knowing glance. 'Well, we can always check out if it doesn't suit,' they said together.

Maureen peered out over her large sunglasses at them both,

even though they were slightly out of focus to her. 'Well, I wouldn't advise anything like that – being a bit hasty. What I'm saying is you've paid a lot to come here and I'm not sure you've experienced everything our beautiful retreat has to offer until your departure date, so to speak.'

'To be honest, Maureen, we've made up our minds,' said Gemma in a demanding tone that Maureen hadn't heard before. 'Can we make plans for tomorrow? Luce is feeling really quite unwell.'

Maureen eyed Lucinda Macintyre through her dark glasses and, even then, they didn't give her a hint of someone with a healthy glow. She was so pale she was almost translucent.

'Let me speak to the doctor... again,' she said.

'I want to speak to Doctor Maguire,' insisted Lucinda.

'Can we have a moment, Maureen?' asked Gemma.

The older woman nodded and made towards the door. She closed it behind her and leaned against it. She had to speak to someone about this very quickly. In the meantime, she wondered if she should have all the drugs removed from the twins' room, just in case.

Having successfully managed to divert Jamie from his line of questioning earlier in the day, Bella now sat with Jonathan Bartlett playing backgammon.

'The twins are lovely girls,' said the man to Bella. 'I find it a bizarre arrangement, but one I can understand.'

'But why not use some of your money to fund research into the disease that is killing your sister? I just want to shake her, look at Dina, what she would give...'

'There's nothing you can do, Isabella; you need to direct your anger elsewhere.'

'I'm sorry,' she apologised as she studied the backgammon

game in front of them. She should be giving him all her attention considering what he was about to give to her.

'Once you've made your mind up about something as dramatic as how your life will end, there's not a lot that people can do to change your mind. That's one of the reasons I kept this to myself. I didn't want people to feel they had to try and persuade me otherwise. I watched my father and brother die of this disease. Their pain and anguish will not be my pain and anguish.'

'Dina doesn't want her children to see her die,' said Bella unexpectedly. 'She was traumatised by her grandmother's death. It took her years to get over it. She doesn't want her boys to go through that. Dina is so sensitive. I understand her decision.'

'When I saw her here the other day, I could see she is a woman on the edge of this life.'

'When did you see her?'

'There's not a lot you *don't* see from this window when you don't move far from it.'

'Hmm,' was Bella's response with a knowing nod.

'Are you sure you're cut out for this job?'

'It's just all come at once – Dina, the twins, you – plus I don't think I see the *aftermath*, if that's what it's called. I see the nice bits, these bits,' she said, waving her hand around the area between them. 'This isn't a hardship. Speaking with people, chatting, laughing, getting paid for it. It's the other bit of it; I'm not sure how I'll deal with it.'

The sharp knock on the door brought them back to reality with a start as Maureen popped her head round with a friendly smile.

'Sorry to interrupt, spoil the party as it were.'

Bella noticed that Jonathan had gripped her hand a little tighter at the appearance of Maureen in her animal print and, after trying to release herself, she decided to stay holding him just as tight.

'Have you got a minute, love? Won't take long.'

The man opposite reluctantly released her, and she made her way to the door where Maureen grabbed her and pulled her into the room that appeared vaguely like an operating theatre.

'Right, we have a small problemo,' began Maureen.

'What?' asked Bella, looking around. She hadn't been in the room before and she found herself staring with her mouth open.

'The girls have brought forward their departure to tomorrow.'

'They're leaving?' Bella said before it sank in, and she said simply, 'Oh.'

'That causes us a bit of a dilemma 'cause that's when himself was planning on checking out,' she went on with a nod back to the room Bella had just left.

'Oh.' Her response was an octave higher, shocked to find that her newfound benefactor would be leaving her sooner than she would like.

'We can't despatch three in the one night. I mean, we can't despatch Gemma at all. It's unethical. Problem is, luv...'

'Uh-huh?'

'I think one of them has had a change of heart, I do,' said Maureen, folding her arms with a look of indignation.

'What?'

'Now this is just me thinking, right? But I reckon Lucinda is trying to persuade Gemma not to make the trip with her, I do.' Maureen spoke in such terms that made you think the girls were going on a fabulous cruise to a far and distant country.

'You see, Gemma wants to speak to that little Dutch troll 'cause he'd tip anyone over the edge, know what I mean? But Luce, well, she wants to speak to your whassisname 'cause I believe she wants him to persuade her sister to stay in this world and not shift over to the other side, so to speak.'

'But what about Jonathan?'

'Oh, he's taken care of, that's not a worry. But Gemma... not over my dead body... well.' Maureen made a face at her own comment, and Bella screwed her mouth up. 'And another thing,' said Maureen, pulling Bella close. 'We might have another little issue, what you lot would call a *wee problem*.'

'Yes?'

'Some of our drugs have gone missin',' she said in a stage whisper.

'Missing? What do you mean, *missing*?'

'Well, you know me and ma macular, I thought I was misreading or something, but I've done another little mini audit,' she went on and handed Bella a folded sheet from her pocket with a list of drugs on it. 'I know I put them out, I'm really particular me, but I've noticed some are way down and some not there at all. Now, you and I both know I like a wee helper now and again, but none of this lot.' She pointed a painted nail at the sheet of paper Bella was trying to decipher. 'And this one, Ondansetron, supposed to prevent nausea in cancer patients – you slipping any of that out for your pal? You can tell me.'

'Absolutely not! I can't even pronounce these names, never mind know what it's good for!' The only drug Bella recognised on the list was *morphine*; she was NOT going to be accused of syphoning out of the drugs cabinet by the woman whose casual use of amitriptyline had not gone unnoticed.

'Moran?' she asked of the woman in front of her.

'Oh, 'e's past all that. I'm sure of it.'

'One of the nurses? Sissy or Sylvia?'

'Not sure, they're shit scared of Angie,' said Maureen, and Bella watched as she bit her lip in concern. 'I don't know how you're going to explain that to Van der Valk.' A moment passed before Bella realised what Maureen was saying.

'Me?' she asked in horror.

'Well, *I'm* not telling 'im.' Maureen pushed her glasses up her nose, leaned back to turn the handle on the door and, before slipping out, leaned over to Bella and said in almost a whisper, 'Let me know how you get on. 'E's a pussycat really,' and she closed the door quietly behind her.

Bella leaned against the wall, gave a deep sigh, and said out loud, 'What the actual,' before heading to the corridor where all that was left of Maureen was the lingering scent of perfume that drifted in the air. She stood for a moment thinking about heading back in to see Jonathan Bartlett, but instead she decided to divert to see the twins. She was trying to find any excuse not to go back downstairs to where she knew Louis De Groot was hovering near the back office.

She knocked as quietly as she could on the girls' door, hoping not to attract unwanted attention. When she entered, the twins appeared subdued and slightly distant, which she wasn't expecting.

'Oh,' they said in unison.

'I thought it was going to be Doctor De Groot,' said Gemma.

'Are you waiting to see him?'

'I was hoping it was going to be Doctor Maguire,' said Lucinda.

'Both of them? That's a rare treat!' replied Bella, trying to lighten the mood, but she could feel a tension in the room between them that she hadn't noticed before. 'Is everything okay, girls?'

'I was telling Gemma, I noticed the way Doctor Maguire was looking at her and—'

'Luce,' interrupted a clearly annoyed Gemma.

'*And,*' Lucinda continued, 'last night we were up all night. I think she should reconsider leaving with me. She needs to continue with her life and learn to love someone else.'

Gemma raised her eyes to the ceiling. 'We've talked about nothing else but this plan for years, so I don't see why we should change it with twenty-four hours to go?'

'What way was the doctor looking at you?' asked Bella.

'It was pity,' said Gemma sharply.

'It was the opposite of pity,' replied her sister.

'Tell her, Isabella, if she has a chance of love. She'll never forget me; she'll love me more!'

'Absolutely,' agreed Bella and knew immediately it would not be a look of pity that Moran had given this woman.

'I think I should leave things as we decided, and Gemma should wait a few days. I don't think we should go together. Once she seeks some solace for her grief, I believe that might change her mind. I think *he* might change her mind.'

'What I think right now is that neither of you is ready,' began Bella.

'Oh, I'm ready!' said Gemma sharply. 'We've spoken to Maureen. Tomorrow evening.' Gemma sat down on the large chair next to her sister and a huge sigh came out of her small frame. 'I've asked to see Doctor De Groot. He knows best. If someone is going to talk me out of it, it would be him, but I know I'm doing the right thing. WE know I'm doing the right thing.' Gemma folded her arms like a petulant child, and Bella realised she was caught in the crossfire. 'In fact, if you know where the drugs are, we can go tonight, do it ourselves,' suggested Gemma.

'Oh, let's not be hasty,' said Bella, holding up her palms in defence. The last thing she wanted was a confrontation in front of Louis De Groot with the girls in the background.

'There's a lot of planning that goes into this. It must all be done very professionally, I'm sure the doctors have told you.'

'If it was legal and above board, we'd have done this at home in Dorset. We're here because all this stuff is still *underground* as it were.' The word was emphasised with air quotes.

Bella was struggling for an answer.

'I mean, the guy that came in to replace the drugs the other day, take away all the out-of-date ones, I'm sure if I'd slipped him some money, we could have got what we needed, and we'd have been gone by now! We wouldn't be having this co—'

'What guy?' asked Bella, cutting her off, suddenly perplexed.

'The handyman guy. Said he was checking the drugs on behalf of Maureen. I mean, I'm not surprised, she's lovely, but, but her eyesight is chronic.'

'Niall?' asked Isabella, confused.

'I don't know the guy's name. The guy with the beard.'

'Short? Stocky? Grey hair?'

'No. Tall, slim, dark hair, dark beard. Black boiler suit or black pants and fleece or something, I dunno.' Gemma shrugged. 'Wasn't like regular staff, but he was in and out pretty quickly.'

So, someone on the payroll *is* syphoning off the drugs, thought Bella. It was a relief to her that it wasn't Moran. But he wasn't out of the woods with her yet if he was eyeing up Gemma.

'You know what we all need? A nice cup of tea,' she offered and sat down.

Once tea had been delivered, drunk mostly in silence and removed by Sissy, Bella made her excuses to leave the twins for a short time. With this latest information about a thief in their midst, who could she trust to tell?

Moments later, in the small cupboard-like room in the hall, Bella struggled to work the CCTV. She was loath to ask anyone for help for obvious reasons. The twins had given her an estimate of when the stranger was in their room removing and replacing drugs. She pressed buttons on the digitised system that she found more than confusing. There was a noise, and she watched as the live feed started rewinding at speed and then she pressed another that appeared to be a Pause button. It jolted the machine into rewinding faster, and she glimpsed a very brief shot of her and Constable Jamie MacKay climbing into the police vehicle and driving off. There were four cameras around the property and this one was clearly aimed at the front of the house. She pressed another button and realised this was pointed in the direction of Sweet Briar. She saw Marcie coming out of the house with a laptop and sitting to work at the wooden table with a pile of papers and a notebook on the chair beside her. Her husband came out behind her, mug of coffee in hand, before bending to kiss her on the top of the head. Simon ran or hiked every day and after a short exchange, he disappeared up into the forest at the back of the house. Then there was a bright light, and her eyes were directed to the far end of the garden. The light had come from a mirror on a motorbike. *What was it doing at the old Drovers' Road – a road that was a locals' secret? Who would know how to get there?* She leaned in, peering closely at the figure, but whoever it was, they were too far away and too blurry.

'Shit,' she said as she automatically put her hands to the screen to open the view wider which, of course, it wouldn't do, and she muttered at her stupidity.

'Well, well, well, what have we here? You'll be on a hiding to nothing if you're found in here, you do know that?' said Moran in a whisper, so close to her ear that it made Bella jump.

'Jeezo!' she replied, hand on her heart. He closed the door of the small room, so small in fact it was no more than a cupboard.

'Now this is cosy.' His arms encircled her waist and embraced her tightly. She tried unsuccessfully to wriggle from his grasp, but he started nuzzling the back of her neck as she leaned over the desk in front of the screens.

'Stop it! We have a problem,' she began. She found the Stop button on the machine and nudged him in the ribs. 'Look!' she demanded.

'What am I looking at?'

'Him!' she said in a stage whisper and prodded the screen.

'Still no idea.' He loosened his grip on her as he leaned over her neck, resting his head on her shoulder, and peered at the screen. 'It's a blurry picture on a screen; you'll have to fill in the blanks, Bella.'

'Have you spoken to Mrs B?'

'I passed her in the vestibule, and she said she wanted to speak to me after she'd spoken to the poisoned dwarf, as she called the boss.'

'Drugs have gone missing from some of the rooms.'

Moran let go of her quickly and raised his hands up in surrender, only managing to put them halfway up in this small space.

'Not guilty, your honour.'

'Well, you were my chief suspect, but the girls remember seeing someone in their room who said he was checking on the dates of the drugs in the cabinet.'

'How would he have got in? It's like a Swiss bank vault in here,' replied the doctor as he put his hands in his pockets and leaned closer to the screen, shaking his head.

'No idea,' replied Bella, doing the same until their cheeks were touching, inches away from the TV in front of them in this small, confined space.

'You know what we should do, Bella?'

'What?'

'Scarper,' said Moran, still leaning only inches from the screen.

'If that's not a guilty conscience...'

'Is that a motorbike? I've seen that down in the village, outside the general store. It's a Ducati Panigale, I'd know that a mile off. Expensive bike. If I were twenty years younger, it would be my bike of choice. That, and if I had twenty grand to drop.'

'Twenty thousand? For a bike?'

'Not any old bike, Bella, it's a Ducati. A Panigale. She goes like a dream.'

The moment was interrupted as they heard a voice directly outside the door. Bella put her hand down to turn the handle so that they could leave, but his hand was on it in an instant, stopping her from turning the handle. He managed to squeeze his hand up to his face and put his finger to his lips and said, '*Shh.*' It was Maureen they could hear outside the door, and Bella put her ear to the thick wood in an effort to hear what was being said, but she could only make out the occasional word. She knew from the pitch of the voices that Maureen was talking to Angelina San, explaining the predicament they were in. Then the door swung open, and Bella and Moran found themselves thrust into Maureen and Angelina.

'So, that's where we keep the CCTV, Bella, not that you'll need to use it or have access to be honest,' said Moran, and he made to walk away before he was stopped in his tracks by Maureen, who took a firm grasp of his sleeve.

'Not so fast, Sherlock,' she said, holding tight to the man's suit.

'What about ye, Mrs B?' said Moran confidently, displaying an air that showed it wasn't the first time he'd been caught in a compromising position.

'It was something we were discussing earlier.' Bella smiled at Maureen. 'Maybe we could continue our chat?'

Maureen stood rigid, changed her glance from Bella to Moran and then back to Bella. She let go of Moran's sleeve and folded her arms.

'I'll leave you to it,' said Angelina and turned to head back to the office.

'Right, you pair, if you want to get up to some 'anky panky while you're on the clock, you better think again!' warned Maureen with a wag of a long painted pink nail directed at them both, in a warning tone Bella hadn't heard before.

'Someone has been in the house and has stolen the drugs that you said were missing – it's not your eyesight or your inventory, it's him; the twins saw him in their room, someone has come in and we don't know what else is missing, but I've seen the person on CCTV and...' Bella blurted out rapidly, with a nod to the man next to her, before stopping just as quickly as the two people turned and studied her.

'Well, you're a little squealer. How did you get on inside with that kinda attitude?' asked Maureen, stepping back with folded arms to look her up and down.

Bella glanced to Moran for support, but he simply put his hands in his pockets and watched Maureen.

'So, I don't know what we can do, I mean, we can't call the police, can we?' Bella went on.

'Hmm. We need a plan, we do,' said Maureen after a moment, and began to hum.

'I'll speak to the twins,' said Moran.

'I bet you will,' said Bella under her breath.

'What was that, dear?' asked Maureen.

Bella simply smiled at the older woman and watched as Moran made for the stairs, taking them two at a time, and leaving Bella once again to explain what had taken place both with the twins and in the CCTV cupboard.

'Be careful. I'm beginning to think you're too good for 'im,' finished Maureen and headed for the office.

Bella followed closely behind.

'And how did you get on inside with that attitude, missy? I've not been inside the clink meself but I tend to keep everything under wraps, if you know what I mean. Well, I told you about what 'appened and all that to me but you should count yerself lucky. I don't go and tell any old bod about me person-als.' She leaned on the desk in the office, folded her arms and waited. 'You?' she asked, but it came out more like an order.

'I got myself into a bit of bother with a young guy,' began Bella.

'Oh yes. Do continue,' said the older woman, pushing large dark Celine glasses up her nose and waiting for Bella to speak.

'I don't know where to start. I met this guy here; he'd followed Heather back from her holidays – bit of a holiday romance. It's how I ended up inside. I thought he could help me get the village back on track but he kind of got in tow with someone else.'

'Who was that then?'

'Marcie's uncle, Callum.'

'Oh, my,' said the woman, raising her eyebrows.

'He had had a problem back home – turns out he was Russian – and was in serious debt to some very dodgy people, so he hatched a plan to do Callum out of his inheritance when his mother died, Marcie's Gramma.'

'Imagine Marple 'aving a Gramma, oh well. Go on...'

'Turns out Lisanne, that was Marcie's Gramma – she lived here, by the way – didn't leave any money of any substance to Callum, so his, um, friend, was quite annoyed as you can imag-ine. He thought if he got rid of Callum then he'd get his hand on some serious money.'

'Oh, I do like a plot twist. So where do you feature in this drama?'

'Well, I'm not proud of it,' began Bella.

'Oh, *tish-tosh*, who's proud of most of the things they've done? Spill.'

'Well, he asked me to help him with some stuff and said he'd give me money to stop my trekking centre being repossessed.

You know, it was just after the latest pandemic – we were all in the shit to be honest. Strathkin then was hardly party central,' joked Bella, but Maureen remained stony-faced. 'So, he had some people who were interested in buying Swanfield Estate for some oligarchs who needed to spend some, um, washed money let's say, and that would get him out of the bother he was in back home, so I showed them around, showed them a good time – not in *that* way – and I was going to get a cut out of any money he made. I didn't know just how dodgy he was, Mrs B, honest. He told me it was Callum who wanted to get rid of some of the property – and he did. They wanted to start a new life abroad and Cal clearly thought he was going to inherit everything, so it appeared legit. Kind of.'

'And it all went south? Sounds a bit fanciful to me.'

'He accidentally, or otherwise, poisoned some climbers who died up on the hills, and he poisoned Callum, tried to make it look like a road accident and he tried to get rid of Marcie...'

'Don't have a problem with that, to be frank. She's got a nose on her that isn't handy.'

'It just all unravelled when Cal didn't get the inheritance and Brodie, well, he was cornered.'

'Who's Brodie when 'e's at home?'

'That was the name of the Russian guy.'

'Doesn't sound very Russian to me.'

'Well, his real name was Poytr but... och, that's a long story, too.' Bella sighed, glad to have brought her previous tale out into the open.

'Russian, you say,' mused Maureen.

'Yes,' confirmed Bella.

'Funny that...'

'What?'

'I'm sure I met a Russian man recently. I said to Angie I thought the guy was Russian. Anyway, I bet you feel so much better now? Got that off yer chest.'

'Wait, what do you mean, you thought you met a Russian?'

'Had to give him a bunch of money. One of those brown envelope car park jobs, except I said to himself, oh no, Doctor De Groot, I'll do your dirty business in the cold light of day, not a problem, but I'm not meeting some random in a car park in Aberdeen at midnight to hand over a wad of cash. Met some guy in Amsterdam airport. He's been actin' as his fixer or summat.'

Bella stared at Maureen, wide eyed and horrified.

'Oh, don't be squeamish, girl. It's 'ow the world turns, innit.' Maureen was matter of fact, while Bella bit her lip. 'Anyway, I only said coulda been Russian... to be honest, with my eyesight he coulda been Clark Gable, wouldn't have made any difference to me. Let's get a move on, I'm in the mood for a nice cup of tea. Chop chop.' She turned and headed to the kitchen at the back of the house.

Bella felt a churn in her stomach. *Surely not*, she thought to herself, *that would be just too much of a coincidence*. Fanciful indeed.


In Lochside Croft a peacefulness had settled. Ruaridh had taken the boys to shinty practice, and with all five males out of the house, all was still. Marcie was peering down at a plastic container that contained cupcakes.

'Well, the recipe did say cupcakes.'

Dina looked into the box then up at Marcie. She shook her head.

'I think it was the baking powder,' Marcie apologised.

'Hmm, I think it was more than the baking powder. You're usually a very good baker. I have Granny Gabs's old recipe books. I decided when I got married, I was going to do a recipe a week. But that quickly turned into a month, then every couple of months.'

'When did you last open it?'

'About eight years ago!'

Marcie burst out laughing, and Dina laughed until she broke into a cough that started as a tickle in her throat then had her gasping for breath. She and Marcie were sitting on the bed in the guest room, both with backs to the wall across the hand-made quilt, legs straight out in front of them. Marcie lifted the cup of water she was holding to Dina's lips, and she took it in an effort to stop the coughing as her doctor told her to do – *divert yourself away from the cough and it'll stop – the more you think about it then it'll have a chance to take over.*

'All okay?' asked Marcie as she rubbed Dina's back.

Dina patted her knee in thanks. If there was one thing the four girl friends of Strathkin were good at, it was laughing and having fun. Sometimes there could be tension like in any friend-ship, but laughter always won in the end. Even though today there were only two women giggling like schoolgirls at Lochside Croft, the missing two were there in spirit. Dina sat back up against the wall and tossed the plastic container of listless sponge cakes to one side. Instead, she began to fill her mouth with giant pink and white marshmallows from a bag sitting next to her. Her mouth was now so full she couldn't close it, and her cheeks were puffing out and she said as much as was audible. 'What if I die like this? It'll take a while, but the children will be able to tell their grandchildren a funny story about how their great-grandmother passed away – death by mallow.'

The tears were running down Marcie's face. 'Dina! Don't! I'm sore from laughing!'

Dina tried to speak again but her mouth was turning into a gooey mess as the mixture melted, and she spat the mallows, now in double figures, out into her palm, still laughing.

'They're absolutely disgusting, but you know I love the sugar rush and always have. Do you want a chocolate?'

As Marcie agreed and put her hand out, Dina squished the spat-out mess into her hand and closed it over.

'Oh, D! Yuck!' complained Marcie as the pink and white mess oozed out through her fingers.

'Don't say I'm not kind to you. I'm just returning them to their rightful owner – you brought them in.'

Marcie made a face like she was about to be sick then sat back against the wall, letting out a sigh with a giggle. 'Thankfully, these are thick jeans 'cause your hands are disgusting! You're mental! Do you know what I think we should do?' she began until Dina placed a sticky hand on her knee.

'Not making plans, Mars. You're only going to be disappointed. And I'm sorry to be the one to tell you, you're going to have to get a new designer. I'm not going to be able to see the renovations through to completion. Sorry about that.' Dina squeezed Marcie's knee. Marcie rested her hand on top of her friend's.

The blunt statement hit Marcie harder than she expected, and she intertwined her fingers with Dina's, the top of which was still a sticky mess. 'Ssh. I don't want to think about it.'

'I can think of nothing else,' Dina said and sat back, once again both side by side, legs out on the handmade quilt, backs against the wall. 'You know how people say, *oh life is short*, and we all dismiss it and laugh it off. Turns out it's true.' She shuffled on the bed and settled herself, her hand still resting on her best friend's. 'What I'm trying to say is that if we need to do something, to change something, to escape from something, we need to do it now. We only get one chance. Don't leave it until it's too late. Trying to talk to Ruaridh about it has been a nightmare. He doesn't want to know. Actually, that's not strictly true. He thinks if he doesn't confront it then it'll go away. You know how he hates change. Likes everything in a steady state. I sat him down and told him we need to have 'that' discussion. That he can't spend the rest of his life grieving me. That he's got to find someone else.'

'You're irreplaceable, D.'

'Well, maybe not a replacement as such but those boys need a mother. He can't be both. I look at you and...' Marcie sat up at Dina's statement. 'Well, you lost your mum and dad, and your granny became your de facto mum and your uncle, your dad.'

'I think I turned out all right!'

'That's what I was meaning. They need both. He can't do it on his own, and my mum has enough on her plate. I mean, you're the twins' godmother, but I'm not expecting you to step in as their stepmother.' Marcie nodded.

'I told him not to be afraid of internet dating. It's all the rage, particularly for people not brought up like us. People in the big cities. I mean, Heather hasn't been that successful but that's by the by.' Dina gave a sharp intake of breath, and it was clear she was still in some discomfort.

'Do you want to sit up?'

'No, no, this is fine. So, I said to him by all means grieve for me but you're too young. Too young to go through the rest of your life alone. The children will keep him busy and occupied, of course, but I know it won't be long until Dax gets a girlfriend, then the twins and before you know it, they'll all have left home, and he'll be sitting in here like billy no mates.'

Marcie laughed at the thought of Ruaridh sitting alone staring into the flames of the fire. The man who was always surrounded by other men, children, relatives and, for some reason, women of a certain age who found him charming and irresistible.

'There will be new women moving into the area. They've approved that planning permission for twelve houses at Strath Aullt so you never know. I'm ever hopeful.'

'I mean, even at that place across the road. I think they'll bring in proper therapists and it would be great to think someone is sorting out that stiff neck of his and he's already said he knows he's going to get arthritis in his knees like his dad – all that kneeling on the hills when they're taking the visitors out stalking.'

*Tell her.*

'He used to call it *early onset rigor mortis* and we laughed about it but now... uh-uh... can't speak about death.'

'Dina...'

'I just want the whole family settled.' Dina squeezed Marcie's hand. 'You'll be the same. Family is everything. I'm just leaving them too soon. I was frightened, Mars, at the beginning, really frightened but then I came to accept it. I just need to sort all this out before I go. I need to know I've done my best for him. For them.'

Marcie bit her lip and she realised this was simply not the time. Not the place. Not the moment. She heard a door slam. Chattering voices returned as the quiet of their time together drifted out the window. She heard Ruaridh shout something from the kitchen and Donald, the eldest twin, knocked the door and peeped around it.

'That's us back. Dad wants to know if you're coming out for tea, or do you want a tray?'

The women looked at each other, and Dina made to shuffle off the bed.

'Are you sure? We can stay here?' asked Marcie, but Dina pushed herself with some effort from the wall to the edge of the bed. Donald held out his hand to his mother and led her from the room. She stretched her hand behind her. When she took Marcie's hand, it was still sticky and she stuck to Dina like glue as they made their way to the kitchen table.

# THIRTY-ONE

'Independence Day,' said Doctor Arshia Brahmins as she sat back with her bottle of Cobra beer, smiling at the man in front of her who had been so effusive about her cooking.

'The movie?' Poytr quizzed.

'No, when we got married. You asked the other night. I was always mad about anything American, and my parents said if we – me and my brother – either agreed to become doctors or lawyers, then they would take us to Disney in Florida. I loved it so much; we went there on our honeymoon! Fourth of July. I had to show Krish that it was, in fact, really *the* happiest place on earth!' She giggled.

Poytr joined in despite the fact he detested anything American and thought the best thing for Mickey Mouse was a dose of rat poison. He told her to stay curled up on the sofa and he would clear everything away and, after the briefest of protests, she agreed. He deftly stacked the dishwasher and put plastic wrap on the leftovers. He continued talking from the kitchen while he rifled in her bag, did what he had to do with the set of surgery keys, replacing them in her bag in the blink of an eye. When he returned to the living room, he sat in the seat near the fire and, despite an encouraging tap of the seat next to her, he remained some way away and they continued their conversation at a distance.

'You never told me what you do?' Arshia asked through a stifled yawn.

'I'm writing a book – that's why I've rented a remote place out of the way, with no distractions... almost.'

'Almost?' She gave him a sultry look.

He got up and walked over to where she sat, curled up like a cat. He lifted her chin and gently kissed her lips until he felt her breathing change. 'I have a deadline tomorrow. My agent is on my case. But the weekend is only days away,' he said and kissed her forehead. She unfastened two buttons of her silk shirt while her eyes didn't leave his. He didn't flinch.

'How about Saturday night? I can come back – I'll even bring breakfast?' Poytr suggested, and he heard her give a little gasp.

'Deal,' she said.

He kissed her cheek, made his way past her and picked up his backpack from the kitchen table on the way to the back door. His plan was coming along nicely.

# THIRTY-TWO

The look on Gemma Macintyre's face could only be described as one thing: *surly*. The recipient of that look was none other than her sister, Lucinda. And, sitting between them, were Doctor Moran Maguire and Jonathan Bartlett, both there to try to change the mind of the girl who wanted to end her life at the same time as her sister, later that night. Moran leaned close to her, his eyes settling on hers, which she found distracting, and she turned her face to the side to try to avoid his intense gaze.

'I know you two have talked it through,' he said in a low, concerned voice, 'but you need to take a step back and look at it from your sister's perspective.'

'Where's the other doctor?'

'He's not here right at this very minute, but he asked me to speak with you.'

'I don't think he did because you're telling me the opposite of what he told me,' began Gemma, 'and he agreed with me, that we could go together.'

'Well, while that might have been true some days ago, your sister tells me that things might have changed, however, since you had a wee chat with that lady across the way,' said Moran with a nod over the water to the white croft that could be clearly seen from the wide window.

'I've not changed my mind – she has.' Gemma eyed her sister opposite. Moran moved his chair a little closer, and Gemma backed away again as she felt him invade her personal space.

He took her hand in his. It was softer than she imagined, and his other hand closed over it. She gazed up into his eyes and realised that it had been at university that she had last been this close to a man. She left shortly after her only dalliance, her degree in Marine Biology still in its tube in her dressing table, unused and of no use for the life she had now. Lucinda had left the year before. Gemma had known that caring for her sister, as her health declined, was now her only goal in life: what was left of it.

'I've spoken to Lucinda, and I know how she feels, that she has had a change of heart. Now you know that. I also know that Mrs Balfour, Dina Balfour, and her story affected you both.'

'It affected me, too,' said Jonathan Bartlett who had remained quiet since joining the foursome.

'I feel sorry for her but...' began Gemma.

'She has five children, Gem. She's only a few years older than us,' said Lucinda in a quiet but authoritative voice. She may have only been a few minutes older than her sister, but it was clear she was the elder in more ways than one. There was silence in the room and Gemma gazed down at Moran's hands which had gently and silently encircled her own.

'What will happen to her children?' she asked after a moment, without looking up.

'Well, I'm sure her husband will have to give up work to look after them. The youngest is just a bairn,' replied Moran.

'But doesn't he work here?' she went on.

'He does occasional work, yes, driving and the like, but that'll have to stop with a five-a-side football team to look after.'

'But what has this got to do with me?' asked Gemma, directly to the man in front of her, still letting him hold her hands.

'You're perfectly healthy, my dear,' replied Jonathan Bartlett who had been watching proceedings. 'What I wouldn't give to have your heart, your soul, your spirit. Like your sister here, I'm ready to shake off my mortal coil. But you? You should be planning your life, not your death. When your time comes you should be in a big bed, in your own home, surrounded by your children and grandchildren, not here,' he finished, gazing around the room.

'Dina doesn't want to die at home surrounded by her children,' said Gemma by way of a disagreement, though she didn't remove her hand from Moran's grip.

'Different circumstances,' qualified the doctor. 'I'm sure if she had your money she'd choose wisely.'

'I'm not changing my mind,' insisted Gemma.

'Well, Gem, I didn't want to bring this up, but we may have a problem. One of our, er assistants, well, he removed the wrong drugs from your room the other day and we have a wee bit of a supply issue,' Moran explained to disguise the recent theft of drugs by someone unknown to them and their tight little group.

'Well, buy more,' replied the woman in a matter-of-fact tone.

'It's not as easy as that this far north, to tell you the truth. You see, that's where the other doctor has gone. He's gone to personally pick up the latest batch. I didn't want to have to tell you that but I'm afraid that's the position we find ourselves in, Gemma,' said Moran with so much conviction, he almost believed the yarn himself.

The sisters exchanged a look. It wasn't the normal loving

glance that he had become used to seeing but instead it appeared to have moved to a different level.

'You know what we need to do?' asked the doctor. 'I think we could all do with a drink.'

Jonathan made his way over to the cocktail trolley and started lining up crystal glasses.

'Who'll join me in a G&T?'

'I'll have one,' replied Lucinda and found herself on the receiving end of a look from her sibling. 'What have I got to lose?'

Jonathan exchanged glances with Moran and began to drop large ice cubes into the four glasses. He handed one first to Lucinda and then to the man sitting next to her and returned to the trolley. When he came back, he handed a glass to Gemma who shook her head.

'It's okay, it's just tonic and lemon,' he said quietly, and she smiled at him before taking the glass, almost reluctantly.

Gemma stood up and walked to the window, taking a sip from her glass which was indeed only filled with tonic. She gazed out at the cottage on the other side of the loch. Moran was up like the wind to follow her, standing so close to her she could hear his breathing.

'Stunning, isn't it?' She felt him lean behind her, his arm reaching to the window lintel. 'Imagine never seeing that again...' His voice was mesmerising, soft and comforting.

'I want to die,' she said in a whisper.

'I don't think you do, Gemma. I don't even think you've started living yet,' he whispered into her ear, and she felt herself shiver and a feeling she thought long dead stir inside her.

'I don't want to lose her,' she said and lifted her hand to let her finger trace the image of the white cottage on the window.

'Sometimes when you lose something, you gain something else,' he said on a breath.

Gemma leaned back slightly to feel Moran's body against her. She didn't move, allowing him to breathe slowly onto the back of her neck. Maybe he was right, maybe Lucinda was right, maybe she was making the wrong decision. Maybe it wasn't too late to change her mind.

# THIRTY-THREE

Encountering Marcie Mosse seething was not an experience you would want to repeat without the aid of a strong libation. Heather was loudly munching from a bowl of sweet and salty popcorn as the battle between her two friends was in full swing. Heather's eyes flitted from one friend to the other, eating noisily, until both her girlfriends stopped and looked at her.

'Sorry, this is delicious. I can only afford the cheap stuff. This popcorn is amazing.'

'Just take a step back. You're now not wanting to buy back your precious stables because you're paying for Dina to move into Swanfield? I mean, what the actual, Bella!'

'It's not like that per se.'

'It's not like that, *per se*? What the feck is it then because I'm really struggling with this conversation?' said Marcie as she strained tagliatelle though a pasta strainer and threw it back into the pot before emptying several spoonsful of homemade roasted vegetables in. She emptied the pasta into a large white bowl, tipping the rest of the vegetables on top, picking up her cheese slicer and shaving off large pieces of parmesan on top of the pasta. She placed the steaming bowl in the middle of the table and started to pour glasses of wine. Finally, she dropped on to one of the chairs around the round beechwood table. Simon sauntered in and removed the empty bottle, swiftly replacing it with a fresh cold wine with the deftness of an experienced hand. He placed a fresh platter of homemade garlic flatbread on the table, and silently slipped out of the room, smiling at the girls. He gave his wife a signal that he was heading out before Marcie started speaking again. She took a very large gulp of the wine and breathed in a deep sigh. She sat back as the other two women sat down, Heather carefully folding the packet of popcorn shut and sitting it next to her cutlery.

'Start from the beginning?'

'Well, I wasn't really sure at first when they asked me to work there, but they do really good end-of-life care...'

'End-of-life care... *at Swanfield*.' Marcie held her hand up, 'Yes, I know it's called something else now!'

Bella and Heather exchanged a look.

'So, it's like a hospice?'

'You could say that, I mean, you've been in it, it's very high-end.'

'Uh-huh?'

'Dina expressed a wish to go there in her final days.'

Another look was exchanged between Heather and Bella, as they knew they were treading on extremely dangerous ground with the black and white lawyer who sat in front of them. Heather reached out and slid her hand into the popcorn, sneaking a couple of pieces.

'It's private?' asked Marcie.

'Yes.'

'How much will it cost her?'

'Well, I'm hoping to get a, er, staff discount.'

Marcie put down her spoon and fork and poured herself another glass of wine, topping up her friends' glasses at the same time.

'I mean, she doesn't want to go to Inverness or Strathdon to the hospice.'

'Can we pay for a private nurse?'

'WE?' asked Heather, between mouthfuls of pasta and popcorn until Marcie threw her a look of, *well, we know we means me.*

'She has a Macmillan nurse. But, really, just at the very end, when *she* decides it's, erm, time.'

'So, let's just rewind. It's more like a kind of Dignitas than a hospice?'

'Hmmm,' replied Bella, sucking in her cheeks while playing with her pasta. 'They promote dignity in dying.'

'I'm really uncomfortable with this. I knew there was something odd going on there. It's all so shady and murky,' said Marcie, shaking her head.

'You're only saying that 'cause it used to be Swanfield. Everyone is so exceedingly kind; people really can die with dignity.'

'If you can afford a helicopter. Are you benefiting from this?' Marcie asked as she turned to Heather.

'Well, I sometimes let them have Adam or provide a bit of a supper – you organised the first one, so you know how much I took in.'

'What exactly are they *licensed* to do?'

'That's above my pay grade, Marce.'

'It's a very grey area,' concluded the lawyer.

The girls opposite each other exchanged another look.

'Look at it this way. Roma, Apache, Flash, Ace, they were all our horses, right? What happened to every single one of them?'

'Cushing's,' replied Marcie.

'So, all our horses got an equine disease, and we had them euthanised. We provided them with a straightforward way out. Why can't we allow people to have that decision?'

'Well, the beasts didn't really play a part in the discussion...' qualified Marcie.

'What I'm trying to say is that don't *we* deserve to make our own decisions about how *we* shuffle off our mortal coil? Yes, there will be a referendum or whatever, but everyone shies away from it. They don't want to bring it up because suddenly they're faced with their own mortality. It's okay if it's happening over there.' Bella pointed into the middle distance, wine in her glass in danger of spilling over the tablecloth. 'I've seen the paperwork that guests must sign. It states quite clearly that it's for people with a terminal condition that's incurable, irreversible, progressive and advanced. Six months to live. It's all overseen by a medical professional.'

'But legally, it's still wrong, it's *murder*,' stated Marcie.

'Are you telling me it doesn't go on secretly elsewhere?' suggested Bella.

Marcie shrugged.

Heather's eyes flitted from friend to friend and decided it was time to interject. 'So, what are we going to do about Dina?' she asked to bring the conversation back round to why they had been invited to dinner. 'And Ruaridh.'

Marcie had thought long and hard about Ruaridh Balfour. She would certainly provide him and his young family with enough money to hire someone in, a live-in nanny or au pair to look after the house and children, otherwise he wouldn't be able to work at any of the many jobs he currently juggled with his terminally ill wife and young family to support. Whether he took the money or not would be a different matter. Marcie knew how proud he was and receiving handouts was not something he would normally ever consider – well, not before he had been dealt such a hard blow. Ruaridh Balfour, the one-time love of her life. The man everyone thought would end up with Marcella Mosse in the big house, master of all he surveyed. But sometimes life doesn't deal you the card you either want or desire and you just pick up and play with what you have in your hand.

No one answered the question Heather posed and forks were noisily thrown on plates as, once again, all three women had only one thing on their mind. Their best friend, Dina Balfour.

# THIRTY-FOUR

Simon's escape from the girls' long and involved chat had come at a price. A walk before bed had now turned into a cat-and-mouse game, he never believed possible. He was breathing hard as he ran the fastest he had ever run in his life. Through gorse and over moss-covered stones, almost falling several times but somehow managing to stay upright. He stopped for a second to listen and the sound of the motorbike appeared to be far away in the distance. He had managed to lose him as he detoured from the road into the forest, but without a landmark or knowing what side of the loch he was on, Simon was unmistakably lost. He had walked in these hills for years but with dusk settling, he was bamboozled. He'd lost sight of the mountain range through the trees, so didn't know whether he was heading further into the darkness of the dense forest or approaching the shoreline. Then he heard the bike again. This time it sounded more like a dirt bike or a trail bike instead of the designer bike that had nearly knocked him off the road. It was when it came round for a second, then a third time that he realised he was being hunted.

His long walk up to the far side of the estate, to Broomfield, had taken him out of phone signal and far from life in this deserted part of the wider area of Strathkin. He hadn't expected to see anyone around, so when he noticed a man walking back and forth from the croft to the workshop situated adjacent to the little white cottage, he knew this was more than an itinerant using the property as a squat. He watched from behind a tree, puzzled about the man's appearance; smart, bearded, lean, well taken care of. This wasn't just a van camper taking a chance. Simon was convinced Marcie still owned the property, so he was momentarily confused. He stood next to a tree and held up his phone, taking a photograph of the man, and he cursed as he heard the phone 'click' loudly like a camera as it took a burst of several pictures.

The man stopped dead in his tracks and gazed around, apparently observing nothing in the still of the late afternoon. His head was raised up like a deer about to escape the inevitable bullet, and he sniffed the air. A red kite swirled above, caught in the thermals, and the bearded man's eyes drifted upwards for a second or two. Simon slid back behind the tree, hoping that his green fleece would allow him to blend into the forest, as he thought to himself, *why on earth didn't you just approach the man? He may be renting legitimately, and you just don't know.* As he stepped back, he felt the branch crunch under his foot, with the accompanying loud noise. He decided to head back now, before the sun began to set and he would have to find the loch road in the dark and spend two hours listening to yet another podcast. It was the sound of a gun being cocked that brought him very swiftly back to the present.

'Is it illegal to take pictures of someone without their permission in this country?' said the voice behind him.

'Listen, mate,' began Simon, who instinctively wanted to raise his hands up in mock surrender, 'my mistake. I deleted it. Thought you were someone else. You look like someone I know.'

'Who?'

'A guy I know in the village.'

'So, you just randomly go around taking pictures of people like some pervert?'

'Listen, mate.'

'I'm not your *mate*,' said the stranger, and Simon noticed a slight accent.

He certainly wasn't one of the Polish workers who had worked on the farm site previously. His English was better and his clothes didn't resemble workwear. Yet, something about him was familiar. Simon turned around slowly and was shocked to see not only how close the man was, but that he was pointing a handgun directly at him. He stared at the gun and realised his life, for no reason, could be extinguished in an instant. Brought up on a farm in Yorkshire, Simon was no stranger to hardware for despatching animals and vermin, but a Glock 9mm was not something you'd see being casually carried on a farm anywhere in this neck of the woods, in his opinion.

'I'm only out for a walk, mate,' he said as he raised his arms. 'I was just taking in the air. I'll be on my way in a minute.' He felt his voice begin to break a little and fear crept over him. The two men eyed each other with the bearded man cocking his head a little.

'I know you. I've seen you,' he said, and Simon noticed that accent again. Within an instant he felt the sweat begin to gather on his back and run down his spine. It was as if someone had suddenly pulled back a curtain to reveal the actors in a play. Simon gulped hard. It didn't go unnoticed.

'You look a bit worried, *mate?*' said the man mockingly, holding the gun steady and with purpose opposite an increasingly worried Simon.

'Well, I've never been threatened with violence over a photograph,' said Simon with a quivering smile to calm down what he saw as an increasingly escalating situation. *If I can't defuse this with humour*, thought the Yorkshireman, *I'm a goner.*

'Thing is, I wasn't expecting you to turn up, I was sure it was going to be your ever resourceful wife.'

*It is him*, thought Simon, *I knew it*. This posed him a problem. *I either must play stupid like I don't know who he is, or I fess up and distance myself from my wife.*

'I just wanted to see who was renting the place,' offered Simon.

A bird squawked above them, and they both looked up sharply. Simon watched incredulously as the man raised the gun and took out the bird that had been flying low in the glade of the trees. It bundled to the ground without another sound, and they both continued their standoff. Simon wanted to run, to take off at speed, but walking boots were not like his running trainers and he didn't know how long it would take for him to stumble and fall and be taken out like the bird so needlessly killed seconds before.

'Mr Marcella Mosse.' The accent was so clear now, it could only be him. The man almost spat out the name and this riled Simon, but he decided to keep his counsel. He realised that keeping his mouth shut may allow him to stay alive for at least a little while longer.


Several miles away, Marcie examined her watch.

'Going somewhere?' asked Heather.

'Simon's been away a while, and I know how particular he is at packing. He likes to pack everything in a set way so that he can capture the *Highland air*. We're a bit tumble dryer forward in London.'

Heather marvelled at these new expressions and couldn't fathom why someone wouldn't put their laundry out on a washing line in the garden to dry and capture all that fresh mountain air. Come rain or shine the laundry at the Inn was dried outside.

'He said he'd be back for something to eat – take some of our leftovers – but he's probably lost track of time,' thought Marcie aloud.

'When does he go back?'

'Tomorrow. Then he'll come back up in a few days,' she replied with a glance to the large designer wall clock. While he wasn't a stickler for punctuality as much as his wife, Marcie knew that it was unusual for him to stray off course in their plans and, as she was staying on, she wanted him back tonight. They needed to talk.

'And you?' asked Bella.

'I can work from home. I can't go back until, well, I just couldn't *not* be here,' she replied, and all three of them found a place in the room to look to distract from the conversation.


At The Retreat, the sound of the ticking clock was annoying Maureen. It had become the soundtrack to her life, every minute leading her closer to the inevitable. She opened the window and breathed in deeply as fresh air filled the room. Closing her eyes, her mind drifted to her last moments with her Brian. Her reverie was cut short as a loud *bang* far away in the distance brought her back to the present.

'Bloody poachers,' she said aloud and snapped the window shut. Glancing around the room she headed to the door, closing it quietly behind her. She tapped the pocket of her dress, reminding herself that she had the required number of drugs secreted away for when the time was right. At the top of the stairs, she met the Macintyre twins, Gemma's arm linked with her sister as Lucinda was clearly struggling.

'Ladies, how many times do I have to tell you that we have a lift? Just give me the nod.'

'It's the only exercise I get.' Lucinda stopped several steps away from the top landing, trying to disguise her panting.

Maureen smiled and stepped aside. She was about to speak when Moran came bounding up the stairs.

'What's all this, ladies? Don't you know we have a lift?' he said as he encircled the weaker of the two women in his arms. Maureen raised her eyes to the ceiling as Moran helped Lucinda up the remaining stairs and guided her to her room. Gemma took in the scene with a smile that Maureen knew extremely well and thought, *here we go again*. Moran gently let her down into the plush reading chair, and Lucinda felt relieved knowing that it would be the last day she'd make the journey up the stairs.

'Are you okay now? Can I get you anything?' he asked, leaning down to her with his concerned bedside manner, and his hand resting on her arm. She smiled up at him and mouthed 'no, but thank you,' in a voice that came out in no more than a whisper.

In the corridor, Maureen had held back her sister.

'How's she doing, dear? We're working on getting our items all delivered in the next few days so that we can get everything organised for you lovelies.' Maureen smiled.

'Thanks, Maureen, but I have been thinking of everything that people have said to me over the last few days. That woman across the water, Diana, I keep thinking of her and her husband and all those children.'

'Dina, dear,' corrected Maureen.

'I just feel so sorry for her. She's so young. Her husband is so lovely. Her children are just, well, tiny.'

'They could do with so much help,' suggested Maureen.

'Am I being selfish, Mrs B?' asked Gemma to the elderly lady standing in front of her.

'Here's the very man to help you decide,' said Maureen as Moran made his way from her sister's room to stand next to Mrs B.

'Ladies,' he greeted, hands firmly in pockets and taking a casual stance.

'Gemma wants a word. I'm going to have a cuppa tea with your lovely sister,' said Maureen and turned to head back to the room that had just been vacated by Doctor Maguire.

Gemma bit the inside of her lip. Moran placed his palm on the small of her back, ushering her quietly forward along the corridor, where he led her through a door and up a small flight of stairs. They entered a stunning modern white room that was almost Scandinavian in appearance. A huge painting adorned the wall opposite the bed: the stunning head of a sea eagle that looked like it was about to swoop out of the canvas and take off through the window.

'It's beautiful up here!' Gemma said finally as she took it all in. She crossed to a door, releasing herself from Moran's tight grip of her hand, and opened it to reveal a stunning bathroom in white marble with a huge double walk-in shower and a giant rolltop bath. She picked up a thick, fluffy white towel that was draped over a huge white vintage towel rail and sniffed it – it smelled wonderful. The whole room had a calming scent with notes of lavender and neroli. When she went back into the bedroom, Moran had positioned himself on a grey sofa that had sheepskin rugs casually thrown over the back, and she sat next to him.

'I never thought for one minute—' she began.

'This is The Eagle's Nest,' he interrupted her before she had a chance to ask.

'It's absolutely gorgeous.' She smiled, and he watched her face light up, a scene he took in before placing his hand under her chin, lifting her head up. She gazed up at him. His lips grazed hers ever so briefly until she closed her eyes and when she opened them, he was sitting back on the edge of the sofa.

'I have a bit of a problem, Gemma,' he confessed.

'Yes?' she said breathlessly.

'I'm not sure I'm going to be able to agree to your wishes. I may have to leave that to someone else, to Doctor De Groot.'

'What? Why?'

He took her hand and moved forward in his seat, clearing his throat. 'I think I'm falling for you, Gemma Macintyre, therefore I obviously can't go ahead with your wishes to help you end your life.'

'Oh,' said Gemma, surprised at this admission.

'I couldn't do it. I'm sorry.'

She waited for a moment. His gaze dropped to look at her small pale hand as he began to entwine his fingers with hers.

'I'm having second thoughts,' she said, so quietly it was like a whisper. 'I've spoken to Luce. We were up all night. I think, *we think*, I should be using my money – *our money* – for good. Someone said we've been so caught up in the process of dying we're in danger of forgetting how to live. Lucy still wants to go, but we made the decision that I'll stay. I want to help the family of that woman across the road. I want to help other people with what Lucinda has and help them live a better life. I could start a small foundation in her memory, promote her legacy.' She blurted it all out at once, as if the very thought of it would change her mind if she didn't say the words out loud and quickly enough.

'You're making the right decision, darlin', I can assure you of that.'

As he spoke, he let his eyes look deep into hers, and she felt a tingle run from her neck to her spine. A noise, like a sharp crack outside, startled a flock of birds, but Gemma was already so wrapped up in the strong arms of this wonderful man, she failed to notice.

# THIRTY-FIVE

Simon felt certain that it would be only seconds before another shot would finally take him down. A distraction had allowed him to turn, to escape. And now he was hiding in a thicket of bushes having run through gorse, machair and grass and had no idea of where he was. It was now dark, and he had completely lost his bearings. He dug deep into his pocket and muttered 'feck' – his phone was still showing no signal. There wasn't a mast for miles and the area was so remote, no location tracker would work so far into the wilderness. He had felt a sharp pain in his left leg and hoped it was the result of him stumbling on to some rocks as he tried to jump across a small stream before falling heavily, and when he reached down, he felt his water-proof trousers damp from, he hoped, the water.

He waited until his breathing regulated and listened with his eyes closed to hear any movement behind him, in front of him or anywhere in the area around him. He thought of his wife still at home, and the fact she knew every part of this estate. He thought of all the times she wanted to drag him out on one of her famous tours either on foot or on horseback and he refused, citing work, or tiredness, or simply finding any old excuse to put it off for another day. Now, here he was, in the middle of nowhere with no idea of where he was or if he would, in fact, ever make it home.

He looked up at the moon and knew, with the mountains on his left-hand side, he would be able to reach the village if he kept them on his left and tried not to veer off course. He had walked for at least two hours before he reached Broomfield. If he could hear anything that sounded like the ocean on the other side of the Drovers' Road, or the loch beating against the shore near the foot of the mountains, he would get his bearings. But apart from the occasional owl, and the gentle rustle of the trees, there was nothing. What he did hear was the crunch of branches underfoot behind him and the click of a gun being cocked. He closed his eyes. He thought of his wife and how much he loved her.

At Sweet Briar, Marcie checked her watch for the umpteenth time.

'Are you sure you're taking him to the airport tomorrow?' asked Heather as she, too, cast a glance at her watch. 'Couldn't Ruaridh step in?'

'Yes, but I'll take him, if he gets back in time,' said Marcie as she peered out the large window, hands now resting on her hips.

Simon was a country boy, but there was a clear difference in the scenery of the north Yorkshire moors and the rugged desolate Highland landscape. It was now pitch black, *black dark* they called it when it was so dark and there was no light pollution, no streetlights and only the moon to guide you. She had every faith in his sense of direction, but five hours was a long time to be away with nothing but a snack bar for sustenance. She had heard the occasional shot from a poacher out on the hill breaking the silence, and she began to have an uneasy feeling, a feeling she remembered all too well from not that long ago. She felt her stomach start to churn and a shiver ran through her body. Despite her concerns about their marriage, she still cared about Simon very much.

'Are you okay?' asked Heather, seeing the sudden change in her friend's demeanour.

'He goes out every day to walk or hike. Just this time. Hmm...' Her face told a story to her friend. 'I'm going out. Let's get the car,' Marcie announced it so loud it startled Heather, and she immediately leaned over to pick up a light fleece jacket from the back of a dining chair.

'I'll come with you,' she said, and she wrapped her pashmina tighter around her shoulders.

'I'll head next door then.' Bella sighed.

'Thing is, I have really no idea where he was headed,' said Marcie to her two friends as they made their way to where Marcie's car sat at the back of the house.

Bella walked around the long garden, past the helicopter pad at the bottom of the grassed area and on to the newly laid road. She waved as her two friends drove past and then turned as she heard a noise coming from the woods far up along the Drovers' Road.

'I'm glad someone is back; I forgot the number for the keypad,' said the person sitting on the Adirondack chair on the back patio.

'Gosh! You gave me such a start!' said Bella, her hand on her chest as the white-haired figure of Jonathan Bartlett came into view, followed by the aroma of an expensive cigar.

'Just out enjoying the peace and taking in the Highland air.' He held up his expensive Montecristo cigar, getting up from his seat to join her. 'I've taken the opportunity of putting that money in your holding account, the one we discussed. I appreciate the time you've taken with me, Isabella. I also appreciate the time you've taken with the twins. Looks like you've influenced our young Gemma. She's changed, or is changing, her mind. I can feel it. I think you've missed your vocation as a counsellor.'

She was about to respond when they were both disturbed by the loud sound of a shot from the woods where Isabella had been earlier.

'I don't know what those poachers are trying to kill but I'm not sure it's ready to die,' said Jonathan to Bella as he took in her puzzled face. 'Is everything okay?' He gave her shoulder a quick squeeze. 'Isabella?'

She tensed under his hand on her shoulder and turned her head towards where the sound of the shot had come from, her face angled to the woods with the knowledge of someone who had lived a country life and knew instinctively when something was just not right.

'I think they might be looking in the wrong place,' she said to herself and dug into her back pocket to find her phone and quickly dial Marcie's number. It went straight to voicemail as they were already clearly out of range. She didn't leave a message, but went to settings, made sure her location services were switched on and put her phone back in her pocket.

'Isabella, may I say, you look like you have just seen a ghost,' said Jonathan, on seeing her startled face.

'I might be about to,' she said and started swiftly towards the Drovers' Road.


Simon Grainger was tall and lithe, but slim and light enough for the man who had shot him to lift him without too much difficulty and throw him unceremoniously over the back of the motorbike. Like an undignified stag being taken from the hill, he was driven slowly down to the cleared site where a large grey truck sat idle in the clearing behind The Retreat. It was a place

Poytr Medvedev had identified earlier as the future deposition site of Simon's wife after he had drugged her into submission. Coming across her husband unexpectedly, however, was a fly in his ointment. He knew he would now have to deal with them both at once, which hadn't been in his plan. But he was nothing if not resourceful.

After dragging Simon from the motorbike, he deposited his quarry in the back of the large truck. After jumping out of the back of the large grey vehicle, he waited for a moment to listen. His victim's breathing was heavy but expected. He decided to walk back to where he needed to be, leaving the motorbike propped up against a tree, hidden away from the clearing. He took off his leather gloves, shoved them into his back pocket, and whistled quietly to himself as he made his way down the hill to Sweet Briar.

High up on the back road Marcie and Heather had reached the top of the hill in the dark and looked around without getting out of the car.

'Where do we start?' Marcie asked.

Heather peered out into the darkness that surrounded them.

'Did he have a bivvy with him or anything?'

'He was just going out for a bit of a hike. The most he had was an oat flapjack or something. I mean, he did leave in time to be back for a late supper. I wonder if we should drive up to Broomfield or Tigh-na-Lochan. He may have gone for a wander and met someone. They're both empty, but what if he's taken ill?' Marcie said and it worried her to think that something ominous may have happened. Not prone to uneasiness or maudlin thoughts, something insidious was creeping over her. Marcie turned to Heather. 'Let's just head back,' she said, and Heather agreed.

They turned the car on to the road that took them away from the short drive to Broomfield and on to the road that took them back down to Strathkin village.

'Let's go around, see if he's ended up back at the Inn, gone for a pint,' suggested Heather to lighten the mood, and they drove quickly down the dark, remote road until they reached the car park of The Strathkin Inn.

It was busy inside the bar, but the restaurant was empty save for a few overnight guests. They went into the back office, where Marcie's phone suddenly flashed to life with a location pin with Isabella's name attached to it. She checked that there was no message from Simon, then replaced her phone in her pocket.

'Anything?' asked Heather who had organised two coffees in tall glass mugs.

'Nada,' said Marcie, taking the latte, and she watched as Heather used her own phone to call Simon, holding the phone up between them.

'Still no signal, text only,' she said, taking a large gulp of the milky liquid.

'I'll head back; he's probably turned up and will be wondering why I'm not there.' Marcie was trying to convince herself that all was well despite an increasingly uneasy feeling nestling in her stomach.

'Sure,' said Heather and finished her coffee, her eyes resting on her friend's concerned face.

# THIRTY-SIX

Preparations had been carefully made. The scene had been set. The room had been staged and lit, and specific drugs, previously missing, had been mysteriously discovered by Doctor De Groot, after a stern phone call with his 'fixer'.

'Where's Bella?' Gemma asked Maureen who was in deep discussion with Moran. The doctor was checking, and double-checking, paperwork. He wasn't keen on anyone bowing out without the final sign-off from Doctor De Groot or his wife, but they were both currently in Amsterdam, phones off, uncontactable.

'I know she went next door to have a bite to eat with our neighbour, but I haven't seen her for a little while,' replied Maureen, reaching deep into the pocket of her tiger print trousers and digging out her phone. She held it out, far away from her, and pressed a single number which took her to a voicemail service.

'Hello, Bella, dear, Mrs B. Need you back at the house, el pronto,' she said loudly to the blank space at the end of the line. She gave Gemma a weak smile. 'She'll be back, I'm sure, as soon as she picks this up,' she said reassuringly.

They all turned as someone knocked gently on the door. Maureen moved quickly to answer it and saw Jonathan Bartlett on the other side.

'I've been invited in for a glass of champagne,' he said as Maureen opened the door wide for him.

He gingerly stepped in and was handed a glass by Gemma after a long embrace.

'Thank you for coming.' Lucinda smiled as he ambled over to her and wrapped his arms around her, glass held high. They exchanged a few unheard whispered words, and he held her out by her shoulders, gazing deep into her eyes.

'Are you sure?' he whispered into her ear.

She nodded and rested her hand on his cheek. 'Very sure,' she responded, and then placed her hand in his, giving it a gentle squeeze.

'It's been so lovely meeting you; I know Gemma will be pleased to have you both around,' she continued, with a glance to Moran. 'I'm so glad to have you here with us.'

He kissed her forehead tenderly and led her over to her favourite chair, where he gently helped her to sit down. She mouthed, *thank you*, and sat back while Gemma placed a cashmere throw over her, lifted her feet on to the long footstool, and handed her a glass of Dom Perignon. Classical music was playing quietly in the background, and there was an air of stillness and calm in the room.

'Did Bella come back to you?' asked Gemma anxiously to a perplexed looking Maureen, who shook her head slowly. She turned to her sister who had taken the merest sip of the champagne and put the glass on the small table next to the chair that engulfed her.

Maureen, an air of serenity surrounding her, approached the two women with a small smile. 'Ladies, we're about to start preparation for... well,' she began, 'so I need to ask if you have any other requests before we start our cocktail mix.'

The twins stared at each other, their secret language dancing in their eyes. Both turned to Maureen at the same time.

'No, thank you,' they said in unison and then their eyes locked again, until Gemma broke away from her sister's gaze to look at Moran.

'And you have had no change of mind, no change of heart about what is about to occur? You're fully aware of what is about to take place?' asked the Irishman.

Lucinda responded with an exaggerated shake of the head.

'It's time,' said Gemma to her sister as her eyes filled with tears.

# THIRTY-SEVEN

Isabella felt the dry branch break beneath her feet as she made her way further up onto the Drovers' Road and, as the moon broke through a dusting of cloud, something caught her eye. As she gingerly walked closer, she saw the outline of a motorbike leaning against a tree and she felt her heart skip a beat. She recognised it – a Ducati Panigale – Moran had pointed that much out to her on the CCTV and for some reason she had taken it in. Few people from Strathkin would own such a high-performance bike and even fewer could afford it. An uneasiness had crept over her and it now began to settle in the pit of her stomach as to why that was the case. There was a realisation that this was neither a visitor nor a tourist and that the person who drove this bike had come back to Strathkin for one reason – to settle old scores. She pulled out her phone, anxious to see if Marcie had responded to her location pin, but she had no signal and no reply from her friend. She turned on her heels and began to make her way back to the side of the loch where The Retreat and Sweet Briar sat side by side, like mother and child.

. . .

All was peaceful in the big house. Tears were being shed. Hands were being grasped. Maureen gazed around angelically at the serene perfection of it all and sighed. Gemma Macintyre was still holding the hand of her sister as her life ebbed away, while being wrapped in the tender embrace of Moran Maguire. Jonathan Bartlett rested his hand on the shoulder of the woman he had admired for her dogged determination in not letting her sister be the second person to succumb vicariously to the disease that had so cruelly robbed her of a long and fruitful life. Above the gentle music playing in the background, an owl hooted loudly, and, for a brief second, they all took in the muted scene before returning to the new normal, one without a set of twins in it, but simply with a vulnerable young woman setting out in life alone for the first time in her life.

Next door, in the low jazz-filled kitchen of Sweet Briar, Marcie had finished loading the dishwasher and took in the near perfection of her newly fitted, expensive kitchen. Outside, an owl noisily announced its arrival in the tree that had escaped next door's brutal renovations, and the sudden clatter of the back door swinging open brought her back to reality. She turned around expectantly as a gust of wind blew into the room. It ushered the dish towel off the counter, and she watched as it floated to the floor.

'Where have you been?' she called out as she went to the back door, expecting to see a harassed Simon full of explanations. While the door swung open in the wind, there was no sign of her husband, which she thought odd. She closed the door and as she made to turn the handle but not the key, she felt the breath on her neck. An absolute chill ran through her body, and she stiffened. There was a familiar smell, an odour, a scent. It was of fresh cologne. Something she hadn't smelled in a long time and one that brought back memories of horror and fear in equal measure. This man had upturned the lives of the people of Strathkin, caused untold harm and almost caused the death of her only living relative. In the dark recesses of her mind, she knew that he would come back at some point to seek revenge. She was glad that Callum was thousands of miles away now that this moment had manifested itself out of the blue. The breath touched her neck still. She was struck dumb and felt an arm encircle her waist, the same arm that had been outstretched to hold the gun to her husband's body.

'Well, well, well,' said the voice.

She gulped loudly and hard.

'What is that expression from a poem? A play? "When shall we three meet again?"'

'*Macbeth,*' she said so quietly he missed it. 'Where's Simon?' she asked as a dawning realisation swept over her. He wasn't late, she now knew, and she began to curse herself for blaming him for his tardiness, for not heading out to search for him sooner.

'Yes, we three, well, two. Your husband won't be joining us. I was thinking I might make him into a seafood salad, but instead I believe he would like his ashes scattered over the loch or the beautiful mountains.'

Marcie tried not to gasp aloud and instead concentrated on not being sick as her stomach lurched at this statement.

'Where is he?' she asked in such a quiet tone, she wasn't sure she had said it out loud.

'As I said, he won't be joining us. He did like what I had done to Broomfield though. Decor wise.'

They were so close to Broomfield, she and Heather, before she had made the decision to turn back. *Would that have changed this outcome?* she thought. *What has he done with him?*

'I've waited for this moment, my dear. Don't worry, I won't drag it out. You deserve to die together.'

In a second, he had flipped her over, hit her over the head, upturning the chair that had her bag resting on it, and rendered her unconscious. He grappled her over his shoulder and then unceremoniously threw her into the back of her 4x4, key conveniently left in the ignition.

It only took moments for the erratic driving up the hill to come to a sudden stop and Marcie to be dragged from the back seat. She was coming to when her attacker pulled her on to the stump of a tree and cable-tied her slender wrists. Her eyes adjusted to the darkness, the black dark of the forest, and what was happening to her. She'd been sure she would come across Poytr Medvedev again at some point in her future. She now realised with his dyed black hair, fashionable thick beard, and trendy dark-framed glasses, she had seen him from a distance in the village but thought him simply another tourist or, with his binoculars, a twitcher coming to check out the local bird life.

'Where... where...' she mumbled.

'Speak up,' he said sharply.

'Where's Simon?'

Stretching to see behind him, Marcie made out the shadow of a large vehicle and tried to squint in the darkness to see what kind of van or truck it was, any sign of livery. Then she realised she had seen it before, but before she could let out a scream, she heard a tearing noise as a large piece of gaffer tape was ripped off a roll and thrust across her mouth, rendering her silent.

'I'm sure you knew we would meet again, my dear. You must have realised I would want my revenge, hmmm? After everything you stole from me. You're such a meddler. You can't keep to yourself, can you? Always interfering in everyone's life. You always have a nose in everyone's business. I knew that before I even cast my eyes over you. Bella told me.' He was talking as he was circling her. 'Your so-called "best friends" call you Marple. An old lady poking her nose into other people's business. Even with *all* your money, *all* your riches, you can't let your friends have the life they want. You must take a piece of their lives so that they owe you.'

Marcie was shaking her head. She was trying to do the best for her family of friends, almost the only family she now had left. Help Heather with her hotel. Look after the trekking centre when Isabella was *away*. And now, despite Dina's imminent death, she was the strongest of all of them.

'All your money,' said the man, encircling the trussed and silent Marcie, '*that should have been mine*, by the way, has it made you truly happy? Has it made your heart swell with joy? Has it?'

Marcie continued to squirm as he mocked her, her eyes on the vehicle in front of her. *Oh please,* her internal monologue was pleading with herself, *please let Simon be OK.* She was trying to move her hands behind her, trying to find some traction, but the cable ties were just too tight, and the tree stump had no sharp edges to try and loosen off the thick plastic. Her eyes were darting around every time he moved behind her, but she was struggling to find an escape route for herself, knowing that Simon could be injured, or worse, and she couldn't leave him to his fate.

At the same time in another village not that far away, Constable Jamie MacKay was dealing with a conundrum inside the Strathdon Surgery with Doctor Arshia Brahmins.

'I'm not sure what you're saying – you have or haven't been broken into?'

Arshia was now regretting her call to the police as she, too, was unsure.

'I just seem really low on some of my medication – I know it doesn't look like a break in.'

'Well, the door certainly hasn't been forced.'

'Hmmm.'

'And you're now saying the drugs cabinet doesn't look like it has been tampered with? Could it have been opened with a key?'

'Hmmm.'

'But you think the CCTV has been shut down?'

'I never switch it off. But it has *been* switched off. Deliberately. I know that.'

'Deliberately,' repeated Jamie with a nod. 'Let's have a look.'

He watched as Arshia switched on the machine that covered the back and front door and the reception area of the surgery. There did seem a shadowy figure at the rear of the premises before it appeared as if, after a glance up by the potential intruder, something was thrown over the camera. Jamie appeared a bit perplexed as only a moment later the entire system seemed to be shut down, apparently from the inside. It was Jamie's turn for a pondering 'Hmmm.'

He rewound the tape to where the figure was at the rear entrance to the surgery and tried to zoom in, but all he could make out was a tall figure, possibly bearded, and wearing a baseball cap. He thought for a moment it could have been Ruaridh Balfour but that was for a brief second before the camera was covered.

'Okay, let's take a statement,' he began and pulled a chair out for her to sit.

'I feel a bit foolish now,' she said. 'Maybe I'm completely mistaken. I met a new guy and my head's been in a bit of a spin.'

'Oh, aye?'

'Yeah, he's new to the area, too. Lives up at Broomfield? Would that be right? To be honest I can't get my head round this whole area and here I am, dragging you out at this time of night on a wild-goose chase.'

'Not at all, better safe than sorry, doctor,' reassured Jamie.

'So, your new man is staying on the Swanfield Estate? I wasn't sure anyone was staying up there, but then with the new owners, who knows!' He smiled but his inquisitive mind was already working overtime on what was really going on.

# THIRTY-EIGHT

Isabella hadn't run so fast since her school years. She checked her phone several times and had seen the yellow band move to a red band, then her phone completely shut down. She knew she had to charge it. Never did. She ran into Sweet Briar and checked in all the rooms. Empty. Running back out through the kitchen she stopped in her tracks. A tea towel on the floor, an upturned chair she hadn't noticed before in her rush. A glance down. Marcie's bag lying with contents spilled on the far side of the floor at the table leg. *He's been here*, said her internal voice, *and he's taken her*. She rushed out as fast as her legs could take her. She cursed the new road round from the cottage to the old Swanfield and reached the back door completely out of breath and panting heavily. The door, as usual, was locked, and she had to wait a few seconds before her mind clicked back into gear and she could remember the number for the keypad entry.

'Six, one, nine, four,' she repeated aloud as she punched the numbers into the box on the wall. It flashed up 'NO ENTRY'.

'Bugger!' she said aloud. She knew the number was changed frequently, and especially, she had been told, if there was an imminent departure, so that no one could inadvertently stumble into a room where preparations were being made.

'Feck!' she gasped as she realised what might have been decided with the twins in her absence. She knocked gently, then more forcefully on the door, but knew that if most people were upstairs, then this frantic knocking would go unnoticed. Her breathing having returned to normal after her gasping run from next door, she ran quickly round to the front of the building, hoping that the door would be unlocked. It wasn't.

She knocked on the door, as quietly as she could, then, with no response, tried with a little more force and listened as she heard footsteps come along the vestibule. She stopped for a brief second and Bella knew that the person on the other side of the door would be checking the CCTV. She turned her head towards the camera with a withering look. A loud *clunk* signalled the door being opened. Sissy lifted her finger to her lips before Bella could open her mouth as she stepped inside, and the assistant pointed up the stairs. Bella knew immediately what it meant.

She leaned on the door lintel and sighed. It took a moment for her to recover. Soft music still drifted from the twins' room as she went upstairs. She gulped heavily before a gentle tap on the door made the people inside realise someone was about to enter. When she gingerly stepped inside, several sets of tear-stained eyes turned to her. Her gaze fixed upon the frail body of Lucinda Macintyre, now tenderly laid out in the centre of the large bed.

She appeared to be simply in a peaceful sleep: her pale, frail body no different to what she has been like in life. Bella's eyes shifted to Maureen, whose gaze was rigidly fixed on the tiny frame of the dead woman. Jonathan Bartlett gave her a brief nod from his seat next to the bed, and she saw that Gemma was wrapped in the arms of Moran Maguire who was gently stroking her back in reassurance and support. She returned a weak smile. *What do I do now?* She couldn't interrupt this serene moment of grief with her own unfolding trauma. She signalled that she was leaving and ran downstairs into the kitchen where phone chargers were attached to the wall and immediately plugged her phone in.

'Come on, come on,' she shouted at it as she waited for an age for the little design to appear on the screen. But there was still not enough charge to allow her to make a phone call.

'Sissy! Sissy!' she shouted as quietly as she could.

'Yes, ma'am,' said the nurse from behind her.

'I'm taking the car,' she said, grabbing the phone from its charger and taking the car keys off the hook.

# THIRTY-NINE

Deep into the Swanfield Estate, Constable Jamie MacKay had his baton out and ready for any eventuality as he used it to push open the door of the croft house known as Broomfield. The cottage, which had been empty on his last drive around the estate some time ago with Marcie, would appear to be now occupied just as the doctor had suggested. His police antennae were bristling as he moved from room to room, initially in the strong beam of his Maglite torch until he then used the tip of the baton to switch the main light on. It was exceptionally tidy in every room, sparsely but elegantly furnished and obviously only recently vacated. He went out to the workshop that sat next to the house and again saw items strewn along the work-bench. He wondered suspiciously what activity had taken place and lifted his police radio closer to his mouth. He felt his mobile buzz in the pocket of his police issue cargo pants but waited until he had finished talking to his police headquarters' control room before retrieving the phone, just as the caller hung up. It was Bella Forrester whose name appeared on the screen as his most recent caller, but he replaced the phone in his pocket and continued his search of the workshop before responding to his friend's call.

'Not now, Bella,' he said quietly and slipped the phone back into his pocket.


Several miles away in the village, the car screeched into the car park of The Strathkin Inn and Bella left the door open as she rushed in. She immediately went in the back door to the office where she expected to see the friends she'd only left a short time before at Sweet Briar. Heather was instead behind the bar waiting expectantly for the tall handsome figure of Moran to join her.

'We've got to go!' shouted Bella, despite being only inches away from her ear.

'It's a wee bit busy, Bels,' responded Heather as she held her hands up before she felt herself being dragged by the arm back into the storeroom then out through the office.

'Slow down!' she ordered, as Bella was talking so fast, Heather couldn't make out a single word that was being said in Bella's rush to get the words out. 'Peter who? What are you on about?'

'Not Peter! Poytr! Poytr Medvedev!' shouted Bella.

'Wha—?' began Heather.

'He's here! He's here!!'

'Where?' asked Heather, her eyes growing bigger at the very thought and looking around frantically.

'I think he's got Marcie from Sweet Briar. There's something not right, H. I think there's been a struggle or something – it must be him, it's all so, all so...' Heather was waiting for the explanation. 'It's all so, just... well, *HIM*! The bike, the, I don't know, just the feeling... Plus, I think he might have taken Simon, too.' Bella was blurting out so much, so quickly Heather felt she was rambling, but her head was shaking at the same time as she listened.

'Marcie? *And* Simon?' She gulped as a chill ran through her.

'We need to go, I think I know where they might be,' said Bella, dragging her friend out into the car park.

'Bels, isn't this a time to call in the big guns? I mean, after last time,' pleaded Heather.

'I've called Jamie, I've left a message,' responded Bella.

'Called Jamie? He's hardly the cavalry! I'm going to call nine-nine-nine. What do I say to them?' asked Heather, while trying to break free from Bella's grip to get back inside to her office.

'No time!' demanded Bella. 'Just bring your phone.'

'Er, I've no idea where it is. I don't think it's charged,' she replied as she was dragged out and forced into the front passenger seat of the Mercedes SUV, and Bella drove off at speed.

# FORTY

While the sound of screeching tyres echoed around Strathkin, at The Retreat all was peaceful and it was just the way Maureen Berman wanted it.

'Just lovely, Bri, just lovely. Did you see it? Peaceful, it were. You had ol' blue eyes on the CD, we 'ad Spotify. It's a newfangled thing, Spotify, I'll tell you all about it,' said Maureen to her deceased husband as she wafted around the room, lighting candles and holding a glass of vintage champagne. 'I'll be seeing you tomorrow, I will, luv. I've made me mind up. Picked the best room in the 'ouse, innit? Leaving 'ere after supper in the evenin', I am – they don't know about it yet, mind you. Can barely see a thing now, me. But you know me, Bri, I'm a finisher and I wanted to get young Lucinda off safely. Gorgeous she was, too. Pretty little thing but a bit on the thin side, if you ask me, and that's coming from *me*. Still weigh the same as the day we got married, darlin', oh yes, still like Twiggy as you used to say.' She giggled to herself at a memory. 'I was just saying to Bella, you'd like 'er. Bella, I said, when she asked me 'ow I keep my figure. Well, Bels, I said, it's easy. I've been on a liquid diet since nineteen sixty-eight. I have the occasional blow out, you know, 'cause I can't resist seafood. That was a luxury when we was growin' up. And sometimes, I have the occasional cheeky little cheroot if I'm feeling a bit *pangy*, you know, but I believe it's the quinine in that tonic water that keeps me going.'

Maureen continued to float around the room, lighting candles and sipping her champagne until she said to Brian, 'Gawd, it's 'ot in 'ere, luv. I'd better go and check on poor Gemma then I'll come back to say good night.' She took off her silk kimono and threw it on the bed, letting its length drift over to the floor until it appeared like a perfectly staged photograph for expensive nightwear.

When she closed the door behind her, a light draught lifted the belt of the silk robe slightly off the bed and over the wick of one of the burning candles. It fizzed for a moment, the champagne that it had accidentally been dipped in causing the small flame to go out, but the tiny spark drifted on to the bed and began to slowly take hold on the expensive dry bedding before it insidiously curled over to the long, thick curtains. Within moments, the room was alight.


Across the water at Lochside Croft, Dina had had an exceedingly difficult day, and her breathing had gone from shallow to laboured then back to shallow again. At her insistence, she had spent the last few nights in the beautiful bed in the guest room. The large guest bed had been turned around and a camp bed set beside it, where the boys had played cards and continued to talk their normal childish nonsense to their mother as she drifted in and out of consciousness. The Macmillan nurse had paid several visits and explained that she had gone downhill very fast. Sometimes, she had said, accepting your fate made you give up the fight. Sometimes it made you fight even more. Sometimes none of it made sense. Dina had started with chemotherapy that had made her nauseous, with sore muscles and mouth sores and a never-ending brain fog. She had been surviving on painkillers and now her nurse had affixed the syringe driver. She was sleeping more and more, Ruaridh was making frequent trips to the toilet both to bang his fist against the wall and fight back his tears in case she woke up, then rushing back to her side, regretting that he had ever left her.

'Is she in pain?' asked Dina's husband of the petite woman standing beside him.

'I don't believe so,' replied Arshia Brahmins, 'but can I suggest you let the boys spend some time with their grand-mother next door for the next little while?' He had told her he wanted them to go away to stay with relatives and friends and, knowing Dina's wishes, Doctor Brahmins had agreed.

Her suggestion was not lost on Ruaridh as he gently ushered the boys to say a soft and mellow 'night night' to Mum and that they'd see her in the morning.

Arshia rested her hand on his forearm.

'I spoke to Dina. I know what her plans are,' she said by way of an explanation, and Ruaridh looked down at this caring woman by his side, eyes filled with tears. 'But sometimes things move along quicker than we would like.'

As the door closed, he went to his wife and lay beside her, stretched out. He wanted to intertwine his legs with hers the way they always did, but she was so fragile he didn't want to risk causing her any more pain. Instead, he pulled her gently towards him, tucking her body into his, her head on his chest, as her heavy breathing began to fill the room.

Outside, in the living room, three boys were curled up against their grandmother, watching an evening children's channel with the volume on low while Dax Balfour had taken a thick fleece blanket and was lying across the door threshold to the bedroom, unseen by his father or grandmother. He had been taken into his father's confidence about difficult days ahead and looking after his younger siblings but, as a deep thinker and careful listener, Dax knew it wasn't only his brothers he would have to look out for. His stoic bear of a father was on the verge of breaking.

# FORTY-ONE

Across the loch, in the clearing at the back of The Retreat, tensions were palpable. Poytr Medvedev liked the thrill of the chase. He loved being one step ahead of everyone which was how he managed to run drugs, stay at school, be a model citizen and look after his grandmother until her premature death from one of his practised 'mixed cocktails'. He simply thanked her, raised his eyes to heaven with a brief point upwards, and knew from there on in, if anyone got in his way, he could dispose of them with a pat on the back and a drink from his full cabinet of choice international drinks. And he was enjoying this game of cat and mouse.

The woman who stole his future. The woman he believed took every penny of her uncle's inheritance that should have been his. He didn't manage to get rid of her the first time. He wasn't going to let her escape this time. It wasn't how he had planned it, he wanted to drug her slowly, a little stab here and there, allow her to bleed to death when she was almost incapacitated, but it was her husband who had moved things up a pace. Was he *really* only out for a walk and stumbled innocently across him at Broomfield, or was he sent out to look for him?

A moan behind him shook him from his reverie. Marcie was waking up from being pistol whipped, a slow trickle of blood running from her ear down to the corner of her mouth then drifting to her chin before slowly dripping on the dry branches below her feet.

He saw her glance down to where her white trainers appeared to have two red stripes on them.

'Welcome back!' He smiled. 'I'm so glad you returned for the final act!' He walked around behind her, and saw how she flinched, waiting for another blow. 'Do you know I can fly helicopters? Yes, I was trained in the army – you didn't know that about me, did you?'

She shook her head. The last time she quipped back at him, he had slapped her so hard on the side of the head that he knew she must have seen stars before she drifted into unconsciousness.

'Well, I could give you a choice. I could take that without the owner's consent.' He nodded behind them to where a helicopter sat idle a few hundred metres away. 'I'm sure you would be dead before you hit the water, but it's the circle of life, isn't it? You become fish food, and I accidentally take all the money out of your bank account. It's so easy to nowadays. You're awfully quiet. I surely thought you'd put up more of a fight,' he said as he approached her, pulling her up by the hair until she was facing him.

He thought better of saying something and instead let her go, effectively dropping her so that she missed the tree stump and landed on her side, letting out a howl of pain.

He thought about picking her up when he heard something behind her and he turned around, suddenly alert.


Across the stillness of Loch Strathkin, Ruaridh stood by the water's edge, arms folded, his children tucked up in bed, well, all except one. They were all going away tomorrow for what they thought was a little holiday. His hands were in his pockets and the tears fell freely from his eyes. He could tell it was getting closer and closer, that moment he dreaded, and out of sight of his children, his tears just couldn't be stopped. He found himself standing in his youngest son's favourite spot for collecting useless items washed onto the shore and already he could hear his wife in his ear as she leaned on his shoulder.

*He'll catch his death, you know. Did he first go into the water at just weeks old? I'm surprised he has feet and not fins. What do you think he'll be when he grows ups? A diver? Do you think he'll bring his own children here and we can sit on this bench, all fat with grey hair, and watch as he teaches them to swim?*

He expected to see his mother-in-law with a cup of strong tea when he turned around, but it was Doctor Brahmins who put her hand on his shoulder.

'How are you doing?' she asked gently. 'I've left Dina's mum with her. She's an ex-nurse. She's just having a moment with her daughter then I'm sure you'll go back in,' explained the doctor softly. They stood in silence, darkness enveloping them like a thick blanket.

'Such a beautiful night. I'm surprised people have lit their stoves,' she remarked and peered down the still, dark loch. Ruaridh lifted his head and sniffed the night air.

'That's not a stove,' he said, questioning her statement just as a flash of light appeared from the other side of Strathkin Loch. 'I think Swanfield's on fire,' he shouted and took off into the house, leaving Doctor Brahmins on the water's edge as a huge fire opposite her began to light up the still night sky.

Screaming and shouting. Chaos and panic. Fire drills easily forgotten. Paperwork being hastily bundled into bags by two inexperienced nurses, and a housekeeper struggling to keep large glasses on her nose and breathing hard.

'Quick! Before the doors close!' someone was yelling with a strain in their voice from coughing. A fire alarm was incessantly ringing, and sprinklers were showering water on to the people running about, but the fire had taken hold so quickly that no amount of water would stop what was going on.

'Where's the fecking car?' shouted Moran Maguire as he ran to the front door and back again. There was no response from the people scurrying about as thick acrid smoke began to drift down from upstairs and a crackle that had started low and quiet became louder and louder.

'Lucy!' shouted Gemma. Moran's grip on her hand became tighter as he saw her try to make her way up the stairs. Loud coughing made them both look up.

'I'll stay with her!' shouted Jonathan Bartlett from the upper hallway to the terrified faces in the vestibule below.

'No!' shouted Gemma as she tried to release herself from Moran's grip, but his strong pull was too much.

'Look after her!' Moran yelled up to him as he ran to the door with Gemma, leading her to the parking area outside. He warned her to stay there and not move. He ran back into the house that was beginning to fill more quickly now with thick invasive smoke and yelled at the two panic-stricken nurses, fear etched on to their faces and blue surgical masks over their mouths.

'Get out now!' he ordered. 'Go to my car.'

With a glance to each other, they raced to the front door where they fell into the open arms of Gemma, whose own panic-stricken face was staring up at the room where her sister still lay.

Looking up, Moran saw Jonathan give him a look of resigned acceptance and watched as he disappeared coughing into the room where Lucinda was already long dead. He continued to stare before he made his way to the back office where Maureen was still stuffing paperwork into bags.

'Leave that stuff. It'll burn to ashes,' ordered Moran as he crossed to the safe, twisting the dial this way and that until it sprang open. There was a meagre amount of money, mostly in euros, and he shoved it into his pocket, and the few pieces of paperwork that appeared to be deeds were also grasped as he began to cough. Two necklaces that were clearly Angelina's, which he found in a couple of jewellery boxes that he opened, were despatched into his pocket. 'Let's get out of here!' he said loudly as he saw Maureen swallow down two pills with gusto with no water.

'I'm going to go next door,' she responded calmly.

'What?'

'Well, the smoke will get me before the flames, like Jonny upstairs.'

'Don't be stupid, woman!' Moran shouted at her.

'You get yourself out, I'll stay with Jonny and Luce,' she stated matter-of-factly and handed him a bag full of paperwork. 'I have a date with my husband.'

'You can't stay here, get yourself out!' Despite his shouting, his plea was in vain.

Coughing, Moran watched Maureen enter the front room, smoke billowing from upstairs down into the hall and swallowing up any air that was left. He could go after her, drag her out, but not without risking his own life. The wide-open front door was fanning the fire. Moran ran out into the hallway and, with a final glance up the stairs, ran out the front door and immediately headed to the side of the house, where Gemma was standing beside the car as ordered.

'Where's Maureen?' shouted Gemma, hand to her face.

'She's staying to take care of Lucinda,' he responded in a calm and measured tone to reassure the woman by his side. His hands fumbled in his pockets for a set of car keys to his own car and he nodded a signal to Gemma to get into the waiting vehicle. He was going to go to the front of the house to reassure the two nurses who had managed to evacuate the house. But Moran Maguire knew that even they would know by now that he would have no intention of coming back for anyone since he had saved himself.

Isabella had no sooner made it back to the clearing when she heard a distant crackle and occasional bang and sniffed the rising smell of smoke in the air. She glanced at Heather, and they both turned to where the sound was coming from as a red glow began to fill the still night sky.

'Oh, shoot,' said Heather as the noise from the building on their right, which now was well ablaze, got louder and a hundred years of dry wood began to succumb to the flames that engulfed it. To their left, fifty metres away, they saw their friend woozy and confused as she was encircled by her nemesis. They crept closer while Bella looked back, torn between two lives.

'What are we going to do?' asked Heather weakly, unsure of a path forward.

'Wait here!' said Bella and quickly ran back down the road towards the house that was now fully ablaze. She pulled at the back door which was security locked and would not budge. She ran around to the front of the building where she was confronted with the scene of two crying women, clinging to each other, fear etched into their terrified faces.

'Where is everyone? Is everyone out?' she demanded.

'Maureen,' said Sissy in a quiet whimper as Bella's eyes darted between them and the house.

'Moran? Is he inside?'

The women shook their heads. Just then, Ruaridh scrambled out of the car and ran towards the tearful women standing in a two-person huddle.

'Where is everyone?' he yelled before one of the nurses pointed to Bella, who was pulling out large pieces of broken glass from a window frame She began dragging a bench to climb on to it to get into the front room. Smoke was billowing out the window as Ruaridh ran to grab her before she manged to climb in.

'Who's still inside?' he shouted to her above the noise.

'Maureen, Jonathan... I don't know!' She was crying, and he pulled her off the bench and began to climb in himself. 'I've called the Fireys,' he shouted, referring to the retained fire-fighters from Strath Aullt, but they both knew that by the time they arrived, the chance of survival would be slim from such a catastrophic fire. Ruaridh pulled his sweater over his mouth, and she watched as he slithered through the broken window to the room which was disgorging smoke out of the only open exit from the house. It only took seconds before he was back at the window with the barely breathing body of Maureen Berman, and he shouted for help from the two nurses. They ran forward and helped to take the woman out of the window and place her on the ground. She was moved into the recovery position, and Ruaridh bent close to her mouth to hear her shallow breathing.

'She's alive,' he stated and went back to the house as one of the women shouted to him that everyone else was upstairs. The oxygen rushing into the house was fuelling the fire and it only took minutes before all the windows upstairs blew outwards, showering them all in broken glass as they heard the roof begin to fall inwards. Ruaridh barely took one further step forwards before he felt the strong grip of Bella on his forearm.

'Don't,' she ordered. 'Think of your kids.' They both watched the entire top of the building being overtaken by the fire and flames. Tears were rolling down her face and she felt herself clinging to Ruaridh as she thought of Jonathan still inside, all thoughts of Moran Maguire out of her head for the moment.

.   .   .

At The Strathkin Inn, guests were standing in the car park watching the spectacle on the other side of the water. Moran had left a startled and shocked Gemma sitting in the car as he ran into his room at the Inn, quickly clearing anything of note into his case, and was back in the vehicle within minutes. His only detour was a brief stop to reach into the bar to grab a bottle of Jameson Irish Whiskey from the gantry. He glanced at the cash register, quite full on this busy night, but knew the CCTV camera was directed above it. *Pity*, he thought to himself, *could always do with a bit of ready cash.*

Moran paused his car at the end of the road to allow the fire tender from Strath Aullt Fire and Rescue to pass them at great speed, men climbing into the protective uniforms as the vehicle drove quickly to the scene of the fire on the other side of the loch.

# FORTY-TWO

In the clearing behind the big house, Poytr sighed.

'It's a pity you can't see what I can see. Your former home looks like a tinderbox.'

Marcie could smell the smoke and thought it was the muir burning at this time of year before she could feel the heat behind her and see tiny pieces of ash floating down in the air, covering her clothes and embedding itself in her hair. Poytr leaned down and brutally pulled the tape from her mouth.

'What do you want from me?' she asked drowsily.

'Is *revenge* too harsh a word?' He smiled at her.

'Revenge for what? You killed all those people, nearly killed Callum and yet *you're* still here?'

'Hmmm, but I could have had so much more.'

'You're a wanted man.'

'You think the stupid police here are going to spend their time looking for me? No, not when they can get a pat on the back from their superiors when they find a couple of sheep rustlers or poachers and then while away their days trying out the farm shops and road food vans?' he laughed.

She heard a gun cock.

'Where's Simon?' she asked, still disbelieving he could be in the truck in front of her.

'Don't worry. I'm sure you believe in the afterlife – you can be reunited,' he stated matter-of-factly.

Marcie gulped. She knew how ruthless he was.

'I like your new house in London,' he went on. 'I've visited it a few times. Unbeknownst to you, of course. Nice – but I'm surprised you went for the lowlier address. A woman of your means.' He was pacing around her again, like a caged animal ready to pounce. She in turn was looking around, eyes darting as she tried to find an escape.

He had secured her tightly and no number of movies she had seen where people could extract themselves from being bound resembled the discomfort and tightness she now felt.


In a different part of the clearing, Heather was watching – with no feasible plan of how to release her friend. She wanted to go back to the Inn where she could get scissors and a posse of locals but aside from that, this was not her forte. She reached into her pocket and pulled out a corkscrew. A butler's friend, it was called, and she tugged both the screw out and then the top cutter used for taking off the collar of bottles of wine. She edged a little closer. She could hear Poytr talking but couldn't make out what he was saying. She was staring down, watching underfoot so that she didn't step on anything that would crunch or crack. Slowly she made her way to behind where her friend, bound and dazed, had been placed on the stump of the tree. She suddenly had an idea and leaned down to pick up a piece of moss-coloured rock and with the strength of a pitcher, threw the piece of stone as fast and as far as she could until she heard a 'clang' as it hit off the large van at the end of the clearing and clattered to the ground.

Poytr spun, arm outstretched with the gun pointing in the

direction of the noise. He edged slowly towards it just as Heather stepped on a dry branch and it snapped beneath her foot. He turned back, eyes ablaze as she crouched as low as she could. She was swearing to herself at her carelessness. Poytr edged past Marcie, after a brief glance, and was heading directly towards Heather, when another clang of something hitting the truck caused him to change direction, and he turned and headed back into the clearing. Heather began to stand up and was working out how long it would take her to creep up behind Marcie, when she gasped as a broad hand covered her mouth and her eyes opened in shock.

'Shhh,' said the man behind her, and she knew immediately it was Ruaridh. She gulped hard, and he released his grip. His mouth was at her ear. 'I'm going to distract him – can you reach Marcie?' he whispered.

She didn't respond but held up the corkscrew with the blade open. He raised his thumb and then crept backwards on his stomach like he was out on the hills, stalking a deer. When Heather turned again, he was nowhere to be seen.

Poytr had reached the truck and leaned up to look in the driver's cab and then walked around to the back of the vehicle, his gun still held out in front of him. In the seconds he was out of sight, Heather had taken a leaf out of Ruaridh's stalking playbook and had edged along on her stomach until she was directly behind Marcie, hidden in the gorse.

'Marce,' she tried to whisper. There was no response. 'Marce,' she repeated a little louder, and Marcie turned her head sharply. 'It's Heather. Don't let on I'm here. I'm going to try and release you but don't draw attention to yourself. Don't move!' she whispered while edging closer until she was within touching distance. She reached out and felt Marcie flinch as their hands touched. Marcie sat up straighter so that she could push her tired and restrained arms down further for Heather to try to cut through the cable ties with the blade on the corkscrew.

Poytr sniffed the air. He smiled at Marcie. 'Wouldn't it be tragic if the flames leapt from one building to the other and your little cottage was razed to the ground, too?' He laughed with a sneer.

'Was that your handiwork?' Marcie asked, and he stopped just a few metres in front of her.

'Me? If I were to set fire to your house, I'd first make sure you were in it,' he spat and moved closer to her.

At this move, Heather had to stop what she was doing and lie completely flat, face buried in moss, letting go of the cable tie that was so close to being severed.


A noise behind Poytr made him turn, and the tall, broad figure of Ruaridh emerged from behind the vehicle.

'I knew I could smell something else beside the fire.' Poytr smiled menacingly. 'We meet again, my friend!'

Poytr's jovial tone set Ruaridh on edge as the Russian turned quickly towards Marcie, Heather still crouching behind her.

'Your ex-girlfriend was hoping someone could save her since I should think her husband is no longer with us in this world.'

Ruaridh said nothing as he loosened the Bowie knife from the leather holder in the belt behind his back before holding his hands up in mock surrender. Poytr laughed and for a moment both men stared at each other in silence. Ruaridh dropped his arm to the side for a brief second and sighed.

'Just let her go. You did enough damage here last time to last a lifetime,' he said.

'Really? You think that? She took away my future – why shouldn't I take away hers?'

'Listen, pal.'

'Pal? What is it with you people and your *pals* and your *mates*? Is it supposed to make us warm to you? Make us like you even though you live in such a desolate landscape, away from reality, lost in your little world in the wilderness?'

If anything was going to rile Ruaridh, it was demeaning the place he thought was the most beautiful place on earth.

'Run!' Ruaridh shouted, and Poytr gave him a strange look, until there was a noise behind him. When he turned sharply, he saw the shadowy frames of both Heather and Marcie making off into the woods and up towards the Drovers' Road. He pointed his gun and fired several shots quickly then must have realised it was a waste of bullets as they were both too far and it was too dark. He coughed as ash still rained down, this time more heavily, and the distant siren from the Fire and Rescue tender grew closer. When he turned, the broad figure of Ruaridh bore down on him and the two men struggled on the forest floor.

Marcie and Heather heard a shot ring out. They ran to the edge of the Drovers' Road before turning to the bridle path then to the road that led to Swanfield, which now had a red glow coming from it like a volcano. They arrived just as the fire tender drew to a screeching stop and watched the firefighters pull a hose from the machine as they saw Isabella bent over the still body of Maureen Berman.

'Is she alive?' screamed Heather above the noise of crackling radios and whooshing water as a firefighter bent towards the woman on the grass, placing an oxygen mask tenderly over her face.

'Is anyone still inside?' asked Marcie, and Bella nodded tearfully.

'Oh, God.' Heather ran her hand through her ash-filled hair, horrified at the thought of people still trapped within the building. One firefighter was being lifted from the fire tender to tackle the blaze from above, one was climbing through the broken window, one was on the radio asking for reinforcements.

The women were moved back into what was now the car park and where an ambulance now screeched to a halt. Paramedics leapt out and began to assess the care needed for those on the ground. Marcie and Heather clung to each other, worry and pain etched into their faces.

'We need to tell them about what else is going on!' said Heather suddenly as if woken from a bad dream.

As she did, she saw Ruaridh's car, which had been parked at the side of the property, take flight, reversing sharply and heading out the main gate. She and Bella glanced at each other then watched as Marcie took off running in the opposite direction, heading back to where she had been held captive in the clearing.

Marcie's mind was still woozy, but her heart was racing at the same rhythm as her feet were hitting the ground, running past the helicopter pad and into the forest beyond. It was there she saw Ruaridh sitting on the same tree stump where she, too, had been taken. As she neared him, he let out a sound that could have come from a wounded animal, a wail that she sometimes heard from the hills, and as she approached him closer, she noticed he was covered in blood. She gasped.

'Oh my god! Are you okay?' she said as she quickened her steps until she was next to him and saw him clutching his side.

'I've been shot, but it's only a graze. I'll be all right,' came his reply. 'Poytr is gone.'

'Simon!' Marcie shouted and stared towards the heavy truck. She was about to run to it, when she felt Ruaridh's hand grasp hers.

'No,' he said quietly, and tightened his grip. 'I need to go first.'

'But I...' she began.

'NO!' Ruaridh shouted, like it was an order, as he struggled to his feet and made his way over to the vehicle, hauling himself up and climbing in.

Marcie's heart was beating so fast she thought it was going to burst through her skin. She raised her hands to her hair then her face, her mouth falling open as she gazed at the expression of her childhood friend as he came out of the truck.

'We need to get the paramedics here, now,' Ruaridh said in a whimper.

No words escaped from Marcie. In front of her, Ruaridh's face was raw as if it wasn't only the fight with Poytr Medvedev that had shaken him. Suddenly a light was on them, a powerful beam from someone running towards them and yelling. When they looked up, Jamie MacKay was speeding in their direction. Marcie struggled to her feet, and Jamie gasped at the blood-soaked shirt.

'Jeez, Marce, are you all right?' he gasped.

'We need to get paramedics here right now,' she replied as Jamie reached out to take her hand. 'Simon's badly injured, and Ruaridh's been shot.'

'It's more a flesh wound than anything else. Just a lot of blood. You should see the other guy.' Ruaridh's attempt at humour was lost on his friends as he held his side.

'Brodie Nairn? Or Poytr, whatever his real name is.'

Ruaridh nodded.

They watched as Jamie lifted his airwave terminal to his mouth to call for paramedics and relay all available details back to his office.

'I think he's got your car, Ruaridh,' said Marcie.

'He won't get far. To be honest, probably a lot of this blood is his. I still have my old Bowie knife... and I...'

'Any idea where the knife is?' asked Jamie. 'I'll need to seize it as evidence.'

'Somewhere over there, unless he took it.'

'Chances of that?' asked Jamie.

'Pretty high.'

'He's definitely not hiding in that thing?' said Jamie as he walked towards the large grey truck.

Ruaridh glanced at Marcie. She took a step back towards the truck, and he shook his head, then, holding his side, walked over to where Jamie was looking closely for the discarded knife. Marcie heard him shout several expletives before raising the radio to his mouth once again and asking for the paramedics to hurry up. She raised her index finger to her lips and let it run around the outline. Whatever her feelings for Simon and what the future may hold, she couldn't bear to think of what this man who had caused them so much grief in the past was capable of. She closed her eyes. Her mind's eye transported her to happier times and more joyous scenes dropped into her head. *Please*, she was pleading to whatever higher power was overseeing these events. *Please*, she repeated again and again until she heard her name as if it was being called in the distance and she felt Ruaridh take her hand. She opened her eyes, and he nodded to the truck with a reassuring look as she heard Jamie make a further request for an ambulance. Her sigh of relief was loud and pierced the silence and she felt herself say under her breath, *thank god.*

In Strathdon, the knocking door startled Doctor Arshia Brahmins as she lifted her head from her laptop while simultaneously reaching over to her printer to gather up some paper. She glanced at her watch then made her way to the door. She was just as startled when she opened the door to the man she knew as Peter, holding his side, with blood oozing from what was clearly a deep wound under his leather jacket.

'Oh my god!' she said, as he moved his hand away from where he was pressing a child's discarded T-shirt, found under the passenger seat in Ruaridh's car, to the wound to stem the flow of blood.

'I came out of the cottage to find poachers on the land outside,' he said by way of an explanation. 'I didn't think I could drive to the hospital.'

'Oh, my goodness. Well, let's get this cleaned up a bit and then we can get you to the hospital. Let's get this top off.'

She eased off his leather bomber jacket, then slowly and gently began to peel off his long-sleeved T-shirt, watching him wince as she pulled it away from the already congealing blood around the wound.

He threw the blood-soaked child's T-shirt in the sink before following it with his own.

'Hmm. This looks quite deep. You're going to need some stitches,' she suggested.

'Can you do that?' he asked.

'Well, it's been a long time. I think I last did this when I was a Registrar in Birmingham. And that was *not* yesterday. Got to be honest with you – I don't really like the sight of blood, it makes me queasy,' she said and followed it with a little gag as if to emphasise the point.

'But you're a doctor,' he stated quite incredulously.

'I know, but, really, unless you're working in trauma or A&E, you never see blood as a GP. You're not going to find me at the scene of a road accident. People who come to me have mostly hidden injuries or diseases.' She turned on the tap and began wiping the wound clean using just water and paper towels that she was discarding into the sink.

'Can you press down on this? I'm going to see what I have in my bag.'

'Where are you going?' he quizzed sharply.

'Just over here. There we go,' she said as she brought the large leather case to the table and fished around in it. 'To be honest, we really need to get you to the hospital to get proper stitches in it. I have some micropore and a dressing but when I've finished cleaning up and putting that on, we'll pop you in the car and we'll be over in the hospital in no time. Do poachers here usually use knives? I would have thought they would trap something. Or were they skinning something? Is that why they would have a knife? We'd better get you some antibiotics just in case of infection. Can't be too careful.'

She began cutting gauze and held it up to the wound and then cut some tape to hold it in place. 'Here, hold these a sec,' she said and handed him the scissors she had been using. 'Careful, they're very sharp. We don't want another accident now, do we?'

He eyed the scissors and then at the beautiful woman in front of him. He smiled.

# FORTY-THREE

The Strathkin Inn was acting as a makeshift reception centre, and Ally was dishing out hot soup and serving cups of strong tea. Another guest had started a tab at the bar in honour of the emergency services, and stunned people were gathered in the dining room now that the police had effectively taken over the bar and reception area. Jamie was on his police radio and mobile phone, sometimes simultaneously, and Heather had given Marcie a change of clothes as the sight of a woman with a blood-soaked shirt was making people uneasy. Ally, however, told Heather in a quiet moment that it was making them spend more as they were confronted with their own mortality. Bella had gone to the local cottage hospital at Strathdon with Maureen Berman in the back of a speeding ambulance, and a police car had taken the two nurses for a check-up and had followed the ambulance along the road.

'Are you sure you don't want to go for a check-up?' asked Jamie to Marcie as they sat in the office while a paramedic cleaned up a shirtless Ruaridh, who was right in his assessment that his injury was only a flesh wound.

'I'll go and see if Moran Maguire has any clean clothes in

his wardrobe that'll at least get you across the road,' suggested Heather, eyes bloodshot from crying.

'To be honest, I'm fine the way I am. It's not as if anyone here hasn't seen me with my kit off.' The joke fell flat, Marcie staring into space. Jamie interrupted them, peeping round the door.

'How is Simon?' Marcie asked urgently.

'That's forensics at the site now,' he began, 'and you'll be able to see Simon in about five. He's in the ambulance outside. He's going to be fine, and you can travel with him to Strathdon.'

Relief flooded Marcie as her hands tightened around the glass of warm, sweet brandy that Heather had insisted she take. *Simon was going to be fine.* Paramedics were working on him in the ambulance in the car park to ensure he was stable enough to be taken to the local hospital to join the others who had gone before them. There had been considerable blood loss, and this was causing them concern. It was clear the medical team didn't want anyone else in the ambulance until they were convinced he had been stabilised.

'Are you okay?' Ruaridh asked over the head of the paramedic kneeling at his side. Marcie simply nodded at Ruaridh knowing that if she did try to speak, no words would come out. And if she didn't speak, maybe this all wasn't really happening to her. Her husband almost dead. Her best friend clinging desperately to life. It was all too unbelievable to be true. The crackling of emergency services' radios continued to interrupt the silence, and the paramedic stood up and tapped Ruaridh's shoulder.

'That's you, pal. All done. You can get it dressed in a few days at the surgery or if your wife's brave enough, she can tackle it.' Ruaridh nodded, bit his lip, exchanged a glance with Marcie and thanked the man who was carefully placing everything into his backpack.

'You're sure there's no injuries?' the paramedic asked to

Marcie who shook her head and mumbled a thanks. The two friends sat silently in the room in a loneliness all of their own as busy people bustled all around them.

'I'll come over tomorrow. Me and the girls will come over in the morning.' Marcie dropped her head to rest it in her hand, elbow on her knee. Ruaridh smiled weakly at her and moved to bend down to hug her but winced instead as a pain shot up and through his back.

'No. I'll text you, eh? Update you on Lochside but don't just drop in, *please*?'

'Sure.'

'What a whirlwind, Mars,' was all he managed to say as he stood up and left the office, going into the vestibule where a flurry of excitement was taking place. He returned and leaned back around the door just as Jamie had done moments before.

'They've found my car -- at Stuart Mooney's old place,' he said, and Marcie stood up.

Heather arrived at their side empty-handed and took in Marcie's tear-stained face open-mouthed. She placed her hand on Ruaridh's shoulder.

'It's all gone,' she said, staring, with a look of astonishment on her own face.

'What's all gone?'

'All his stuff,' she replied, her lips quivering.

'Whose stuff?' asked Ruaridh as Ally passed and placed a freshly laundered towel over his shoulders like a cape.

'Moran Maguire's. His room's been cleared out. He's only gone and bloody left.'

The three looked at each other in shock and surprise as if the day they had just endured could not get any worse. And, on top of that, who was going to tell Bella?

# FORTY-FOUR

A very drowsy Doctor Arshia Brahmins was found inside her house, bound and tied to a kitchen chair, the bruise on the side of her face showing that she had put up a struggle with her assailant. By the time the police arrived and prepared for a standoff, Jamie noticed that, while Ruaridh's car was outside, clearly abandoned in haste, Arshia's was not, and his worst fears had been realised. The interloper who had caused so much damage to the village on his last visit had continued in his trail of destruction and fled, once again evading law enforcement and justice.

In the early hours of the morning, Arshia was taken in the same ambulance that had transported Bella and Maureen the night before to the cottage hospital. When Bella sat up from her seat beside Maureen's bed, she saw Jamie walking past while Arshia was stretchered into an assessment cubicle. Bella jumped up and was heading to the door just as a nurse came in and handed a phone to her.

'That's you all charged. Can I just check on Mrs Berman?'

Bella agreed and shouted after the police officer, who was weary and flagging as he trudged down the corridor.

'Jamie!'

'Oh, you're still here? How's the patient?'

'Och, she'll be fine. Listen, what's the latest? Did they find anyone else in the house?'

'Just the two bodies. A man and a woman. They'll be going to Inverness for post-mortem.'

'Just the two?'

'Yes, upstairs front bedroom. From initial enquiries, and from what you said, it looks like one of the twins and an older visitor, would that be right?'

'Yeah, but definitely no one else?'

'Not so far. No. Fire assessors are still there, mind you, but the upstairs of the building has all but collapsed. You think there may have been other people inside?'

'I'm not sure,' she began and ran the phone over her fingers.

'Oh, another thing. The doctor that was staying at the Inn, Doctor Maguire, I believe, the one who was working at Swanfield? You knew him well?'

'I knew him a bit, yes.'

'He seems to have done a runner from the Inn, according to H. Not paid the bill. I'll be hunting for him for Theft, Board and Lodgings, as if I don't have enough to do. Cleared out his room, too. One of the guests thought they saw him with another woman in the car. Any intel on that?'

Bella stepped back slightly to lean on the wall for support. The police officer shrugged, patted Bella's shoulder and walked down to the nearest cubicle, while Bella tapped on her phone to find her bank app. Her worst fears were realised as the phone sprang to life and she checked her account, and a number flashed up on the screen: £84.07

The sum total in her bank. She gasped. So, Moran Maguire must have persuaded Jonathan Bartlett to put the promised money into a holding account in his *own* name. He'd taken every last penny. She returned to Maureen's room, where she found the woman sitting up in bed talking with the nurse who was taking her blood pressure. Bella gave a weak smile to both and threw herself down on the chair next to the bed. She felt empty inside.

'I'm not supposed to be here,' stated the elderly woman, hair slightly singed, sooty, and looking older than her years without her signature expensive dark glasses and wearing a hospital gown instead of Gucci.

'I'm glad you are,' stated Bella and reached out to take the woman's hand.

'Did I dream it all or was there a fire?'

'Oh, there was a fire all right.'

'Oh, my days!'

'Everything from upstairs is gone,' stated Bella.

'All my lovely clothes. I thought I was goin' to join my Brian. Funny 'ow things turn out.'

'Moran's gone.'

'Oh, I'm so sorry, dear,' said Maureen with a squeeze of the younger woman's hand. 'Hope 'e didn't suffer.'

'Oh, not in the fire. He's done a runner with Gemma.'

'Big Irish shit. Told you 'e was a bad 'un,' said Maureen indignantly.

'He's taken the money.'

'What money, dear?'

'The money Jonathan Bartlett had sent me. He sent it to Moran for *safekeeping*,' said Bella with air quotes. 'I'll never see that again. I've been so flippin' stupid. Again.' Bella sat back and sighed heavily.

'That man's problem, and I've known Moran Maguire a long time, is the fact he is only interested in two things. Money and women. No, women first then money, then his own self-importance. Hang on, let me get this right. Bear with me, love, I've 'ad a bit of a trauma to meself. 'Av you seen my glasses?'

Bella shook her head and smiled and gave Maureen's hand a little squeeze.

'Here's a deal, Bels, luv. You 'elp me get better and I'll see you all right.' Bella smiled at Maureen wondering where this new conversation was going. 'I mean it. I've got nowhere else to go. I planned to end my days 'ere, as it were, so as soon as I get better, I'll be off to see my Bri. I'll leave you a little nest egg. I syphoned a little bit away, you could say.'

'Syphoned?'

'Well, truth be told, love, I didn't give all the money I should have to that new partner, that little squirt. Someone he met at an airport muscling in on my doings. Had to give him cash, didn't I? None of this internet banking whassisname. Too trace-able, he said. That Russian guy I was telling you about. He was getting all sorts. Dodgy creature, if you ask me. Him and De Groot a couple of chancers. Never took to him, I didn't – Ange could have done so much better.'

Bella knew there had to be a reason Poytr Medvedev had come back to haunt them, and she knew deep down there was no chance meeting with Louis De Groot. She knew anything and everything that he did was carefully planned. She shook her head and knew at this point she could not reveal any of this to Marcie. Their current relationship was hanging by a thread, and this was something she would keep tucked away for the time being.

'So, what do you say, Bels?' asked the woman from Streatham currently lying in a remote Highland hospital bed. Bella felt Maureen squeeze her hand a little tighter, and she nodded, a single tear running down her cheek.

'Enough of that nonsense. Get a grip, Bels. Plenty more fish in the sea. Listen, any chance you can find me a pair of my glasses and, while you're at it, could you see about a gin in a tin? Medicinal purposes only, of course.'

# FORTY-FIVE

It was only days since the fire and the disappearance of the man who continued to cause chaos in everyone's life and then, like a will o' the wisp, was gone. But slowly things were returning to normal, or as normal as they could be in these strange and straining times.

For Ruaridh, his current circumstances were difficult to comprehend. The speed. The deterioration in his wife's health. The difference in so few months that turned to weeks that turned to days. Then it seemed to be minute to minute. He was on edge as Dina's tiredness and fatigue worsened, and he felt sick to his stomach in a way he had never experienced, that no one in his position should realise. The younger children had been despatched to friends, only Dax remaining. He was sleeping gingerly next to his mother when his father left the empty space only to return, stoney-faced and drawn as each minute ticked by. She had instructed him firmly that she didn't want the usual Bible readings, psalms and quivering voices around her bed. So, instead, she had asked him to read her favourite gossip magazines. Ruaridh lay on the bed next to her, nursing his own wounds, quietly talking about people he had never heard of who were doing things he didn't understand. People he thought were leading a vacuous life without meaning except chasing money and fame. Lives full of emptiness according to Ruaridh. Unknown people frolicking on Caribbean beaches. Royal family fallouts. Women with strange pulled faces and puffed-up lips and huge black eyelashes. Girls who looked like dolls and not real people. Her fingers were entwined in his as the magazine sat on his knees, and he commented on the descriptions of these people from head to toe as he turned each page quietly.

Dina's last breath took him by surprise. A sharp, loud intake while he was still talking, and then nothing else. He put down the magazine and sat up, wide-eyed. He pulled her gently towards him and started to sob, then cry, then roar so much that Dina's mother came rushing in from the kitchen, tears blinding. And there they stayed for what seemed like forever, as time stopped. Dax was invited in while his father left him with his mother and grandmother, because Ruaridh had done something he had rarely done in all of his married life. He had defied his wife. Gone against her explicit wishes. Done the opposite of what she had asked him to do. She wanted her girls around her in her final moments, but he knew he could not share these last precious seconds with anyone. His last chance to touch her and to hold her and to stroke her and to kiss her. He wanted that for himself and no one else, so when he sent the text, he knew he would have to tell the littlest of white lies to all these wonderful women who had been with her so much in life.

Please come now.

The message pinged its arrival to the three women who were in The Strathkin Inn, sharing coffee and stories, and they leapt up without a word said. Heather had a huge bunch of flowers and Bella a giant pack of marshmallows.

'You must have gone to The Aizle early?' Marcie asked of the woman disappearing behind an abundant bouquet.

'I was there before they opened. I knew a delivery was coming in today, so I wanted the best of the bunch – quite literally.' Heather's voice was quivering and agitated, and she blurted out, 'She's not going to be in pain, is she? I couldn't bear to see it.'

Marcie squeezed her arm. They were walking the short walk to Lochside Croft, each step taking them closer to the moment they were all dreading. Bella decided to try to make it sound normal.

'Do you remember when they moved in here? What a state. No one thought they'd be able to move in before the baby was born. They worked day and night on that place... this place.' They had stopped abruptly outside and exchanged a brief look before walking down the path at the side of the white cottage.

It was Marcie who saw Ruaridh first, standing at the water's edge. But as she neared him, a feeling of dread took over her. She knew immediately as he half turned. His face was immovable. Strained. And Marcie opened her mouth in shock, unable to let any words escape. She turned to Bella and Heather who were standing at the door and Bella, reading Marcie's mind, raised her hand to her face, covering her mouth.

Inside there were gentle *I'm sorry's* to Dina's mother, who took each girl in turn to hug them tight before grasping Marcie's hand to lead them into the room. The bed that had been against the wall was now in the centre of the space, chairs from around the dining table on each side. Heather was sobbing, the other girls with quiet tears running down their cheeks. Dina simply looked as if she was asleep. Marcie felt like if she waited long enough, she would wake up. Her hands were on top of the quilt, fingers entwined, a sprig of heather from the garden between them. A Bible upturned on an open page was on the side table next to a family picture, her precious magazines piled up on the floor. They all sat down and held hands, Bella and Heather on one side, Marcie on the other with her hand resting on the bed. Dina's mother took the spare seat next to Marcie and took her hand to place it on her knee. Heather's gentle sobbing was the only sound that broke their silence until Bella started humming. She started to sing 'Wild Mountain Thyme', quietly at first as if it was just to herself. And then Dina's mum joined in and soon the sound drifted out the open window to Ruaridh, still on the water's edge, his arm around his growing eldest son. The song that meant so much to them all was a fitting end to a life well lived.

In his mind's eye, Ruaridh was at his wedding in the village hall. The song so softly blowing in the air was swirling around his wife as they danced their first dance as man and wife. Dina was glowing like he had never seen, and he felt his heart was about to burst. A heart that now felt as if it was shattered into a million pieces, was so full of love for this woman in his arms that it felt as if they were the only two people in the room. He hadn't yet known the secret she had kept from him. That their son was already growing inside of her, and her smile was as wide as the moon gazing up at this man who had swept her off her feet. Her hands in his, he was twirling her round and round and round, both knowing they had the world at their feet and a lifetime of love to look forward to.

He gazed down at his son, Dax, *the leader*. He pulled him close and wiped a tear from his soft young face. He was so like her, the curve of his cheek was her face, her gentle mannerisms, and he would see her in him every day. He turned to look out at the loch as the gentle singing was taken off in the wind.

# FORTY-SIX

Visitors always remarked on the silence that surrounded this part of the western Highlands. A deep silence that edged across the water, the hills, the mountains, the small winding roads, the vast landscapes. A silence that became the background noise to village life. In the distance, a small boat putt-putt-putted its way from a near-derelict jetty. Its movement in the water left a trail of ripples that slowly reached the sand and shingle shore. Then the sound was swallowed up as the tiny vessel hit the open sea and the silence descended once again like a cloak over the village of Strathkin.

Marcie sat on a bench taking all this late afternoon in. The high ridge had always been a place of solace for villagers and visitors alike and over the years had become her place of quiet contemplation and peace. Her eyes were drawn to what had once been the family home. Its roof was now caved in, but the building had remained more intact than they initially thought. All around, however, because the day was so still, the smell of acrid smoke remained in the air. No wind was carrying it away and no rain was dampening the small clutches of embers that still glowed in pockets around the building. She closed her eyes, tilted her head upwards towards a weak sun and gave a long sigh that made the man sitting quietly beside her turn around.

'Do you wish you could sometimes wind your life back, not to change it really, just to play back the best parts?' asked Ruaridh. 'Like you do with the TV. Rewind, fast forward it, pause it. Take a snapshot and just freeze the frame?'

'Always.' Marcie was transported back only a few years to when she had returned for her grandmother's funeral. Sad as the occasion was, it was a chance for her to reconnect with her childhood friends. In her mind's eye she played back a night at Swanfield, *when it was still Swanfield*, with them all sitting round the fire, chatting, gossiping and laughing. Bella falling on Marcie's shoulder in fits of giggles, Heather standing and swaying in front of them impersonating her uncle Callum. And then there was Dina. Beautiful, serene Dina, with the glow from the fire casting her in a billowing light like she was surrounded by an aura. She had cocked her head to the side, joining in the fun, and her pale smooth skin was translucent, as if she were truly made from angel dust. Dina was watching everyone, listening to them all recount their funny stories, but sometimes when Marcie caught her off guard, she appeared as if she was in a world of her own, so far away was the look in her eyes. Ruaridh had said the doctors told Dina she had been living with her illness unknown for a long time. Maybe that night, she knew but had wanted to have one more try at providing Ruaridh with the longed-for daughter, the one thing she had said to Marcie that would make his life complete.

'I'm thinking of the future...' Ruaridh began then stopped as he searched for words. 'What's in your future?'

'We need to wait for the report from the hospital. I've been there every day. I'm only back to Strathkin today to pick up more clothes. Simon's parents arrived last night. She's hard work, his mother. We've never really got on. He's being assessed by a clinical team, but it seems more mental than physical at this stage. He's physically healing but *they* want to take him back to Yorkshire and, despite *my* protestations, I don't seem to be included in the plan.'

'I could have picked them up from the airport,' interrupted Ruaridh.

'Oh, they drove up the road. That way they can tell me again how far away we are from civilisation and how much better he'd be wrapped up in the bosom of his own family. Well, *her*.'

While she and Simon's father had always agreed completely, and she had Callum's influence for that, his Italian born mother could not see anything that redeemed Marcie especially where her son was concerned. He was her world, and, it became very obvious, *her* future. It was inevitable, Marcie thought, it was a future world that would not include his wife, not when his mother was still around. Maybe this was the best way for their relationship to play out.

'Dina?' Marcie asked but was still partly convinced what had happened had not really taken place.

'Funeral is a week next Tuesday,' he replied.

'I'm so sorry. She was so peaceful, so beautiful. Like she was asleep. It was so quick, Ruaridh, so quick,' Marcie said all at once as if saying it like this meant it was still untrue despite being so unbelievably real. 'I – *we* – can't believe it.'

'So, I spoke with my big brother Ross last night. He's hoping to come over from New Zealand for the service and all. I'm thinking of going back with him.'

'For a holiday? A break? That would be good.'

'Maybe. Or a new start. Take the boys and the wee one. New life away from here.'

'Leave Strathkin?' asked a shocked and startled Marcie, turning to him. 'You can't!'

'I don't see why not. His kids are thriving out there. His girls are amazing. It's an option I'm considering. Seriously considering.'

'You can't go, Ruaridh, you can't,' Marcie insisted as she turned towards him.

'Give me one good reason why. Now.'

Marcie gazed down at the half burned-out house she used to call home and across the water of Strathkin Loch to the small white picturesque Lochside Croft. Her eyes rested on The Strathkin Inn and then the trekking centre and beyond the village hall to where the small road began to meander its way to Strath Aullt and Strathdon. The mountains were rich in colour and reaching skywards as if trying to absorb the white wispy clouds.

'Because I'm coming home.'

Marcie waited for a response that didn't come from the man beside her who continued to stare into the middle distance as if lost in a moment of his own. A gurgle from the sleeping child on the grass in front of them caught their eyes for a moment as they were distracted from their own dilemmas. Ruaridh stretched his foot out to rock the man-made cradle from the papoose that he had carried up into this place of peace. Together they watched as a bevy of swans made their way gently out of the reed bed at the corner of the loch with two swimming away from the rest and floating gently into the still water. Marcie placed her hand on the bench and Ruaridh placed his own on top. They sat in silence, watching as the birds below them finally took flight, the two separated from the rest, now in unison on the wing, and together disappeared into the sky.

# EPILOGUE

The woman crossed her fingers, sighed and looked up with bated breath as the electronic Arrivals board listed most arriving trains as now *cancelled*. The train from Inverness was still listed on the board at Edinburgh's Waverley Station, and she felt herself glance quickly to one side as she felt the closeness of an unknown person appearing next to her.

'It's a waiting game,' said the handsome stranger, hands clasped around two cups of warm coffee on this cold wintry day.

She smiled.

'Waiting for your husband?' he asked, eyes fixed on the board, knowing what train was about to be cancelled and what was to be delayed as his train app refreshed faster than the station staff could adjust the board.

'No, my mother. From Perth,' she said with another glance to the side.

He had already noticed no wedding ring on the finger. She had been easy to spot. Tall, expensively dressed in a long, fitted camel-coloured cashmere coat from Max Mara. Her skin was no stranger to an expensive facial, and he reckoned she was in her early thirties, her honey-blonde hair cascading in homemade curls over her shoulders which he imagined were tanned from a recent Caribbean break with her equally attractive, and wealthy, girlfriends. He had, in fact, been watching her for a while, after accidentally bumping into her as they crossed paths coming out of a convenience store in the New Town almost ten days ago. He called it research; some people would call it stalking.

Another train cancellation lit up the board.

'Oh no.' He sighed. 'My sister will *not* be happy. All that way from Aberdeen. So close and yet so far.'

'The weather is pretty grim, I heard, with landslips north of Perth. Mummy will just not cope with a bus replacement service again,' said the woman with a shrug of her shoulders.

And then the board lit up as he knew it would; Inverness train cancelled, buses only from Perth. She saw the cup of coffee appear in front of her, and the man cocked his head to one side.

'May as well not let it go to waste,' he said, and she pondered this gesture for a moment. 'It's a skinny mocha, no cream,' he offered, 'my sister's favourite. It'll go to waste otherwise, seriously.'

She turned, and he smiled broadly with perfectly straight teeth.

'Just happens to be my favourite, too!' She smiled back, and the carefully planned meet-cute was complete.

'Victoria.' The woman smiled as she took the cup of coffee from him, extending her hand in greeting.

He almost blurted out 'Brodie', then 'Peter', as he was caught unawares standing close behind her.

'William Henry Smith,' he said as his eyes drifted across the shop front, 'but my friends call me Will.' Quick, but rather stupid thinking, he mused.

He gave the woman one of his broadest grins and stared

directly into her eyes, watching her blush. He reached out and took her hand in his, kissing the back of it, and watched as the other hand gripped the coffee cup a little tighter. She'll be telling all her friends about this moment later, he smiled to himself.

And another one was caught in his trap.

# A LETTER FROM THE AUTHOR

Huge thanks for reading *Escape to the Highland Retreat*. I hope you were hooked on Marcie's journey. If you want to join other readers in hearing all about my new releases and bonus content, you can sign up for my newsletter!

www.stormpublishing.co/elayne-grimes

If you enjoyed this book and could spare a few moments to leave a review that would be hugely appreciated. Even a short review can make all the difference in encouraging a reader to discover my books for the first time. Thank you so much!

At the start of last year, I was a writer hoping for a publishing deal. I ended the year not only with an Amazon bestseller on my hands but with another two novels in the bag and ready to be released into the wild. Proof that there is a real hunger out there for a good story with engaging characters and a hint of a burly Scotsman in a kilt.

Once I had found my subject matter, the differing opinions on it amongst friends and family were fascinating. Debates raged and battle lines were drawn on the issues raised, and if anything, it brought a contentious subject out into the open and made people talk about it. Even more engrossing was the fact that couples had differing opinions but had never discussed it, each one thinking their opposite number would agree with their own thoughts and decisions. I'm sure you'll have your opinions. I would be keen to hear how you came to your own conclusions.

Thank you again for being on this incredible journey with me, for your reviews and blogs and for sharing your love of both the front cover and the words inside. Your affection for the characters and their community is incredible and I hope to bring you many more stories about their lives in such a beautiful part of Scotland.

Elayne x

𝕏  x.com/ely_438
📷  instagram.com/ely_author

# ACKNOWLEDGEMENTS

I am absolutely delighted to be writing acknowledgements for my second book. It has been an incredible journey so far. I realised very quickly after publication of *Secrets of Swanfield House* that I had missed one person I meant to mention. As a writer, you desperately seek a book deal, an agent or publisher, publication, recognition of the massive achievement of actually writing a book, physically holding your own words in your hands and – if you're like me – *sniffing* your first novel.

Imagine then if that moment of joy was snatched from you and your book launch was suddenly out of your hands. That big day you've waited all this time for was just another date in the diary to come and go like all the rest. For those debut novelists who had the unfortunate timing of their books coming out in the Covid years – in stepped walnut-swigging Emma Christie to save the day. Emma, herself an extremely successful crime novelist, started an online festival called Diary of a Debut Novelist from her home in Barcelona to promote and showcase authors and their novels who through no fault of their own were suddenly reduced to only meagre offerings. She gave up her own time to produce a regular online feature with authors who could have their own moment in the spotlight and tell us their stories of how they got there – some with luck on their side and others through sheer grit and determination after years of rejection. It was fascinating to listen to everyone's journey and gave hope to those of us who were starting out on our own paths to publication. I mentioned in my previous acknowledgements about writers supporting writers and here it was again in action. Thanks Emma.

My thanks once more to my lovely Scrittrici, Susan Tackenberg and Moira Black who celebrated with me at my own mini launch in London over delicious cocktails and who continue to be both a support and inspiration to me. Kristin Burniston too who is on track as a screenwriter; we all knew you would go on to great success. To my pre-readers known joyously as The Hartnells who are so disappointed that Strathkin doesn't exist, and they can't visit – sorry guys. Kirsty Mooney and Helen Sturrock who read the early drafts of *Escape to the Highland Retreat*, thanks ladies. My wonderful neighbour Maureen Stoneman who was the inspiration for the fabulous Maureen Berman. Her stories are legendary, and it is a pleasure to call her a friend. To Claire MacLeary, a guiding light and co-conspirator and of course the gorgeous Jac Morrison. I can't forget all the published and fledgling authors at Edinburgh Writers' Forum.

Once again to everyone who has allowed me to steal a little bit of their life. I hope I have done you justice, and you enjoy my version.

To the team at Storm, all those working tirelessly behind the scenes, but particularly my editor Kate Smith who has made me a better writer and has the patience of a saint.

Finally, to my sister Juliet who is a mine of information and has a keen eye for a good story as well as a great sense of where to go on holiday. And Skips x

Printed in Great Britain
by Amazon

59622275R00182